THE *Plan*

QWEN SALSBURY

OMNIFIC PUBLISHING
LOS ANGELES

Omnific Publishing
1901 Avenue of the Stars, 2nd floor
Los Angeles, CA 90067
www.omnificpublishing.com

First Omnific eBook edition, February 2014
First Omnific trade paperback edition, February 2014

Library of Congress Cataloguing-in-Publication Data

Salsbury, Qwen.
   The Plan / Qwen Salsbury – 1st ed.
   ISBN: 978-1-623420-68-0
   1. Office Romance — Fiction. 2. Romantic Comedy — Fiction.
   3. Contemporary Romance — Fiction. 4. Diary — Fiction. I. Title

10 9 8 7 6 5 4 3 2 1

Cover Design by Micha Stone and Amy Brokaw
Interior Book Design by Coreen Montagna

Printed in the United States of America

To Deb for the welcome,
Chantel for the spark,
Heather for the gauntlet
Rie for the shoulder,
and Kellie for the shove.

PROLOGUE

Day of Employment:
372…381…maybe 495…something. They all run together.

2:00 AM

❀ CHAMPAGNE: I'm covered in it.

❀ PETALS: Litter my entire room.

❀ BALCONY DOOR: Open.

❀ ROOM: Effing freezing.

❀ NIPPLES: Probably hard enough to puncture this silk camisole.

❀ MY HEART: Who the hell knows at this point?

THE CURTAINS FLUTTER OPEN. It's not the breeze. It's him. He steps into the room, watching his own feet move.

He barely resembles the man who makes grown men cry, who barters lives and livelihoods like wares at a flea market, who I have fantasized about for over a year.

His hair is slick and dark and drips champagne. A single, thick lock escapes, flipping forward as he rakes his fingers through it. His gaze never leaves the floor.

"Just tell me why," he whispers, barely audible over the street below.

Every instinct in me screams to run to him, to wrap my hands around him, to lose myself in his touch…in him.

I would do just that. Lose myself.

It has all been make-believe.

"You don't know me," I say as softly as I can, as if for the first time I consider that I need to be soft, that he might actually be breakable.

His head snaps up, and his eyes — oh, God, his eyes! — they swim, an unfocused torment swirling in their depths.

"How can you say that? After all…after everything?"

"This is not me. I'm not what you think I am."

"You are everything I want." He moves to me. I move twice as far away.

"Alaric, I'm not who you think I am. I'm a liar. And I can't be what you want."

DAY OF EMPLOYMENT: 359

7:25 AM

✽ LOCATION: Bread in Captivity Bakery.
✽ BREAKFAST: Early coffee date.
✽ DATE: As compatible as arranged ones typically are.
✽ IT: What I am not into.

IT IS A FACT, UNIVERSALLY ACCEPTED, that a single man in possession of a fine ass must be observed like wildlife.

Like how Marlin Perkins watched wildlife for *Wild Kingdom*. Catalog. Thorough. Precise.

Constant.

Not that this is an edict. It is simply unavoidable.

And twenty feet in front me is the equivalent of a one-hundred-car pileup wrapped up in a pair of pinstripe pants.

Regrettably, three feet in front of me, and blocking the view of aforementioned ass, is my date.

He forks at a spinach leaf in the quiche that I would lay money down he's ordered primarily to impress me.

I would be far more favorably impressed if he had ordered bacon I could swipe.

Over his shoulder, Mr. Pinstripe sits down to a working breakfast with the potential clients I watched arrive in our office yesterday afternoon. I can't see his plate, but I know he's having his usual fare: peanut butter cinnamon roll with crushed nut topping. Locally sourced milk. Take-out order of hot rolls to be delivered with check.

"So, Emma, you're friends with the girl who owns this place, right?"

The word "girl" makes me twisty-eared. My date gestures casually with his fork to a few points around the bakery, which is indeed owned by my best friend. The offending piece of spinach finds its way to the floor.

I nod yes and note that the table behind him has, even before the to-go hot buns are delivered to their namesake, already erupted into deal-sealing handshakes. Looks like I will be entering some new orders this afternoon.

"These are great," my date says and tears off a bit of maple long john. "You know, Emma, our firm will be looking for an intern after the first of the year. You've been taking classes long enough to qualify, haven't you?" He speaks around half-masticated pastry. "If you're going to go into tax law, I can put in a good word for you."

"Yes, great," I say. The party behind him appears close to wrapping things up. "Erm, uh, oh, sorry. No, but thank you. I'm not really interested."

That phrase works on so many levels.

"Emma, you seem distracted. Was this place not all right? You should have told me you didn't want to come here when I suggested it."

The place is perfection. Scenery especially.

"It's fine. My apologies. I'm just distracted by…something at work."

The table behind us adjourns.

They will be heading back to our office. My legs twitch.

"Actually, Matt, I—"

"Mark," he corrects. His mouth skews.

"Oh, Mark, pardon me. I really have to get on the clock." I smile, hope I manage to look a bit embarrassed. I know his name. I also know that I would rather go get a high velocity mammogram than have another experience of being regaled with tales of his new partnership at Crusty, Dull, and Dusty, LLC, so fumbling his name seems less confrontational than telling him as much.

7:57 AM

THE ELEVATOR INTO WHICH I'm sardined cannot hold another soul.

Good thing the guy trying to squeeze on is reputedly not encumbered with one.

"Morning, Mr. Canon." A random coworker steps off and gives up his spot. Canon and his pinstripe suit slide in and regard the man in much the way one would jetsam.

The elevator whirs upward. Everyone looks dutifully forward at the climbing numbers.

Everyone except Canon, who stares at his phone, and me, who stares at Canon staring at his phone.

I will savor the next eleven floors just as I do the hint of cinnamon roll that still emanates from him.

7:59 AM

❦ FLOOR: 8.

JUST THE TWO OF US.

This has never happened.

In 359 days of working in the same office with him, I have literally never happened to be in the same proximal location as the man before.

Red numbers climb. The floors. My body temperature. Not going to quibble.

He continues to assault his phone and a few of my favorite senses.

Wintergreen. Pumpkin spice and coffee. Sunshine.

I swear, heat actually rolls off of him. Scorches. Vibrates. We are riding up in a stainless steel, solar hot-plate box.

I inch closer. Tilt my head and try to break into his peripheral. Waste a few moments distracted by angular jawlines that put a 1980s Rob Lowe on notice. Gesture toward the elevator keys in a motion as if I mean to verify that his floor button has been already pushed.

You know, as if it would've escaped mine or anyone's notice that they work in the same place as this guy. You could pick him out in a Cecil B. DeMille crowd scene.

This was not the most stellar plan. I just wanted to steal a moment. Get a tiny bit of eye contact. It would be a welcome pick-me-up after such a dud date. Plus, I must admit I put in a little extra effort today; it's a rare Good Hair Day with big, fat waves rather than motley curls. The kind of day where you'd refer to your hair in terms of descriptive endearment such as "auburn" or "chestnut" rather than most days when you just want the brown lot of it out of your way in a hair band and be done with it.

I have even broken out my favorite turquoise wrap skirt, plus eye shadow put on in front of bathroom, rather than rearview, mirror.

No judging. Text and drive is a big no-no, but to commute and multitask is an aged and revered tradition which must be upheld. These are dark times. Darker still if we must forego the snooze button.

His phone continues to be the most interesting thing ever.

Frustrating. Another oh-so-casual sidestep and I'm positioned well within his radar zone. In a last ditch effort to generate a blip, I let my keys hit the floor and fail to bend fully at the knees while retrieving them.

I will chastise myself later for stooping to such adolescent, second-string cheerleader tactics.

And by chastise, I mean snarf a Reese's.

Not even tinny, metal clanking sounds break his concentration. Unfazed. He either doesn't notice or could not care less.

The doors swoosh open on our floor, and he exits swiftly. Not even a sideways glance.

II:05 AM

❈ LOCATION: In my box, like a good Schrödinger's kitty cat.

"WHAT'S THE SOONEST YOU'VE GOT?"

Madeline, with a pencil behind her ear and looking not unlike a real bookie, peruses her chart. "Bert has end-of-day…today." She laughs and shakes her head. "Wow, that'd be a record. He's got confidence."

Still peering over the cubicle wall Madeline and I share, I look out across the office tundra to spot and evaluate the personal assistant who walked through the doors for the first time approximately twenty-seven hours ago. Tidy, strawberry blond bun; pencil skirt; gray shirt with only top button undone. All in the positive column. It appears she has managed to read the past assistants' file on Canon's preferences, and brought the right coffee, and kept out of his way. She looks perpetually busy and nervous.

All signs indicate that she is going in the long-term column.

I dangle a twenty over the partition.

Madeline snatches it and huffs in playful exasperation. "What's your bet?"

I purse my lips as I contemplate. "When did you say the board meeting was?"

"I didn't." She half-smiles and looks at me knowingly.

"That's a lunch meeting today," Bert pipes up from across the aisle. "She already booked Bread in Captivity for the food, but your friend said they're understaffed this afternoon and can't squeeze in another delivery. So that assistant is picking it up herself." A snort escapes him as he tries to keep his laughter contained.

"Wha—? She's going off-site right in the middle of a meeting?" I feel the blood drain from my face. That is a disaster in the making. "I can't watch. Don't you think we should warn her?"

"Oh, Emma." Madeline tsks up at me. "You're such a softy."

My heart clenches. Just thinking about the tongue-lashings I've heard reverberate through those walls for lesser offenses causes me to cringe. No one deserves the kind of hellfire that would come from being absent without leave during a critical meeting.

And it appears Canon considers all meetings critical.

Critical. Maybe that's what *Alaric* meant in ancient Gaelic…

In my estimation, the person who these personal assistants were assisting was not completely unreasonable; of course, it's easy to be objective from my safe vantage point. I'm not interested in loitering on the Grassy Knoll.

Canon is particular and demanding. He's busy and paid to think. The few times I have heard him dress down someone—and, let's face it, if he is speaking to someone, he is insulting them—it's all centered on talk of "impacted productivity" and "wasting" his time.

I have never spoken a word to him, nor has he to me, but I have studied him every day for going on a year. He has high standards

7

and low tolerance. Very low. Subbasement low. Everyone knows it. Everyone stays away.

Everyone who can, that is.

I can't look away.

Alaric Canon is the single most attractive man I have ever seen. Bar none.

He's the guy you wish Jennifer Aniston would be with just to get back at Brad.

Scientists should extract his cells and use them in electromagnetic experiments. Those tubes that can destroy the planet if the particles align improperly. Something along those lines. I would look that up if I had time. Maybe when I'm researching ancient Gaelic.

When he passes through the lobby on the way to his corner office, it's like looking into the sun — in all the good ways and the bad.

From what I can discern, he's also the most stern and unforgiving individual ever to grace the world with his glorious presence.

He is hard and fierce. There's something both hawk-like and leonine about his features. Predatory. A lightning storm of power, terrifying and beautiful.

Thankfully, most of the office has a fascination with him as well, albeit a different one, so my fixation doesn't stand out like it might otherwise. Others watch in morbid curiosity to see how long those who work for him last and what they have done wrong to get their asses handed to them. Madeline runs the pool for PA terminations. There's a separate pot estimated at around $400 waiting for the day one gets their pink slip and is not reduced to tears. Canon is legendary for cutting to the quick. He made a former Navy SEAL cry.

I have the luxury of distance. I'm certain a few moments behind that thick, cherry door and I would be quite over my little crush. Surely someone who tore through people like so much silt is grating to be around.

He has to be an ass of epic proportions.

He has an epic ass.

I'll take "What is Irony?" for $200, Alex.

The (non)incident in the elevator this morning continues to irk me. I'm deeply considering squeezing some lemonade out of it and using his lack of attention to my…details in order to motivate myself, for personal progress. Just once I would like to have him notice me, to look appreciatively at me, a chink in his armor of sorts. I want to see if I can coax a glimmer of humanity from him.

It is a goal. I have a plan.

While I can afford to observe him from a safe vantage point, those poor PA suckers are a different story.

They are the ones in the trenches. I learn from their mistakes. I tell myself it's so I can play along, place winning bets, supplement my meager income through their misfortune, but honestly, it's primarily to support my shoe addiction.

I know his favorite coffee, its substitute, and the proportions of cream and sweetener. I know he prefers oat to wheat and never, ever rye.

There's something he favors about conference room C; I suspect it's the projection equipment. For all his perfectionism, he manages to drip on his tie fairly often. He never sends red roses. No one gets the chance to interrupt him twice.

All in the name of winning the office pool. That's what I tell myself I watch him for.

I know I'm lying.

Madeline waves the tattered green bill in front of my face, breaking my reverie. "So, Emma, what am I putting you down for?"

"I just cannot stand idly by and let anyone go through that." I start toward the redhead's desk.

"If you fix it, I reserve the right to change my bet," Bert says and bolts out of his chair.

I nod in agreement and smooth my hair and skirt as I approach the PA's desk.

The air crackles thickly the closer I get to her desk, to Canon's door. Behind her, behind those solid walls, I picture him in his crisp white shirt, pacing while on a conference call.

"May I help you?" The PA *du jour* doesn't even bother to look up from her papers.

"Actually I think I can help you."

This gets her attention. She turns her head and narrows her eyes. "Oh, really? And just what makes you think I would need your help?"

Wow, she is brusque. I shrug it off. "I can run out on my break and pick up the lunch order for you." I force a smile. Her demeanor is so off-putting. I tell myself that anyone would be on edge in her position.

"That won't be necessary," she snaps and spins in her chair.

"Oh." I'm not prepared for this from her at all. "I had heard you were going to have to pick it up yourself. It sounds as though you have made other arrangements. Good."

She's so defensive, and I can't figure out why. But she's going to let me know.

"Don't think I didn't notice you, missy." She stands and pokes her long fingernail in my chest before I can shrink back. Her red polish glares up at me from her peep-toe pumps. "You staring over here, salivating. You want this position. You think you can show up with the delivery and take the credit. Well, you're out of luck. I have done my homework on him, and I am not going anywhere."

Oh, sweetie. I wouldn't do your job for anything. I swallow back all the things I would like to say to this crass and unpleasant woman and depart, giving her a simple nod.

It's not really a nod. It's a goodbye.

"Put me down for twenty bucks and two p.m.," I say to Madeline as I pass her desk. "Today."

"What?" she and Bert say in unison.

"She doesn't want any of my help." What I don't say is that she's got acrylic nails, is chewing bubble gum, and wearing open-toed shoes with hosiery.

I don't know about her, but I have done my homework.

DAY OF EMPLOYMENT: *360*

10:18 AM

YESTERDAY, A TEARFUL MISS STRAWBERRY BUN collected her personal effects and left the premises at 2:30 p.m.

I was off by about half an hour with my bet, but I still took that money and added it to my shoe kitty while Bert shook his head. Poor guy got wrangled into taking notes during the board meeting. During that time, I made sure I was as scarce as intact hymen the morning after prom. I can only imagine what that atmosphere was like. It seems the lunch order took longer than expected, and the PA was late getting back. Shocking.

2:58 PM

* LOCATION: Break room.
* CAFFEINE DEPENDENCY: Approaching twelve-step program territory.

TODAY, THERE IS A THINNED CARPET PATH worn between here and the cubicle in which I spend the bulk of my days tethered like veal. I have never ventured to the coffee machine this often before. We're forming a bond. We may have to be introduced as Mr. and Mrs. Coffee at this weekend's upcoming office holiday party.

Alternative Dispute Resolution class last night coupled with two final take-home exam briefs due tomorrow have Nosferatued the life from me. My get-up-and-go has got up and gone. Of great concern is that this end-of-semester stress coupled with demands at work and life in general may invoke the lanky, bearded spirit that manifests in my nightmares during periods of turmoil. Beside the coffee pot, a collection jar of shiny silver and an inordinate amount of patina tinged copper catches my eye.

I shudder. Put a fistful of coins in that jar and a pin in that thought. I have been lucky thus far. No need to jinx it.

Down the hallway, I can hear the telltale rumblings of an international conference call. On a hunch, I peer out of the break room entryway just in time to see the door swing open. Canon exits and makes straight for his corner of the office area. Just before the conference room door clicks shut, a collective sigh reverberates from within the room, as if the tension of the entire place decompressed upon his departure. I doubt it is a cheerful call. Our numbers are down. I don't know this for a fact because I don't generate those particular reports, but I have observed the general morose climate and that the volume of requested estimates and orders are on the decline.

That, plus an announcement that the office party is not going to be an open bar this year. Always a surefire clue to economic downturn. One doesn't exactly need to be a resident of Baker Street to arrive at such a deduction.

Having noted that Canon is without the barnacle of his phone, I decide to venture out in the hopes of encountering him without the distraction when he's on his way back to the meeting. I'm annoyed that I could not get so much as a blink out of him yesterday, and far more annoyed with myself that it seems to matter to me.

I just want a glint or glance and maybe a little nod in greeting customarily extended to another member of the human race.

Just need to get that and then put this foolishness to bed. Wait, no. That invokes some seriously dirty thoughts. Just need to put this behind me. Speaking of behinds...

Ugh. I really *have* to quit fixating on buttocks.

This is going to be the end.

rimshot

Okay, I give up.

Halting my sense of humor's complete metamorphosis into that of a pubescent boy, Canon enters the hallway. I aim for nonchalance and walk evenly into his direct path. He deftly steps aside, eyes fixed straight ahead and never breaking stride.

I might as well be a puff of smoke.

This crap is fast getting on my reserve nerve.

8:02 PM

❧ DINNER: Being eaten on sofa.

❧ ROOMMATE: Inquisitor, it seems.

"So," I SAY, SOUNDING TOO DELIBERATELY CASUAL even to my own ears, "there's this guy I keep seeing at work—"

"A guy? What guy? You never mentioned a guy." Clara stops mid-carrot-bite. "You're seeing a guy at work?"

"I *see* him at work. Not 'seeing' him." My fork runs through the rice. I like Clara's idea better.

I think.

"Aren't there a lot of guys that work on your floor?" Clara talks around a mouthful of food. Somehow, she manages to still be cute. I would look like a cow with cud.

"Not like...not like him. They're guys. He's a...well..." I hadn't really thought about this before. Guys wear ball caps. Sometimes backward. This I cannot picture. Guys swill beer and slap buds on the back and often can be observed being pleasant and have even been known to smile. I have never seen this man smile. "He is a man."

"*Man.*" Clara hums the word. Chomps a bit of zucchini. "Sooo how long has this succulent slice worked there?"

I fidget. "About five years." ...*two months and nine days.*

Silence. I really do not know why I brought this up. Why I couldn't contain it.

Clara wears a look that I have learned over time is a sincere attempt to mask supreme annoyance. "Of course. Emma Baker has the hippity hots for a man she works with for a year and just now sees fit to open up and let her best friend in on it." She sighs and sounds hollowly cheerful. "That is what BFF stands for, you know: *Best Friend Forever*, not *Being Frigging Forgotten*." She chucks a carrot at me playfully. That's the grand extent of her capacity for irritation.

I clear my throat and hopefully the air as well. "I don't work with him." We interrupt this message to thank God. "He's got a corner office and a commanding presence and wears suits so very, very well."

Clara quirks an eyebrow.

Another bite. She squirms in her seat. "Go on. What makes this one so special?"

I shrug. "He's not special. He's an asshole."

"Oh, yeah. Assholes are not special, Emma. Assholes are, however, your specialty."

I chuck a snow pea at her. But it's true.

She lobs it back to me.

"So...probably not my Prince Charming then, you think?" I smile.

"You know, Emma, you kiss enough frogs and you end up with HPV."

"Pretty sure that's only toads and warts."

DAY OF EMPLOYMENT: *361*

10:30 AM

❃ Dress: Same red sheath number as my first day.

❃ Wardrobe: In need of upgrade. One that does not run on a two-week repeat cycle.

❃ Desk: Clutter-free.

❃ Cactus: Withering away.

"Already?" I'm in shock. I didn't even get to place a bet on this last one.

"You snooze, you lose," Bert says, fanning himself with the small handful of bills and looking disturbingly akin to a cotillion darling.

Across the floor, a red-faced man (with the potentially fakest blond dye job I've seen possibly ever) packs up his belongings from the desk outside Alaric Canon's closed office door. Not his desk. The desk. No one has it long enough to lay claim.

"I was not 'snoozing.' I was discussing the profit and loss reports with Rebecca in her office ever since I got here today."

Bert remains unruffled. "Snooze, schmooze. Same diff." We all watch Clairol #103 chuck a knickknack dead center against Canon's door. Then Bert continues. "All I know is I'm going to be buying some new shoes, and you are still gonna be wearing those BOGOs." He looks askance at my feet.

Well, perhaps he is always a tad bit ruffly.

But, I note my shoes definitely are of the sensible heel variety. I smooth my skirt and tuck my feet under my desk.

Easy, Breezy, Beautiful PA flips his now former boss the bird and snatches his freshly cut check from Rebecca's hand as he flies out the door.

1:03 PM

❋ LUNCH: Skipped.

❋ SAVINGS: Dipped into.

"WHOA." BERT NUDGES MADELINE. "Somebody skipped lunch." He points toward me.

She looks down. "Ooo, nice shoes. You went shopping? Without me?" She feigns hurt.

Spinning a quarter turn in my chair, I allow myself a moment to admire my shiny, distinctly non-sensible shoes. The shoe fund is earmarked for a particularly gorgeous pair of boots, but these Gianni Bini platforms were drastically clearanced. Their siren song could not be denied.

Whether or not impulse purchase resistance levels are low due to increasing irritation with heedless corner office occupant will not be taken under consideration in this matter.

I head over to give Rebecca the reports before her meeting.

Unfortunately, she's not in her office.

She is also not to be found in the supply room, copy room, or bathroom. By the time my search reaches our deserted break room, I regret not breaking in the new shoes before wearing them at work.

I take a moment to lean over a table and take the weight off my feet. Just a second. Please. Ugh. A moment of relief, that's all I'm asking.

I'm pretty certain I look a sight: my face plastered onto the cool table, and my ass up in the air, feet swinging in the wind.

Thunk. One heel slips to the floor.

My toes fumble around until I feel the leather, twist into it, and oh-so-carefully lift it up behind me like a crane until I can reach back and put it on properly again.

I stretch and grunt and twist and probably channel all the grace of Cloris Leachman performing Swan Lake.

Well, that was certainly…relaxing.

Grabbing the reports, I leave just in time to see one Alaric Canon round the corner, gorgeous jaw clenched.

All the air squeezes from my lungs.

He doesn't even spare me a glance.

Whew. A few moments earlier and that would have been supremely embarrassing.

4:45 PM

❀ EMAIL: Empty.

❀ SPREADSHEETS: Done.

❀ MIND: Preoccupied. To say the least.

ALARIC CANON.

His door stares back at me.

I watched him go in there about five minutes ago.

Or twenty.

Black suit, sky blue tie.

Outline of his frame burned into my retinas.

"Emma? You okay?" Madeline peers over her cubicle wall.

"Hm? Oh…oh, yes. Yes, I'm fine." Shake the cobwebs from my head. I need to do the same for other parts of me. "Long day."

"They all are," Madeline says and performs her end-of-day station shut down shuffle. "I'm heading out after I run over to HR with the picture that PA left today."

"He was in a hurry to get outta here, huh?"

"More likely, to get away from Canon," she says, laughing. On the betting pool chart, she makes a winning mark for the day under Bert's name. "Be ready tomorrow, Emma. Bert is taking us to the cleaners."

She's right. Bert is winning all the time. He must have a system.

Or—I think back to his comment about my shoes, my whereabouts, everyone's happenings—he's just observant as hell.

I am the quintessential, definitive portrait of observant.

Why I'm not winning these bets every damn time is bizarre.

Hell, no one is more observant of Canon than I am. Need to get my head in the game and apply this recon I have been doing in a more constructive manner. Often these betting pools turn into some serious money, and I am not exactly living the type of life in which Robin Leach is going to show up with cameras in tow.

I look at the closed, hardwood door.

There are worse things to look at.

Oh, I will be ready tomorrow.

Thinking about Canon, I'm ready now.

Madeline leaves.

The office sounds fade away.

No clicks. No buzzes. No chatter.

Nothing but me and that unforgiving door.

Clearly, I have read far, far too many trashy romances in my lifetime—because I cannot help myself. I imagine it opening.

Canon would emerge. Starched white shirt. Crisp.

Jacket over his arm. Hair…doing whatever the fuck it is that it does.

I would be at my desk.

Fans blowing my hair back. No. No, that's a bit much. Scratch the fan.

I would be at my desk. Pretending to work.

Pretending not to hear him approach.

"Miss…Baker, is it not?" His voice would spill over my shoulder, warm like coffee along my neck.

I shiver at the thought alone.

I'd spin, look up at him through my lashes. Suppress the urge to say I will be whoever he wants me to be.

"Yes. Mr. Canon, is it?" As if I don't know.

He'd look down at me. Tongue darting. Lips glistening.

"I'm told you handle—" stepping so close I could feel the heat of him "—spread—" hand running along my chair "—sheets."

"Yes, I do." I'd cross my arms, pushing my breasts together. Subtle. Or maybe not. "Anything you want me to handle, you can put in my box."

"I need to whip it out by five."

"Well, that will be hard." My eyes will dart to his zipper. "I'll need you to give it to me, right here on my desk, now."

I want to assume an entry-level position.

He'd look around the empty office and then to me. Like a predatory cat, he would make a final move forward, lean around my body, breathe into my hair, as his white linen-clad arm swept the papers from my desk. Rather than cascade down en masse, they would flutter around us like feathers. Our own private, ticker-tape libido parade.

His hand would slide under my hair, fingers digging into my neck. He'd bend me, bowing my back. I'd crush into him, part my lips, and breathe in the scent of him. He'd lean in, searching my face, eyes to lips to neck, then he's on me. Pouncing. Covering my mouth with his. Again. I'm open and swallowed up.

Underneath his tongue would be smooth and sweet.

My ankle would wrap around his leg, and he'd lift me against him before pushing me down against the desk that I would henceforth never be able to look at again without thoughts of Alaric Canon.

Hands everywhere. I'd feel him at my ribs.

I'd fumble with his buttons. He'd tear mine free.

I would touch his face. He'd wrap my legs around my waist, grind into me. Deep. Hard.

Even through clothes, it'd be better than any of my real sex.

One hand at my throat, thumb under my jaw, lips parted and panting down on me, his fingers would tear through my hosiery, slipping, slipping—

"Emma?"

Wha—?

"It's after five." Rebecca looks at me questioningly. "Are you having difficulty completing all of your work? I haven't overloaded you, have I?"

"I'm fine." Load-free even. Regrettably so.

We both turn to the sound of Canon's door opening. He looks to Rebecca briefly then goes on his way.

I feel my cheeks burn.

It's no big deal.

One more office daydream.

Not like I'm going to let myself get even more obsessed with him.

I clock out.

DAY OF EMPLOYMENT: 362

8:11 PM

* ❧ DAY: Different.
* ❧ SHIT: Same.
* ❧ WORKLOAD AND COURSE LOAD: Big, steamy load.
* ❧ CONSIDER: Pro v. con of liquid diet.
* ❧ SHOPPING LIST: One bourbon. One Scotch. One beer.

MR. THOROGOOD, YOU SIR, are a culinary genius.

Inebriated academia is not in the mix for me. High alcohol tolerance and low fiscal flow preclude sufficient acquisition of libations.

In summation: What is commonly referred to as "broke."

Clara is in my room and, with all her traditional subtlety, suggesting I get gussied up to go out with her and have gentlemen buy our drinks. That's just not my thing. My bar crawl phase was short, sweet and sour.

Not to say I no longer have scandalous, wild times now. Example: I routinely spend long, late night hours having as many as four men entertain me in my bed. *Men like Fallon, Kimmel, O'Brien, and Letterman.*

"Do you even own fancy duds anymore?" Clara says, scavenging through my barren closet.

I shrug. Turn the page in my textbook.

"Emma," she faux whines. "Let's get stolen."

Stolen? My brow furrows. "That doesn't sound pleasant."

"Then you have never been properly stolen." She sticks her tongue out playfully, then winces. I am pretty sure she just realized she smudged her lip color; however, this setback, much like everything else, doesn't ruffle her for long.

"What has become of my fine, feathered friend?" A few hangers slide against the rod in punctuation.

There is no point in pointing out the ludicrousness of most of Clara's asides. If it were my job, my 401(k) would be fully vested.

Further, my personage has not, at any point in my longer-than-I-care-to-admit existence, been either fine or feathered. I may have, however, recently allowed Canon to make me cuckoo for Cocoa Puffs.

Jury is still out on that.

Ha. See? And they said law school is not a joking matter.

What really is not a joking matter is the $1,800 in textbooks that, conveniently for the university's budget, never ever, ever seem to be used by any instructor the following semester. I have given up even venturing to the campus bookstore for buyback.

Clothes shuffling racket stops abruptly. On the uppermost shelf, a black box seems to hold Clara's attention.

"Hey, when is your company's yearly shindig? In just a couple days, right?"

My left eyebrow lifts. Clara fishes the box down with a hanger.

"Oh, no, you do not. Something along the lines of what I wore last year will be quite enough." Heck the identical outfit as last year, more than likely. It's not like anyone is gonna notice.

"People will notice," Clara says, as if she can hear my every thought. "I know what you're thinking, Emma."

I wasn't even kidding.

"It does no good for Emmarella to acquire fabulous shoes if she never wears them to a ball." One half of a pair of crystal adorned strappy heels is a pendulum from her index finger.

1:03 AM

♣ TEXTBOOK: Pillow.

❀ OSMOSIS: Needs to be a viable study method.

I AWAKE TO THE SOUND of my bedroom door being knocked on. Well, beaten on. Repeatedly.

Needlessly, too, I might add as it is wide open.

Clara bounces on the balls of her bare feet.

No other parts bounce. She is disgustingly fit for someone who spends all day surrounded by baked goods.

"Gooooood morning, Emma," she half-slurs sarcastically and points back toward our living room. "I have something for you!"

"Is it a sleep?"

"What?"

"Never mind. What is it?"

"Inspiration." She smiles beatifically, spins, wobbles, and commences to tromp about the house.

On the sofa sits a shopping bag filled to the brim. It bursts with items ranging from satin to silk to what I hope against hope is not white latex. Predominantly lacy, uncomfortable looking underthings. Frederick's of Hollywood kind of things.

I do wish there were assless chaps. Not that I would wear them. But there is nothing funnier than the words *assless chaps*.

But, tangentially, answer me this: Do any chaps actually *have* asses?

I enjoy lingerie even more than the next person. Don't get me wrong.

That being said, I am exhausted and have no wish to humor her and go through these items. Clara would never allow me to go back to sleep if I deny her this. So, with as much desire to handle objects as is typically reserved for radioactive isotopes, I reach in and grab out whatever is nearest the top.

Electric blue coordinated bra and panty set. Nice.

Plum and lavender inset bustier with matching cheekies. I will wear this one some day soon just for me.

A bra so padded it could double as a Muppet. I would have to refer to my breasts as Kermit and Fozzie.

Hot pink fishing line.

Oh, wait. It's a thong.

I cannot be expected to wear a thong. I am not a stick figure. Thongs ride up my butt crack. The removal of undergarments is not supposed to launch a full scale search and rescue operation.

I refuse to go spelunking just take off my undies.

"I am *not* wearing these," I say.

Clara snatches them away. Snorts.

DAY OF EMPLOYMENT: 363

1:11 PM

❀ PERSONAL ASSISTANTS WHO STARTED TODAY: 3.

❀ PERSONAL ASSISTANTS STILL EMPLOYED: 1.

❀ FIT TO BE TIED: Rebecca.

❀ ACTUALLY TIED: Bert and I. We placed identical bets.

"HOW CAN I BE EXPECTED TO ACCOMPLISH anything constructive if I have to replace personnel every damned minute of every damned day?" Rebecca fumes. She must be very upset; her blotter and stapler no longer run at perfect, intersecting lines. She buttons, then unbuttons her suit jacket on repeat.

Madeline smartly tucks the betting pool notebook behind her back. "Wonder why Mr. Canon is acting nastier than usual. Do you suppose it's the holiday blues? I always hear the holiday season can cause depression and loneliness."

Bert laughs. "If that guy is lonely, he has only himself to blame. He probably ate all his young."

Oh, low blow. That hardly seems fair.

There is no replicant technology that affords androids procreation.

8:59 PM

❀ FINAL EXAM: Impossible to complete in the
three hours allotted.

"EMMA! EMMA!" A PARTICULARLY NICE GIRL from first semester study group snags me in the hallway immediately after I leave the classroom.

"Hey, lady," I say, as I try to cover for being unable to recall her actual name. Anything would be preferable to calling her what I remember her as: Age Inappropriate Pigtails.

"Are you taking Klassen's Divorce and Child Advocacy intersession course?" She scoots to the side to allow others to pass, ringlets swaying below her ears.

"Yes, I rented the texts last night."

"Great," she says. "We're forming a study group. We'll probably meet right after class every afternoon in room one-nineteen. See ya!"

She leaves too quickly for me to tell her that I have to use all my vacation time every morning just to be able to attend the class. I won't have enough time this year for any real vacation. Or study sessions. Or a life.

DAY OF EMPLOYMENT: 364

8:41 AM

❀ LAUNDRY: Sorted. Categorized. Pre-treated.
❋ BASICALLY: Everything but actually washed.
❀ KITCHEN: Suffers from an appalling lack of donut.

POUT. I AM HENCEFORTH REIMAGINING THE WORD as more than a mere verb and noun. It denotes my entire state of being at this moment. My outlook.

It's a good thing today is Saturday. I've expended the bulk of my waking moments foraging for the day-old goods that are the greatest perk of being Clara's roommate.

Erm, I mean, apart from her being my oldest and dearest friend. My sister from another Mister. My Sole Sister — highest of honors between us Heel Hoors. Yikes. Must sort priorities.

But seriously: Homer has a point. Donuts equal yum.

"Clara, are you trying to torture me? Quash my will to live?" Cabinet doors bang. I rummage and search to no avail. Not a single cream puff to be had. Not even a stale apple spice cake donut to soak in my black gold. I mean coffee.

Clara is missing.

I will earmark a few minutes later in the day today to rationalize why I noticed that fact after the donuts. About forty minutes after. And a hunt that would've located D.B. Cooper if he had the misfortune to smell of cruller.

She's always home long before now. Her workday starts around 2:00 a.m. weekdays and as early as midnight for the extra heavy Saturday sales.

That Time to Make the Donuts commercial guy was a fairly accurate portrayal of Clara's nocturnal adventures. The more successful her entrepreneurial efforts, the more zombie-esque she has become. Which is not exactly an insult in her mind, either. One of the eccentric things that endears her to me is an inexplicable affection for the extraordinarily terrible film *I Walked with a Zombie*. Which, I must admit begrudgingly, may have grown on me over the years of coerced viewings.

There are days I half expect to find a check from the Sadist Sleep Study Institute in the mail. Compensation to us both for being participants in a long-term deprivation experiment we are both far too exhausted to remember signing up for.

Clara's text tone sounds out. Her shop is slammed, and the help went home sick.

No need to ask.

My successful lobbying at work helped nudge her catering bid to victory. Even fully staffed it was shaping up to be a huge production day for her. In under three minutes, I tie my hair up, throw on blue jeans, a white T-shirt, and Keds, and back the car down the drive.

I better at least score beaucoup donut holes for this.

10:16 AM

❊ HERE: Flour.

❊ THERE: Flour.

❊ AND EVERYWHERE: Flour.

"HOW'S IT GOING BACK THERE?" Clara peeks into the prep room.

I'm up on a pallet, working at the cutting bench, giant mixing bowl on an old storage drum that sits waist high. Beside me, several metal racks await donuts to be cut from Clara's secret recipe dough.

She guards it like none other. It's all very Super Secret Squirrel. Fort Knox could take tips. Colonel Sanders would tell her to relax.

"You tell me." I finish another roll through the dough with the cutter. She watches me pop the centers out of donut rings two at a time and place them onto a proof box screen.

I touch the one in the lowermost right corner. "Dibs."

"Looks like you've got it under control. Reminds me of ye olde good ol' days when you used to help out at my mom's store."

"Just like riding a penny-farthing." I poke out two more holes in her direction for emphasis.

Clara runs back up to man the counter. Display case is all but barren. Neck deep in customers.

"What time exactly does the demand for donuts taper off?" I call up to her. Desperation is evident in my tone. Though tonight's catering goods are mostly complete, we still have to do the finishing flourishes and prep for transport.

She smiles crookedly over her shoulder at me.

I have flour in places where flour ought not be. Where people typically only complain about having sand in.

Flour has gotten farther than anyone I've dated in recent memory.

Flour needs to buy me a dozen long stemmed homophones.

1:35 PM

Clara calls me to the front counter because she says she needs me to sack orders.

Clara: Is full of shit.

Canon is here.

I regret telling her his name.

He towers over Clara. Peers over her shoulder, inspecting the individually wrapped, ornate cookies she spent the past two days making. I presume he is verifying the party order.

I'd like to verify his parts are in working order.

He's wearing slacks and canvas brogues, long sleeve white shirt. Biceps strain the fabric slightly. Hair styled the same is if he were ready to take the podium and address a shareholders' meeting.

Coming in person is hands-on, in the extreme. Surely this could be delegated. Well, if said delegee stayed employed long enough, anyway.

"Emma." Clara waves me over. "Please finish up with Mr. Canon, would you?"

I slide in. He looks over and draws back fractionally.

This is when it occurs to me that I am coated in a layer of flour thick enough to be easily mistaken for a geisha.

His head shakes in the negative. "No need. Everything appears to be in order. Good day." He's gone before the white, powdery dust cloud settles.

"Ooo la la papa ooo mawh mawh, Emma," Clara teases. "You can sure pick 'em. He is gorgeous. And, oh so very proper," she says, puffing her chest up and tucking her chin in, "and stodgy." She marches mechanically. Drops her voice low. "Very good job indeed, I dare say. Indubitably. Say, could you be a brilliant chap and help me to extract this board from betwixt my bum cheeks?"

2:00 PM

❧ BAKERY: Closed.

❧ ARMS: Sore.

❧ SHOWER: Ineffective.

❧ ALSO: Superfluous.

WHAT, PRECISELY, IS THE POINT of bakers showering off with vanilla and warm sugar scented body wash?

I collapse back sideways onto my bed, hair wet and hanging over the edge.

3:40 PM

"EMMA," CLARA TRILLS FROM MY DOORWAY. "Let's Beau Brummell the hell out of you."

I don't bother to lift my head. "It doesn't even start for over three hours."

"Listen. This fixation of yours with the aloof man on your floor just isn't like my Emma. What are those annoying words you're always saying you do at work? Be proactive. Facilitate. Solution focused. What else?"

This gets a partial sit-up. "Clara, I am putting it behind me, because, as you well know, that man pays me no heed. And furthermore, I'm probably lucky for it as he is the hugest of jerks. This situation doesn't feel good, and as a rule, things that cause pain should be avoided."

Coincidentally, that also is my outlook on running. I think it's a healthy outlook. Irony is chock-full of fiber.

Clara shakes her head and smiles disbelievingly. "You? Avoid a challenge? I cannot believe such a thing." She tames an errant curl with the hot iron. "Emma Baker. I have known you this side of forever and have never once seen you back down from a challenge."

"I am not going to talk to him, Clara. Exactly what have you gotten in your head that I'm going to do? Saunter right up to Canon and strike up a conversation? Dazzle him with witty banter? My rapier wit? Feign insight into world politics or whatever it is that might actually appeal to him?" My rant steams on. "Anything I have to say to him is magnificently inappropriate, at best. Like 'Hey, now that you have a few beers in you, are you loosened up enough to speak with one of us plebes?' or 'Greetings, Mr. Canon, how lovely to finally meet the owner of my favorite butt cheeks.' Or...or...or..." I stumble over a few words, sounding more upset than I feel. "'Are your beer goggles thick enough to make me sexy?'"

"You finished?" she asks, drumming her fingers against the door-frame.

Squinting, I dare to ask, "Your point being?"

"Just walk up to him and say whatever comes naturally. Whatever you say will be either brilliant or unnecessary because you are smart and beautiful, so you don't exactly need a killer pick-up line. An annual office party is the ultimate place for people to cross corporate barriers. We're talking drunken grope sessions under the receptionist's desk. Copy room fornication." She whisks a set of hot rollers out from behind her back. "Let's make some regrets!"

I flop back on the bed.

5:23 PM

ONE MIGHT THINK THAT HAVING several hours to get ready for a party, even a rather dressy one, might be plenty. One might also think that a person such as myself who has managed to get up every day and leave the house fully and appropriately attired for multiple decades could be entrusted to accomplish the task of achieving said state of being clothed.

Clara: Not amongst the collective "one."

"I happen to think I dress quite nicely, as well as on trend, thank you very much." I slide out of the third outfit I've nixed.

She holds up a women's white tuxedo. Intended to be worn shirtless.

I can't say no fast enough.

"Yes, of course you do. That's not even in question. I would never borrow your stuff if you looked passé. And you know perfectly well that's not my point, so stop your fidgeting." She plops a set of false eyelashes down on the vanity. "But if your normal gorgeousness isn't cutting it, crank it up to eleven."

I look at the lashes. They look back at me.

"I will dress to the nines, but it will be for *me.* I used to love the holidays, and I used to take the time to make them special. So this year I will decorate me." I half-laugh, unwinding a roller. "Say, do you still have those silicone bust extenders?"

Clara squawks, "You wanna borrow my chicken cutlets?"

I wince at her accurate description. "The very same."

7:26 PM

❄ Official Party Start Time: 7:30.

There is nothing fashionable about being late.

Crimson satin dress so shiny and bright red that dalmatians may try to ride around on top of me.

Sparkling shoes strapped on. Dark curls cascading over my shoulders and down my back. That shadow trick with pearlescent powder finally worked.

I may even keep from ripping these false lashes off.

Not likely. But still. The possibility exists for the first time in the history of ever.

"Well, helloooo, nurse." Bert shakes his wrist like he has handled a hot spud.

I smile and give a tiny curtsy for good measure.

Off to the bar. Belly up.

Rebecca is already here, resting her elbows on the bar. Shoulders hunched slightly. The constant upheaval at work may be getting to her. Overturned shot glasses line up single file in front of her like good little soldiers.

Plus, she runs the committee that puts this soiree together every year. I'm sure it's a thankless task. Nobody really wants to come to these things or buy presents for coworkers instead of having more money for loved ones.

I stepped in many an afternoon to run interference, keeping all the people who had "the perfect idea" for everything from music to theme to food. She would have gotten nothing done if she'd listened to each individual pitch. I sorted through the onslaught, separated wheat from chaff so to speak, and prioritized the best according to cost.

This year, Rebecca instituted a White Elephant gift exchange, that passive-aggressive method of conveying just how little the people you see more often than family mean to you via the splendor of craptastic gifting.

She also set the fun additional requirement that we all wear, or in some other manner utilize, our gifts at work on at least one day prior to New Year's Day.

I drew Bert. I shall bestow upon him a ninety-percent-off-the-clearance-price Team Jacob shirt and a defunct Borders Book Store gift card with a one dollar and seventy-eight cent balance. Adoringly gift wrapped in junk mail. Bow crafted from plastic grocery bags.

Reduce. Reuse. Recycle.

Regret.

Regret bagging on my shoes, Bert.

After an exchange of a few pleasantries (read: gossip) with Rebecca, I head to the bathroom to readjust my bra and all the things that currently threaten to no longer dwell within.

7:45 PM

♣ VICTORIA: Spilling all my Secrets.

❀ HOLIDAY PARTY: Secular.

THE EARLY SOJOURN TO THE BATHROOM was perfectly timed to miss our comptroller's announcement that our company is in distress and there would be minimal bonuses this year. Most staff will get spiral sliced hams.

Oh, joy to the world.

Way to set a festive mood there, Jeremiah Bullfrog.

Rebecca and Madeline fill me in. It's not entirely dire. There is a huge merger deal in the works.

If the contract comes together, not only will it save the company and our collective livelihoods but create a few new production jobs as well.

Mr. Personality himself, Canon, will be devoting all his time between now and Christmas to sewing it up. The man of the hour has not yet darkened the door this evening.

His involvement sets me at ease as well as most other folks who can see how effective he is at his job. It should also come as a huge relief to the residents of Whoville since he will be too preoccupied this year to steal their Christmas. Enjoy your roast beast in peace, Cindy Lou.

8:30 PM

❧ WHITE ELEPHANTS: Exchanged.

❧ NOT BEING DISCUSSED: Other pachyderm in the room.

❧ BERT: Team Edward.

❧ CANON: Still not here.

I WISH I DIDN'T FIND MYSELF watching for him every few minutes.

So let us properly assess this situation: I am trussed up like a Thanksgiving turkey and just about as relevant at this moment, surrounded by a drunken crowd of people who may or may not even know my name despite having gone to work in the same building with me for upward of fifty-two weeks.

I have relied upon the guidance of a friend, who is well-intentioned but flaky enough to think everything from cup-size to prepositions are interchangeable, and who thinks my rather illicit designs on a man who has never deigned to look directly at me is not only *not* a cause for psychological counseling, but rather a call to arms.

Received a pair of ninety-nine-cent-store Crocs and a back scratcher in the shape of a brown nose. So I have that going for me. My life is complete.

They were from a person in human resources who I don't think I have ever laid eyes on before. Touché.

I wish I had kept the same frame of mind all night tonight that I had while getting dressed. To come out and have fun with my friends and enjoy myself, not be concerned with some a-hole who would not cross the road to spit on me or my chicken cutlets.

This is ridiculous.

I am ridiculous.

9:15 PM

HE'S HERE.

Deepest midnight blue suit.

I want to get this accomplished and behind me.

I want to squeeze his behind. Whichever. I'm flexible.

It comes in handy.

He mills around by the large red and white poinsettia arrangement doubling as a present depository.

I inhale. Move into position.

I schedule a much needed self rebuke at eleven.

9:21 PM

❀ ME: By the poinsettias, being generally creepy.

A PARADE OF FEELINGS MARCH through my mind. Dozens of them. So many that I almost expect to spot Robert Preston high-stepping it through here, singing about trombones.

Canon is alone. Solo.

I circle around, a lion to his gazelle. He sips from a highball. Stops. Straightens. Ears perk.

I move closer. Closer.

Into his personal space.

He shifts on one leg. Turns, angles away.

I clear my throat. The glass stops short of his lips. He straightens impossibly more. I catch a whiff of scent I can't label but need to find and douse my pillowcase in.

He turns to me, one eyebrow lifted infinitesimally.

Here's where I spot a fatal flaw in my design. I have walked up to him. I have his attention…and what do I do with it?

Say hello? Or shake his hand? Or rip the buttons off his shirt and commence with defiling the flower arrangement?

This is my moment.

The world around us goes on spinning. It's just Canon and me in the doorway. He looks amazing. (And, I must admit, I look darn decent myself.) He smells amazing. He is amazing…ly annoyed-looking.

So yippee-ki-yay and *carpe diem*, as Clara said while zipping the back of my dress earlier.

Say something that opens up the discussion I have wanted to have for a year. Be eloquent. Be confident. Be a goddess.

"Hi."

You know those funny moments in movies where things get all uncomfortable and the editors splice in the sound of crickets in the background? Yeah, those are so not funny when they really happen. And this is merely the DJ playing crickets of the "Buddy Holly and the" variety.

Canon pivots back away, handing me his empty glass in the process.

"Johnnie Walker. Neat."

Flames. Flames out the side of my head.

Not only do I not ring any bells with him after twelve months of working together, apparently, my makeover result is that I now pass for waitstaff at this restaurant.

Rather than the day, I seize any reason to hightail it out of there before I'm motivated to stomp my heel directly onto his big toe.

I walk his glass to the bar.

Place his order, specifying Blue Label because I know that's his preference. Even though I'd love to see his face if he were delivered an umbrella drink.

Point out the jackhole to whom it should be delivered.

This will not do. This simply will not do.

10:01 PM

❧ DJ: Karaoke: "I Will Survive."

❧ DANCE FLOOR: Barren.

❧ BAR: Drained.

I SPOT HIM ACROSS THE WAY, being chatted up by the vice presidents of sales and marketing.

Canon appears to barely stifle a yawn. He isn't paying attention to the VPs in the slightest.

Turnabout is fair play; the VPs' lines of sight pass over Canon and fixate on the area immediately to the left of him.

To his date.

She is made from the same mold as the other two dates I have witnessed, the ladies who have also rested their hand in the crook of his arm.

Flawless up-do. Ivory column dress. Diamond drop pendant of the Tiffany, not QVC, variety. Makeup job so perfect she looks as though she isn't wearing any at all. A single beauty mark to highlight, rather than mar, faultless, olive skin.

Teeth so white they could potentially blind oncoming traffic.

My lip snarls up like I'm about to belt out "Rebel Yell."

If pride cometh before a fall, then I am slip sliding away. I pride myself on being observant, so how did I not take into account how very different "his type" is than what I am?

All the extra effort we put into my appearance this evening has moved me even further away from the real bull's-eye.

Well, Pooh.

And Tigger, too. I am trashy, flashy, brashy, splashy. And oh so bum bum bummed.

This is not a one-size-fits-all kind of man. Casting a wide net is not the solution.

A precision strike is needed. Pinpoint accuracy.

As I speed home, my eyelashes take flight out the car window.

DAY OF EMPLOYMENT: 365

11:00 AM

SUNDAY.

    Couch.

    Fuzzy blanket.

    Remote.

    Today is the one year anniversary of my first day at work.

    Final paper was submitted two days early. I'm good, but I am not usually that good.

    As it is a Sunday, I mark the occasion with a John Hughes movie marathon and eat directly from a jar of Talenti raspberry sorbet until my hand loses all feeling.

    When feeling is regained, I dig into the vanilla bean.

5:02 PM

HE DIDN'T NOTICE.

    One whole year.

    Not even a blip on his radar.

    Not that I find this shocking.

    Not in the least.

    I have been utterly invisible since I started. I was not really expecting any acknowledgment of my anniversary.

I have now officially crossed that threshold from new hire to old hand with little fanfare. By "little" I mean none. I won't even stand out in the crowd as a fresh face now.

So I'm changing this. I'm changing me.

His radar will no longer be blipless.

Tomorrow I start over. I don't expect him to notice me right away. It is a process. I have a plan.

DAY OF EMPLOYMENT: 366

6:00 AM

❀ AWAKE: Already.

❀ THUS FAR: Plan sucks.

❀ CLOTHES: Laid out night before.

❀ LUNCH: Salad. Yay.

I EAT SALADS ALL THE TIME; however, I maintain they are not truly food. They are food's food.

My feet hit the cold, hardwood floor and I fight the urge to creep back under my duvet. Sleep is my friend.

Not as faithful a friend as cellulite. It is so loyal. Always there.

The treadmill groans right along with me as it whirls to life. It probably thinks I have sold it to someone who will actually utilize it. Maybe it will miss its life as my coatrack.

It's slow going. I'm walking on an incline. Walking, not running.

It's slow going, but that is okay. It's a process. I have a plan.

7:45 AM

I HAVE NOW LOST AN ENTIRE HOUR of my life to exercise and a shower. Time better not be the only thing I have lost.

I'm one of the first to arrive at work.

He walks to his office.

He's wearing the blue suit.

He looks around behind him before he enters. Midway, his gaze floats across me as if I'm not even there.

Invisible.

No blip.

2:18 PM

✿ PA: Old Mother Hubbard.

✿ POT WON: $96 and change.

REBECCA'S STRATEGY to place a septuagenarian in the hot seat fizzled out.

I can't really fault Canon for this one. She had great phone skills, but was technologically challenged. Got cursor and mouse confused. Kept placing the mouse in direct contact with the screen, right on top of the item she needed to click on.

Maybe you had to be there.

Anyway, she's cleaning out her cupboards and headed back to the Blue Hair Group in time for *Wheel*.

DAY OF EMPLOYMENT: 367

6:00 AM

✿ AWAKE: Again.

✤ PLAN: It still sucks.

✤ LUNCH: Salad. Again.

✿ HAIR: Flat-ironed into submission.

✤ CLOTHES: Tan pencil skirt, ivory blouse, flesh-toned stockings, brand-spanking-new taupe suede pumps courtesy of yesterday's winning bet.

LAUNCHING THE NEXT PHASE of the plan, I have shoved my teals, pinks, lavenders, bright blues, and all other colors in the Roy G. Biv spectrum to the back of the closet. Even indigo. I'm considering that a unique blue.

I'm a big blender full of subdued. So beige Helen Hunt would be envious. Total corporate drone, all business.

Plan forecast: Nothing but black, navy, and beige, with scattered gray and a slim chance of red.

7:30 AM

OUT THE DOOR.

The new shoes feel like walking on a big ol' poofy cloud of air... until about three-quarters of the way to my car when my toes go numb. *Too late to turn back now.* I sigh and look mournfully down at them. Too bad; I do like the way they make my calves look. I make a mental note to see if I can take them back tonight.

I scratch through the note just as quickly. These shoes look like hers. Example B.

I have seen Alaric Canon with two women: Company picnic. Christmas party.

Example B (name unknown) wore similar shoes to last year's party. No hair out of place. Everything about her was subdued. Colors. Manners. Refined.

Company Picnic Chick was so similar. She wore capris and a blouse, but somehow they looked like a power suit. Immaculate hair, unaffected by humidity. Grace personified.

True to form, this year's Holiday-Party Model was no exception. Made from the same seamless mold and polished to perfection.

My plan might've benefited from a stint at finishing school.

I picture myself balancing books on my head as I slip into the car.

Incoming text: My office ASAP — Rebecca

Weird.

I know this is the sort of thing that sends others into a tizzy. Rebecca might come off like a bitch, but she's really just assertive. Her praise is usually in the form of silence. I know she values me, and she knows I do my job, do it right, and never question anything. The only time I have ever feared her was when I went to her about starting night classes. But she appreciated my full disclosure. She seems to trust me even more since then. She knows this is not my forever.

In no time, I sit in Rebecca's office and listen, dumfounded, to her explain what's happened and what she wants me to do.

"I think there has been some sort of mistake."

"Your reaction doesn't surprise me," Rebecca says, as she leans over her desk and straightens an already straight stack of files.

Perpendicular angles everywhere. Without sparing an upward glance, she continues, "Try to see the genius in it. This is the plan. Adjust...and don't embarrass this department. Here's his itinerary for the week." She hands a stack of papers to me, which I nearly drop when I see the look she has leveled at me. She's terrified.

Rebecca.

Terrified.

I may soil myself.

"This department has a lot riding on you. And by this department, I mean me." She clears her throat and manages to assume something close to her normal, chilly demeanor. The cracks in the ice are still there.

"Emma, you've been here long enough to know how this shakes out. No one expects you, or anyone, to last long. Every Canon PA is really a temp position. Help him prep for the trip and make it until he leaves and I'll give you a raise when you get back here. Make it a month and you'll come back to this department with a promotion."

I want to say something about her lack of confidence in me, but I know it's moot. No one does last as his assistant for long, and I should know. Watching the unbroken string of broken assistants leave his employ has been my hobby for a solid year.

They always screw up. Wrong coffee. Wrong outfit. Right outfit, wrong day. Misdirected memos. Hygienically challenged. Wheat bread instead of oat. Flirting. Tardy. Speaking. Not speaking. Offensive perfume. Desperately in need of perfume. Being in the bathroom at just the wrong moment.

March A had tapped her fake nails on the desk.

March B was personable and professional. Misplaced trust in spell-check had her gone in two weeks.

Early April shut his phone off at night.

After the infamous Indianapolis Incident, during which three PAs had revolving-doored their way to the unemployment line in under a week, a secret back-up assistant had been at-the-ready ever since.

"What about the back-up? Why me?"

"She's on bed rest as of Monday. High risk pregnancy. Emma, I need a pro in there. We simply cannot afford any mistakes, and Canon needs to be able to focus. You have proven communication skills, a degree in writing, an impeccable performance record, a professional demeanor, and frankly, your obsession with him makes you far and away the best-prepared for the job."

"Rebecca!" My knees give, and I sit down gracelessly. "I'm not obsessed. If anything, it's a gambling problem."

I clasp my hands to hide the shaking. *How obvious have I been?*

She laughs softly then says things that make me glad I'm already sitting down. "Emma, I consider you a friend, and more importantly, a colleague. A trusted colleague. I don't know if you realize, but I'd have you as my right hand if you were planning on working here longer. But you're too good for that job. Hell, you're definitely too good for a personal assistant position…and that is precisely why I am entrusting you with it. You see everything. You know when to speak up and when to keep your mouth shut." She hands me the itinerary that seems to have slipped out of my hand and drifted down to the floor.

Kneeling in front of me, in her closed office, Rebecca looks up at me. I can't help but notice where she has placed herself. "Emma, please. So much is riding on this deal."

"Fine," I hear myself say.

She closes both of her hands over mine and squeezes warmly, a shake of sorts. She opens her mouth to say something just as the sound of her door opening behind me stops her.

"I'm still waiting on that report." Canon's voice slides along the walls of the room. I feel it wrap around my spine. Rebecca's eyes go wide, but she covers quickly and stands. Wordlessly, she grabs a file from her desk and hands it over my shoulder to where I assume he takes it from her. A pause. Rebecca narrows her eyes.

The door shuts.

A gust of air leaves my lungs. I didn't realize I'd forgotten to breathe.

This does not bode well. Surely oxygen will play an important part in performing my new job satisfactorily.

She manages to wipe the confused look from her face and sits on the edge of her desk. "Go gather up what you need at your new desk and meet me back here in twenty minutes. I will officially introduce you to Mr. Canon then."

8:20 AM

- Hair: Pinned back.
- Buttons: Top only undone.
- Bladder: Empty.
- Shoes: Killing feet slowly.

THIS WAS NOT MY PLAN. I'm not under the radar at all now. The plan has changed from generating a blip to being directly in his sights.

"Ready?" Rebecca asks as we approach Canon's door.

"No." I wanna hurl.

She laughs and knocks once.

"Come in." His deep voice pierces the door. The last of the free air fills my lungs.

Rebecca walks ahead into his office as if a 2×4 is strapped to her spine. I stay behind her, plotting how to use her as a human shield.

"Mr. Canon, this is Ms. Baker." She steps to the side and exposes me. "Your new assistant."

He's standing at the window, his back to us. Without turning, he sighs loudly and gestures toward a chair.

I sit and hear the door click; Rebecca has already abandoned me. Coward.

"Tell me." He continues to look out the wall of windows. His arms are crossed and long fingers drum his sleeve.

I wait for a moment. I wait for him to clarify. His jacket is draped over his riveted-leather desk chair. His pants are light gray, and I force myself not to focus on any portion of them. The slope of his broad shoulders is also not a safe focal point. Light from the window catches golden strands in his hair; that is off-limits too. I don't know where to look.

I become acutely aware of the silence.

"Pardon me?" I really feel at a loss, as if I have walked into a conversation midstream.

He huffs and continues to stare out the window. "Tell me everything. The who, what, when, where, why, how. Who you are. What you think this job entails. When you think your workday ends. Why you took this position. How long you think you will last."

My throat is a desert. I've already exhausted his patience. It never occurred to me that he would ask me anything about me. I'm an expert on him, not on myself.

I launch into a dissertation on my education and credentials. Masters in English. Intern and job experience.

Scholarships. I omit any mention of my current law school scholarship or enrollment; I doubt he's the type to be receptive to divided priorities. I make sure all this takes no longer than thirty seconds. I skip right over anything that relates to why I think I can do this job—I don't think I can pull off confidence.

"The job expectation is that I make you available to perform your job at optimum level. I need to learn and anticipate your needs in order to ensure this. Any distraction or delay has a negative impact. My workday began when I walked into this room, and it will end when I leave your employ." I keep talking, but I notice a shift in his demeanor. His fingers still. A few moments later, he moves to his desk chair. I know I'm in. Maybe, just maybe, I've even impressed him.

Words continue to spill from my mouth. I explain that I've been with the company for a year. I'm flexible and a good observer. Performance stats.

"Finally, Mr. Canon, I understand there's a critical contract on the line, and there is no time to prep a new employee. I bring to the table a solid understanding of this company and am committed to its success."

My speech has taken under two minutes. Brevity. I feel good about it. My face is hot, but I'm still breathing.

The win column gets a tick.

"Ms. Baker, I have no illusions about my reputation. That being said, I consider myself fair. I do not expect miracles, but I will not tolerate mistakes." He leans back in his chair and levels his gaze at me. His eyes are a gray-green. If he ever blinks, I miss it. I'm caught in their pull.

"It is my understanding that there is a CYA file on me. It would be in your best interests to familiarize yourself with it."

My eyes are probably bugging out. *He knows about the file?*

He must misinterpret my surprise for bewilderment and explains further. "Cover Your Ass. A cheat sheet," he seethes. Clearly, he thinks I'm playing dumb.

"The COYA file?" The words are out of my mouth before I can think better of it.

One corner of his mouth turns up. It might be a burgeoning smile. It might be irritation.

He gives me a look that tells me he wants an explanation. I want to show him I get non-verbal communication. I want to show him I'm honest. I want to show him my matching bra and panty set. I sure as hell do not want to tell him what COYA stands for.

There is no escape.

"Canon Owns Your Ass."

He blinks. Finally.

I hasten to add, "I feel it is important to point out that I did not name the file, sir."

Without looking away, he writes on a paper and walks around his desk to hand it to me. "My number. Call me so I have your cell." He pauses for a moment, his face unreadable. This is unsettling. I thought I knew him better than this. His gaze falls to my shoes. I can't understand why as they are completely nondescript. "Check the calendar and itinerary. Leave word in human resources about the trip departure date and phone extension change. IT will need to reroute your calls. I take lunch when and only when it does not impede my job. You will follow suit. You take lunch when I do, for as long as I do." I know I look surprised, and it doesn't get past him. "This does not mean, however, that you and I have lunch together.

"Emma, I'm aware that this is all short notice. You'll need to make arrangements for the upcoming trip. I will handle the bulk of my own this time. Get yourself ready and familiarize yourself with the material. An ill-prepared assistant will be a distraction and an embarrassment to me."

A flick of his wrist dismisses me. Immediately before I open the door, I hear his voice behind me.

"I will not let you be either."

12:00 PM

❀ FILES: Downloaded.

❀ CALENDAR: Set.

❀ DESK: Conspicuously free of my personal belongings.

❀ BERT: Sufficiently guilt-tripped for getting spotted slipping a bet to Rebecca.

❀ SHOES: Pooled with the blood of my innocent toes.

"I'M OFF, MADELINE. See you later, right?"

She pats my back reassuringly. "Of course! I'll be by with every-thing you asked to borrow. Call if you think of anything else."

I do my best to smile at her but can't help feeling like I'm off to meet the noose.

One last item of business before I head out remains incomplete. I have procrastinated over calling him. Now I can call him and check in before I leave without facing him again. This is pointless craziness because I will be neck-deep in Alaric Canon for the next seven days. Just one less encounter.

I program the digits into my phone then shred the paper so no one can stumble across his private number.

He answers on the second ring. "Canon."

"Hello, Mr. Canon. This is Ms. Baker. You said to call."

"Yes."

Cue awkward pause.

"Let us hope you endeavor to perform future tasks more promptly."

Oh…he wanted my number right away? Even when I was still in the office? Okay. Noted. Do everything right away whether it makes sense to me or not.

"If there is nothing else, Mr. Canon…"

The line goes silent. Barely a click. He's probably already reading an assortment of potential PA applications.

DAY OF EMPLOYMENT: 368

4:00 AM

IT IS FOUR O'CLOCK ON THE DIME.

Or, more appropriately, the penny.

Because, while I had fervently wished to avoid it, it has happened.

The nightmares are back. My private monster sits at the foot of my bed. Addressing me.

Lecturing me. Giving me a speech.

Getting his two cents in.

7:30 AM

✽ EARLY: Happens so frequently now that it feels like on time.

✽ OUTFIT: Bland mixture of tans.

I'M NOT EVEN CERTAIN it's buttoned straight at this point. I am thoroughly and utterly exhausted.

Perhaps Canon will take my first day as his assistant to break the shrink-wrap on his sick days.

One can dream.

On a good, fully rested day, I would have my work cut out for me just trying to stay upright and form coherent sentences around him.

He appears as if from thin air. I never heard a door open or the elevator ding.

Reports in one hand. Phone in the other.

His leaves his office door ajar. Unspoken expectation that I enter.

Once inside, I await instruction. My feet begin to shuffle from one side to the other, and I continue to inspect the wall. He still moves around behind me.

I tell myself to stare at the wall. Stare at the wall. The wall does not have piercing eyes, or an unholy, defined jawline, or six creases—four long and two short—that form in its bottom lip when it gets dry. The wall is plain. The wall is your friend.

"I will be out most of the day tying up loose ends before my trip." He never looks up as he speaks. "Should it prove too difficult to manage a few calls, you have my number." With that, he brushes past me.

Then a moment of clarity. Sanity sets in.

Focus on his personality.

Oh, yeah. Pass me the Irish Spring. It's like a cold shower.

5:01 PM

❀ OUT: Clocked. Patience.

❀ SHOULD BE OUT: Me—the door.

I SURVEY THE BATTLEFIELD, er, office as it empties. I have survived.

That wasn't so bad.

I have outlasted predictions. Beaten the odds. Madeline's number book has never seen such an upset.

Piece of cake.

Doubtless, tomorrow will be an even greater challenge. Canon and I might actually be inside the same building.

7:10 PM

❧ DINNER: Comfort food.

✤ CLARA: Treading softly.

"SO, HOW GOES THE DREAM JOB?"

Unfortunately, it's more like Clara is treading softly in steel-toe work boots, shattering eggshells everywhere.

I do not favor her with a reply.

"That good, huh?"

"He was out of the office all day."

Clara plates up our salmon in Veri Veri Teriyaki sauce. "That sounds ideal. So why the frowny face?"

"If you think I'm acting sullen because he wasn't around, you are wrong. I just feel a bit disjointed from the change and, well...no one would come near me today."

She looks at me and rolls her hand as if asking me to elaborate.

"I was my own private leper colony today. No one came by except Rebecca. A couple of distant waves from Madeline."

It's not a big deal, really. It just felt weird. I might need a day or two to adjust to life on death row.

DAY OF EMPLOYMENT: 369

7:10 AM

♣ Me: Low-rent Nancy Drew.

I ARRIVE A BIT EARLIER TODAY. Want to solve the Mystery of the Magically Appearing Boss.

Can't catch a break or a clue. He is already here in full business mode. Fluorescent bulbs shine from his office out across the darkened cubicles. He may never actually leave.

Maybe his office en suite is a pod chamber in disguise.

8:00 AM

UPON MY RETURN TO MY DESK, I find a written to-do list.

Canon is milling about in his office.

I dive in.

Item number one: Hand collate a twenty-page handout a previous assistant failed to copy correctly.

What a flagrant waste of wages. It would be far more efficient to have me recopy the set and cut the others down for scrap paper.

I knock on his door. Silence.

I knock again. He initiates a phone call.

Confident in my assessment of the situation, I set off for the copy room. Of course, all the paper trays are empty. When I open the cabinet for more, I am met with a bright orange Post-it note. It reads: Ms. Baker, Do NOT make new copies.

I can't even…

Shaping up to be my least productive day. Ever.

10:35 AM

❀ LOCATION: Conference room B.

UP TO MY GIZZARD IN SORTED STACKS of corporate propaganda. Reams and reams of it. The Lorax would be impressed with our tree carnage.

It now makes sense to me that it was both a) important not to waste this much paper by reprinting, and b) a mistake by a former personal assistant worthy of at least reprimand, if not quite deserving of dismissal.

Make personal note to propose we use a short-run printing house to produce similar future projects.

"So this is the tower that Beast has been keeping you toiling away in?" Madeline teases, entering the room.

I greet her with a withering look. "It's not so bad, actually," I say and imagine what it will be like to have to spend eight hours a day working closer to Canon, in the scorched earth outside his office. "It could be much, much worse."

She starts to set down a fresh cup of coffee and a piece of her homemade banana bread near a few sorted paper stacks. I suck up half the air in the room as I imagine coffee stains ruining the project to which I have dedicated my entire day thus far.

"I'll just put this down over here," she says, placing it on a separate table. "I thought you could probably use a pick-me-up, and I wasn't sure Mr. Canon allows breaks. I wouldn't want to see what would happen to you if you incurred that man's wrath."

Wrath of the Tight End. I'd watch that movie. I might even buy the DVD. It couldn't be any worse than the remakes.

I know I'm legally entitled to a break, but I didn't take one. Not sure why. But I sincerely appreciate Madeline's thoughtfulness. She's like a USO pilot, dropping a care package behind enemy lines.

4:10 PM

❧ MINDLESS TASKS: Causing me to lose mine.

I'M IN THE BASEMENT, hunting for the market trials we did on preteen pseudo-cosmetics years ago.

It's a wild goose hunt, and I'm dangerously close to cooking Canon's.

I get the distinct impression that Canon is avoiding me.

Why, I do not know. Maybe he wants to avoid the hassle of hiring yet another PA before his upcoming trip. Never being near me definitely limits the opportunities to irritate him.

I have had far too much time to myself down here. Like, life-evaluating time.

I feel like my life is on hold, in limbo. Do this. Accomplish that. Work. School. Rent.

Clara says I don't leave time for love. I won't argue. But it's not accurate.

I don't exhaust time on relationships or people who aren't worth what little time I have.

Which sounds bitchy, now that I put it in so many words. It's probably more…cautious. I want a love like my grandparents had. Grandpa saw my grandma on the first day she started at his school and said, "That's my girl." They never parted until their dying days. An inexplicable aura of caring.

A hollow clunk from the basement door startles me, and I drop a file. Papers scatter in two hundred directions. I begin playing fifty-two pick up. When I'm a few papers away from done, I can see a person's shadow move against the far wall.

I stop short.

"Hello?" I force my voice out, quashing most traces of fear.

"Ms. Baker." Canon steps out from behind a rusty file cabinet. If he brushes against it, he's gonna need a tetanus booster. "You've been down here a long time. I wanted to make sure everything was okay."

Make sure everything is okay down here? Or that I am okay here?

Huh. That is…nice.

I don't know what to do with that.

He's standing to the side, apparently surveying the place. I can't see his face, just the outline of his frame. I note, appreciatively, that his voice has a calming effect. Which is good since he was skulking around down here like the Ghost of Christmas Party Blow Offs Past.

He's wearing the norm. Suit. Button shirt. Designer tie. It's how he's wearing them that stops me.

Let me make it through a week at this job. Oh, I won't last long, but I can make like a Young Gun and go down in a blaze of glory.

DAY OF EMPLOYMENT: *370*

9:22 AM

❊ OLD DESK: Makeshift Vegas.
❊ CANON: Add an "N" in the middle and launch him out of his own name.

HE HAS LEFT ME ANOTHER LIST.

Madeline has turned my old desk into a veritable gamblers' oasis. There are side bets on everything ranging from what I will screw up to get fired, to how long it will be before Canon deigns to interact with me.

Lists are a favorite tool of mine. I don't have anything against lists.

I am, however, beginning to resent being left a list of tasks a mentally compromised orangutan could complete with minimal difficulty.

He must think I am a grade-A dolt.

Nothing can get me righteously pissed off faster. Do not pass go. Do not collect your teeth from the floor.

Visit my old desk. Rest and recuperation in the old stomping ground.

Bert assaults his keyboard.

"How's your workweek going?" I ask him. "Anything new or exciting going on?"

"I work in a box. My weeks are all pretty much the same."

Fair enough.

12:19 PM

❀ LUNCH: Cold. Mine. His. Both.

❀ DEMEANOR: Icy.

I WAS BID TO GO AND FETCH HIS LUNCH. Which I did. I delivered it to an empty desk over twenty minutes ago. He did not bother to share his whereabouts with me. Even setting aside how impossible not knowing such an important detail cripples the ability to be an effective assistant, that makes the dropping of everything and dashing off to retrieve his hot food pointless.

Now, I am told to set it outside the conference room door.

I am not a labrador.

However, I am closer than ever to lifting a leg. I'd cheerfully whizz in his Cheerios.

5:00 PM

HE IS WITHOUT A DOUBT, bar none, the most infuriating man on the planet. If I didn't need this job so desperately, I would tell him where to stick it. I could draw a detailed, relief map of it. Describe it so well that a police artist's sketch artist's rendering could look like a sixty megapixel image.

How long have I worked for him? Three days? Three full days and not a single word spoken to my face. Not a syllable or a gesture or even a yawn. The most I get from him is a condescending look now and again, as he shreds another file.

Earlier this morning, just when I had begun to consider that he was perhaps stricken with acute onset laryngitis, I overheard Canon on a call, clicking his pen, and talking to any damned person but me.

And now, he is looking at me, staring at me in the corridor by the time clock, as if someone who looks like him has never seen a woman like me in a dress before. As if my clothes are not suitable. Well, hell. I ran out of dishwater-dull duds and had to resort to a short, black column dress.

I look pretty good. More than good, actually, but I'm not a teenager anymore. Caution: Contents may have shifted during flight.

No doubt he has his pick of women — young and old. All remarkably artificially enhanced, preternaturally preserved, toned bodies likely the product of countless Pilates sessions for which I'd have little time and even less inclination. That's the way, now, is not it? Strong, hard, and lean seeks same. Not that it matters. Not that I want him to want me. Not at all.

Ugh, stupid hormones.

Clock out. Eat. Sleep. Drink.

DAY OF EMPLOYMENT: 373

7:57 AM

❧ OUTFIT: Mennonites wear more exciting things.

❧ CLARA: Still unforgiven for her holiday party "help."

❧ CINNAMON ROLL: On my desk. From Canon.

❧ LOCATION: Canon's office.

I ARRIVE AT WORK AND AM USHERED into Canon's office by the man himself.

Feast or famine with this guy. Never see him. Now all up in my face.

"I will gone for several days," he begins, walking around to sit on the edge of his desk. "Please be seated."

I remain standing. Mostly because my knees have locked in shock.

His head tilts. "Very well." He coughs. "Access codes for my home as well as instructions for the items that need attending there in my absence are in a secure email I sent you this morning. Do you have any questions for me?"

This gets me. I sit down gracelessly.

Okay, I do not understand this disturbing, beautiful man.

I came in here fully intent on laying down the law about communicating with me.

I spread my notepad in my lap. Deep breaths. The thoughts I have collected on the subject are few. I acknowledge that I do not know about the nuts and bolts of the upcoming deal or about production operations. What I do have is the ability to make plans and research.

But none of the hassle of me working for him matters if he and I can't work together for the short term. I'd never been in a position to admit that someone else knows better than me at anything, but it is my belief that, in this, he does…and he's not giving me anything to work with.

I reach for the pen and notice him looking directly at me.

We make direct eye contact for what might be the first time.

I expect to find the same aloof judgment, like all the previous sideways glances he's thrown at me. I expect to feed the fire of anger that threatens to blaze. What I don't expect is to find him gauging me, a near light in his eyes.

Before I can process the moment, he's piled my lap with files.

"Mr. Canon," I say and watch him open up and peruse a file from his own stack. Under his white shirt, the tendons in his arm dance with each turn of a page. "Things need to change." I swallow hard. "Tomorrow, I'll be at your beck and call all morning, as has been the case since I started."

I cough softly, clearing a lump in my throat that has materialized and decidedly will not be contemplated. "I would appreciate it if you would speak with me rather than leave me a list. I am neither a handyman nor a husband; I do not respond well to honey-do lists. After lunch, we should sit down and go over — together — what I have found in their business records. If we don't do that soon, you will be gone on that trip and I will have gone blind reading their numbers for no good reason."

I straighten my skirt and notice that he is still sitting on the side of his desk. The file is closed. His look is unreadable.

Hot, but unreadable.

"Ms. Baker, you somehow feel you know better how I need to be assisted than I do myself?" he says flatly.

"To be frank, Mr. Canon, I'm the one with the history of being able to play well with others. Maybe it might be high time to try something new."

10:15 AM

♣ MERGER: In doubt.

REBECCA WHISPERS THAT THE BOARD is under the impression that the production company that's on the other side of our merger may not be on the level. At least, they may be hiding some numbers.

I look back over to my desk just in time to see Canon slip one of his famous lists onto it. He ducks back in his office.

Honestly, how did other assistants ever have the opportunity to upset him?

Sauron gave more face time than this guy.

11:25 AM

I OPEN A DESK DRAWER AND REALIZE everything I want to use will require a trip to the supply room. It's a major inconvenience to traipse all the way to BFE to get a fourth highlighter color. But I am not the fastidious fart who must have his items color coded just-so.

The rest of the day is spent downloading and combing through business records our potential partner emailed over at Canon's insistence.

He is serious about doubting them, but professional enough to mask it in his tone with them. I overhear him move his trip departure up.

It might not be easy to be around the man, but it is impossible not to respect him. Nothing gets past him. Focused like a falcon.

Gee, whatever will I do without his smiling face and cheerful disposition to brighten my workday?

DAY OF EMPLOYMENT: 374

3:15 PM

- LOCATION: Rebecca's office.
- REBECCA: Fast becoming my least favorite person.
- WHY: See below.

REBECCA IS AN IMMORTAL.

I know this because I have been giving her a look that can kill for the past three and a half minutes.

I move to cross my arms in front of me in an exaggerated display of my unexaggerated disgust.

My arms are already crossed. Because, on instinct, my stance is guarded. Protective.

I clear my throat. Try to dislodge the cotton that materialized there once Rebecca told me what she had up her tailored sleeve.

"Tell me, again, why exactly is it I need go on this business trip with him?"

Rebecca rests her chin on the back of her hand. "Because Mr. Canon will need to continue to go through their business records while on site there. He will be party to their board meeting and at least one international teleconference. Plus, if he concludes that a merger is still in our best interests, he will essentially be selling them on the idea."

I start to ask why that is, but stop myself. Of course. Our request for their business records this close to the line must throw up red flags.

If they aren't cooking the books, we have now insulted them by treating them suspiciously.

Judging by all those reports I printed, if there's any cooking going on, they have fire pit and spit roasted a whole library.

"What about my intersession class? I was going to use my saved up vacation days. I-I don't think I can miss classes for a week for this trip." I get the words out, but I can hear my voice begin to stammer.

"Emma, this deal he's setting up means well over a thousand jobs in this community. We really cannot afford to gamble." I feel a wave of guilt mix with my trepidation. Rebecca must sense it, too. She softens and places her hand on mine. "I have called your school. I hope you don't mind. As a part of an already economically depressed community that will be only be more so if our company downsizes or—" she sighs for effect "—if we completely shutter, they stand to benefit from this deal, too. They will video the lectures and email you URLs."

I know I must be gaping at her.

I do not want to go on a trip with him.

Absence may make the heart grow fonder, but proximity requires a change of panties.

4:59 PM

"THE CAR WILL PICK YOU UP AT FOUR," Canon says without salutation.

Four? As in 4:00 a.m.? Oh, holy sh…

"Four o'clock," I confirm, and the line clicks.

I hope he ended the call. I contemplate calling him back to check but decide against it. I would call back anyone else; it's in my nature. Mr. Alaric Canon would call back if he had been cut off.

But he would definitely be pissed if I interrupted him needlessly.

9:00 PM

❋ SKIN: Buffed.

❋ NAILS: Filed to nubs. Clear coat.

❋ CREDIT CARD: Dangerously close to limit.

❋ KITCHEN TABLE: Covered in supplies for every occasion.

❋ SUITCASES: Packed. Everything from Rebecca's best suit to my roommate's cocktail dresses.

❋ WARDROBE: Looks like I have robbed a stranger.

❋ FEET: Raw. Stupid shoes.

❋ ROOMMATE: Bouncing off walls.

"CLARA. CALM DOWN."

"Emma. Calm up."

"That doesn't even make sense."

Clara zips around the kitchen. "Here's a bag of meds and one for late night emergencies," she says, tossing bags in the suitcase with the other items.

"Eagle Scouts are less prepared." I roll my eyes at her. "Clara, I appreciate all of this, I really do."

She shrugs. "Are you going to eat the rest of that stir-fry?" She's rummaging in the refrigerator, tiny ass in the air.

"Nope," I say, "help yourself." Then, unbidden, melancholy hits.

This is not what I dreamed about at all. I wanted him to notice me. To just be kind. See a light in his eyes. Or a smile on his lips. A moment of friendliness or appreciation — or, just maybe, flirtation — from the consummate SOB.

It's a sick need. I get it. I know it.

I still wanted it.

And I feel that dream die.

I had a process. I had a plan.

DAY OF EMPLOYMENT: *375*

12:23 AM

STILL AWAKE.

Wide freaking awake.

If there are butterflies in my stomach keeping me awake, then it's not from delicate little flutters of nervousness. Their wings are like thunderclaps. These are rabid, fanged, snarling butterflies beating their way around under my ribs. These are the Mothra of butterflies.

3:00 AM

NOT AWAKE. MOST ASSUREDLY NOT AWAKE. No sleep would have been better. My God—so groggy.

The snooze button beckons me. Such temptation.

I want to snuggle down into my toasty pillow and to doze and dream of a time when Canon was still a pretty, shiny thing to admire from a shop window. When I was naïve enough to think the PAs who got fired immediately were the unlucky ones.

I get up. I don't give in.

3:58 AM

✽ LUGGAGE: One large, rolling suitcase.

✽ CARRY-ON CONTENTS: Travel documents for myself and one Alaric Glenn Canon. Motion-sickness meds, just in case. Gum. Mints. Purse. Laptop. Magazines and new book by favorite author of new boss. Miscellaneous.

✽ HAIR: Stick-straight, clipped back.

✽ CLOTHES: Gray pantsuit. Gray pumps. Gray everything.

✽ MOOD: Gray. Natch.

A BLACK E-CLASS PULLS UP, sloshing through the overnight moisture. It waits silently.

I heave the suitcase into the trunk. The empty trunk. *What the hell?*

The driver offers no immediate explanation. A fender bender on the highway slows traffic to a crawl for several minutes. He takes an exit off the route to the airport and appears to do some winding around in an impromptu route. The rocking motion threatens to lull me to sleep.

In a neighborhood so affluent all that can be seen are wrought iron gates and ten-foot hedgerows, the car glides to a stop outside one such gate. He punches in a code, and we meander up the winding lane. Canon is outside, suited in deep charcoal. Three-button. Some ridiculous, cool-tone paisley tie that only he could make look as imposing as hell. He walks to the car while punching the keys of his phone.

I note the driver actually deigns to put Canon's bags in the trunk.

Canon sits next to me in the seat now, never taking his eyes off his screen.

"When I give you a time to be ready, it is not an approximation."

My mouth drops open. Do I defend myself in a situation such as this? I was on time.

"Sir," the driver says, proving himself un-mute, "there was a wreck on the turnpike. It was necessary to double-back through the Hammond district."

Beside me, Canon's jaw visibly tightens, but he never stops typing. "Tell me, do you believe that you are paid to arrive at a certain time?"

"Yes, Mr. Canon, I am."

Canon slides his phone into a pocket and looks out the window. "Wrong. You were."

I study the reports I have been pretending to read for all I'm worth. I don't hold my breath for an apology.

5:20 AM

❋ LOCATION: Airport, Terminal A.

❋ CANON: Coincidentally, also such a huge "A" it's going to be the death of him.

"YOUR TICKET, MR. CANON."

He's standing near a pillar at our gate. He has been standing there, still, robotic, since he finished the coffee for which I had to sprint to the far end of the terminal. Sprint. In heels. Try it sometime.

He takes the ticket from my hand, and I'm glad I move quickly or I would have a Guinness-worthy series of paper cuts.

We have checked our bags, but there's still his briefcase, laptop, and my carry-ons to contend with. Priority boarding is called, and it looks as though I'm meant to carry his things, too. He walks away with a hand in his pocket, suit jacket slung over his arm.

Please, don't break a sweat or anything, mister.

He throws a glance my way. "Today." He lays on the last syllable as if the sarcasm might've escaped me otherwise.

Faked grace gets fifty pounds of junk and me down the breezeway without banging his hoity-toity briefcase against the walls. Leather. Probably from the pelts of newborn puppies. Or a giant panda. Anyone seen Ling-Ling lately?

Our seats are in the very front of the plane. I have heard this is not the safest place to sit. But it occurs to me Canon would simply tell the plane it could not crash, and it would begin to flap its wings like a great, metal bird.

He sits nearest the window and utilizes a final few minutes on his phone. I don't think he even realizes I'm here.

I wrestle most of our items into the overhead bin while trying to not block the path for every single person who comes on board. Because we're sitting right up front. Have I mentioned that?

It's a weird angle. To reach up into the bin but keep my ass out of the aisle, I feel like a question mark.

My shirt has come untucked, and I'm hyper aware of the strip of skin at my waist that is now meeting cool air. I slide in my laptop bag and feel a shove from behind, and suddenly I'm no longer stable. I teeter for all of a second before hands clamp around me. All I can feel is heat on my exposed skin.

Slowly I gain my bearings. His face is inches from mine. Hovering. His breath swirls between us. Canon breath. It is coffee and something more. I resist the urge to inhale deeply. His brow furrows, and he swings and plops me down into my seat. I blink again and again.

"I believe you owe someone an apology."

He steps out from under the bin. The bustle of passengers halts. I'm staring straightforward, observing the textured paneling.

"You." His voice booms.

The quiet feels like forever, but it is probably only a few seconds. My torso feels seared, as if I will find two handprint brands on my skin when I undress later.

His crotch is also level with my face. My perception of the world at large is affected.

A reedy male voice carries back to me. "I apologize."

Canon returns smoothly to his seat.

How does one process a situation like this? That was gallant. And kinda hot.

"Thank you, Mr. Canon."

"There is no time to change if you get your suit dirty."

Ah, chivalry.

7:34 AM

"NOTHING MORE THAT CAN BE COVERED NOW."

We have been going over the proposal and possible concessions for the longest ninety minutes of my life. And I saw *Battlefield Earth*.

I know there is more to go over, but he doesn't want to compromise security...or some BS. Whatever. I doubt that silver-haired, golden-anniversary couple behind us are actually corporate spies hanging on our every word.

I understand our current operations, but this is a new venture. New products and production capabilities.

We outsource most of our product line; the level of integration that is on the table would make us manufacturers. What I understand generally is not going to be much help here. I want to push for info.

I doubt anyone pushes Canon for anything...not successfully anyway.

His buttons. I would love to push those. Or pop them.

"Very well," I say as I put my notepad back in my bag. In my peripheral, I see his jaw is set. Tense. What have I done? Not done? He was as personable as he gets until...

...until I spoke just now. Until I said, "Very well." And a thousand thoughts hit me at once. Oh, shit...is this guy thinking I'm going to address him as "sir" or "Mr. Canon" every blessed time I speak? That I'm going to subjugate myself at every turn? That I'm mousy and meek and mild-mannered? I bet he gets off on...*Oh, great dandelions and unicorns—the son of a bitch might be one of those guys.*

His jaw is still tense. *You are gonna chip a molar at this rate, buddy.* Let's test the theory.

"Very well, sir."

His jaw is still set, and a little bulge at the hinge flexes. Then he shifts away from me and presses his index finger near his ear. Cabin pressure is affecting his ears. Jury is still out on the other issue.

"Gum?" I offer him a stick.

He straightens—seems surprised—but reaches over and takes the proffered gum. It's wintergreen.

Hopefully acceptable. Cinnamon is a deal breaker.

I get the universal guy nod as substitute for an offering of thanks.

Roughly five dozen chews into the gum and the atmosphere is full-fledged awkward. Quiet. Unsettling.

Weird.

He begins sifting through the in-flight magazines. I dare say he looks lost without his omnipresent phone.

"Have you had a chance to read this yet?" I hold out the book I purchased for him yesterday. I feel confident he hasn't read it; it just came out.

It is a Kodak moment, tired phraseology be damned. This might be the closest I ever get to seeing Alaric Canon at a loss for words. Taken aback. Discombobulated.

Well, no. Not quite that far.

But he is surprised and surprised enough to not completely mask it. There is an adorable twinkle in his eye. Or the reflection of the emergency exit lights. Whichever.

He takes it from my hand slowly, almost like he can't believe it's not booby-trapped. He looks at it for a moment then lifts it up in a strange salute to me before he starts reading.

That's all right. Just go ahead and be above verbal expressions of gratitude. I will get you to say the words someday, you ungrateful mother...

The pilot has long since turned off the seat-belt sign, but I'm not certain that I'm free to move about the cabin. Upward of a gallon of coffee has gone down Canon's gullet without a single bathroom break. Inhuman.

I, however, do not have a retrofitted industrial bladder.

I touch his armrest in hope to get his attention. His eyes flash to it, then me. I gesture toward the restroom. I tell myself that this is out of courtesy, but I feel pretty sure he thinks he's granting permission. I'm not going to trifle, to split hairs. I just need to survive this trip.

Close this deal. Last a week, or a month if I can.

I can play. I can deal.

Perfect. Quiet. Docile. Opinionless. Sterile.

Act as if the COYA file created me in a lab.

Whatever it takes. Whatever he needs.

30 days. At most.

An Emma-ectomy.

That is the new program.

I have a new plan.

9:45 PM

- Location: Hyatt—Top floor. Room 928. Across from Canon's.
- Room: Could not be more beige.
- Laptop: Charging.
- Suitcase: Unpacked.
- Bath: Drawn. And cold.

Why is my bath cold? Because I, purchaser of sadist shoes, needed to soak after wearing cheese graters on my feet yesterday and then traveling and walking and sitting through meetings and touring facilities and impersonating a pack mule today. 'Twas not meant to be.

Instead I have spent the last two hours typing up messages as Canon rattled them off in rapid succession.

He asked for bar charts. I generated them while he shaved.

He changed his mind to line graphs. I converted them while he took a phone call out in the hall.

He complained that he had left his blue tie at home. I produced the spare one I'd brought from the office.

Ten minutes ago, he'd loosened his tie, wrung his hands, and made an aside that he couldn't relax. I prepared a cup of chamomile tea and texted Clara that I owed her big time for all the ridiculous stuff she packed. He began drinking it and asked why I was still in his room.

You're welcome.

"When would you like the day to start tomorrow?"

"Their offices open at eight. We will get there at seven."

No fashionably late for that guy. I tried to cover my surprise but failed.

He explained, "It's best to see who arrives when, who's dedicated. Actions over words." His fingers twisted and pulled free the already loosened knot in his tie. His upturned chin and neck stretched above the shirt collar. He swallowed, Adam's apple bobbing smoothly. I swallowed too.

I nodded and gathered my things. "Pleasant dreams, Mr. Canon," I said, turning to face him from his doorway.

He tilted his head almost like a dog that is pretty sure you have something behind your back. "Good night, Ms. Baker."

Now I'm draining the tub while I hang the rest of my clothes. The cocktail dresses go in the bathroom in the hope that steam will help with the wrinkles. Suits go to the closest.

While the tub refills, I place our breakfast orders. The hotel supplied coffee is a total loss, as they really don't have a large selection. I order the cream and sweetener anyway. Because my middle name is Prepared, I brought a bag of his coffee. Muffins and eggs and some type of pig. I have no way of knowing if he is a protein or carb morning person, so I'm covering all the bases. Orange juice for him. Grape, apple, and cranberry for me in case he hates OJ.

They send up the in-room coffee pot, and I consider brewing a practice pot, but I don't want my whole room to reek of it.

I bring my cell into the bathroom because I just have a feeling.

The psychic network needs to recruit me because about three-point-five minutes into my well-deserved bath, he calls.

"Hello." I hold still, trying not to slosh water. I have suddenly become conscious about the drawbacks of being in the tub.

Tub means nude.

"Why would you take the second quarter P&L with you?"

"I didn't, sir. It's in your case, behind the personnel lists."

"If I had it, I wouldn't be calling you."

"Everything is in alpha order in your case. It's been in there all evening."

"I need it."

"Fine. I will be there in under ten minutes."

"That is an especially long time to walk across the hall. No matter. It is not here."

"I will look through my things and call you back, sir."

"I will wait."

"Oh, surely you have better things to do than listen to me look for papers. I will call you back in a few minutes."

"Are you unable to interpret certain social cues, Ms. Baker? It should be obvious to anyone that I am irritated, and yet you persist."

Sigh. I look at my bubbles. *So long bubbles.*

I learned this on the day I took this position, didn't I? Do what he wants when he wants it even if it doesn't make sense.

"Of course, Mr. Canon," I acquiesce…

…and then stand right the fuck up in the bath, water sloshing and splashing and then gurgling loudly when I hold the receiver down near the drain. With a metallic thump, I flip the lever so the water starts to go down.

I pinch the phone between my ear and shoulder while I dry off. The terry is soft, but it still rustles against me. I might've made sure it brushed across the phone a couple of times, too.

"Ms. Baker, um, I will check here again. I will call back if I find it."

"As you wish, sir. I will finish looking here, and then, if need be, come to your room," I say, and smile what is probably a very wicked smile before adding, "as soon as I get dressed."

I throw on the first thing I find and get myself into his room almost immediately.

The file is there. Slipped down in his case. It actually is hard to see, and I'm a bit panicked as I first begin to look.

Not sure what he expected me to show up in when I went to his room, but I don't think it was pajama pants and a tank. He's still in his slacks and dress shirt. I think he might sleep in them.

Hell, he may not require sleep. The advances of cyborg technology and all that.

DAY OF EMPLOYMENT: *376*

4:45 AM

❋ BEDSPREAD: Back on bed.

❋ COFFEE: Set to brew in one hour.

❋ CLOTHES: Yoga pants and Mr. Bubbles T-shirt.

❋ LOCATION: Hotel fitness center.

I'M WONDERING WHAT COSMIC MISSTEPS I've taken to now find myself perpetually awake before God.

I have committed myself to making personal progress. Hitting the gym early enough to be done and leave it before the sun cracks over the horizon tests my resolve.

Further, the object of my resolution, the point of it, was to get Canon to notice me. That boost of confidence that puts a spring in one's step. The positive aura that translates as sex appeal. That is what I was going for.

It's all for naught now. Reminding myself that I was merely trying to garner his attention for motivational purposes — that it would be really sick to otherwise hitch my star to such a dysfunctional wagon — is getting harder to reconcile when the alarm goes off.

How did it come to this? To this point of a desperate, pitiful, embarrassing type of thing you would only admit to yourself and the last amber drops echoing in a bottle of what used to be Jack?

Memory blocks rearrange and stack as I recall my initial time at the company, time when I was centered and the existence of one Alaric Canon was comfortably part of the vast unknown. Surely I was not so transfixed immediately. Surely not...

DAY OF EMPLOYMENT: 1
7:55 AM

❉ BAG: Wallet, picture of best friend and self, makeup, notepad, lunch, hairclip.

❉ CLOTHES: Red wrap dress, red pumps.

❉ HAIR: I don't even want to talk about it.

I LEFT TWENTY MINUTES EARLY TODAY. That should've been plenty of time for normal traffic and most emergency circumstances.

But no.

The lot was scraped down to glaring ice. The windshield would not defrost. Time out in the wind has taken a toll on my hair; it is now inexplicable. Everyone drove too fast or too slow. Hit every light. Encountered a school bus route that I didn't know about during my route test run yesterday.

I should learn not to even bother with being prepared.

The best laid plans oft go awry. Oft? What the fuck is *oft* all about? Too much going on to finish the entire word?

That's all just a nice way of saying one is screwed regardless.

Life's a bitch, and she has several sisters.

Now I'm riding the elevator while it stops on nearly every floor. People file in and out.

One person gets on and rides it up one whole level. I suppress a scream.

Some guy behind me huffs irritably. I keep my eyes trained on the numbers. Climb. Stop.

We're over capacity at one point, I'm certain of it. I feel my backside get pressed into the person behind me.

"Sorry," I mutter.

"Not your fault." A deep voice. A soft reply. The flesh behind my ear tingles. Instinct, for reasons I don't want to examine, tells me to fold into the man behind me.

Then I realize that this man is probably getting a face full of my frizzy hair. Mortifying.

The doors open for my floor and I bolt, never looking back.

10:11 AM

"THIS IS THE BREAK ROOM," Madeline states the obvious. I don't mind. It's comforting.

"The coffee is on the honor system. There's usually a fundraiser for someone's school children if you want snacks, otherwise the vending machines are here to price gouge you." Madeline goes on explaining and tosses a handful of change in the collection jar next to the coffee pot.

"The refrigerators are cleaned out every Monday," she says and begins to pour a coffee from one of the pots. "You can get some really nice st—"

A blond woman with a severe look barrels through the room toward where we stand. The crowd parts like the Red Sea, clearing a path for her, but conversation continues without pause. Madeline stands to the side, holding her coffee pot aloft and smiling cryptically at me. I'm sure I look confused.

The blonde reaches for a pot with a masking tape ring on the handle, pours a cup swiftly with one hand while adding what looks to be specially reserved creamer and sweetener. She turns, lips pursing tightly, and heads out of the room.

"Damn it!" The blond woman switches the cup to her other hand and sucks her now free—and probably scalded—hand into her mouth, then shakes it off, all the while walking swiftly away.

My hands float out, a silent request for explanation.

Madeline, smiling, resumes pouring her coffee. "That is Mr. Canon's assistant." She pours in enough sugar to trigger early onset diabetes and leans back on the counter. "Well, for the moment."

"Oh, has she been having trouble?" That explains why she seemed so nervous, why everyone got out of her way.

"Heck, no. She's doing exceptionally well. She's lasted for almost a month. May even set a record."

I decide I need to stay far, far away from this Canon person.

2:58 PM

"PAY UP." A THIN YOUNG MAN LEANS over Madeline's cubicle wall with his palm up.

"Hold your horses there." Madeline is chewing on a marker and looking over a colorful chart. "Yep, it is you." She looks up at the guy and then hands him an envelope from her desk.

I do my best to acclimate myself to this new computer program, but their exchange has definitely piqued my interest.

"Sweet!" He fist pumps and then looks back at me rather shamefacedly. "Oh, you must be Emma. I'm Bert Stiles." He extends his hand, and I shake it. "You also must think I'm terribly morbid, benefitting from the misfortune of others."

My mouth opens, but I don't really even know what to say. Out of the loop here.

Madeline rolls closer to me and whispers conspiratorially, "We have a betting pool for how long Canon's assistants last."

My head pulls back. That *is* rather cold-hearted. Bert fans through several large bills.

Cold-hearted…and profitable. I have loans to pay. Shoes to buy.

Heels on Deals. Pumps before Chumps.

"How does this work?" I ask, but suddenly everyone seems to have heard some cue that I've missed. They straighten and begin a flutter of activity.

Self-preservation instincts are not kicking in; I stand up to see what's going on. I imagine that I stick out like a sore, red thumb over the tops of everyone else.

That is when I see him.

Whoever he is.

Except, I know.

I just know.

Oh, my good God.

There are not enough words.

Beautiful.

Ineffable.

Utterly F-able.

He's a few feet from a set of large, dark wooden doors in the far corner. The desk outside that office is empty. He moves smoothly past it and scans the room.

His eyes fall on me. I'm incapable of movement under his gaze. Held. Matador. Bull.

He straightens his collar, never falters in his long strides. Looks away from me.

And then he's gone.

Everyone resumes their normal lives and conversations, and I'm left standing still and dumbstruck while the world happens around me.

SHAKING FREE OF THE MEMORY, I speed the treadmill up.

I will feel better for this. Definitely. Maybe. Definitely maybe.

I sit at work all day and study all night. It's not going to do me any good to finish school if I keel over dead.

Runs in the family.

This is the problem with treadmills. Too much time to think.

6:00 AM

* ❋ BREAKFAST: Arrived 15 minutes ago. Gone.
* ❋ HAIR: French twist.
* ❋ CLOTHES: Beige suit. It's like keeping a little piece of my room with me all day.
* ❋ COFFEE: Blue Mountain Jamaica. Freshly brewed. Go, me.

CANON'S BREAKFAST ARRIVES as I exit my room. The server smiles at me; he knows he'll be getting a stellar tip for splitting the delivery.

He knocks, and the door opens as if by magic. I duck in behind the cart, hot coffee in hand. Not that I have to sneak in. I have a key.

Clangs emanate from the bathroom while the table is set up, and I make quick work of the sugar and cream.

"Will there be anything else, sir?" The server speaks loudly to a closed bathroom door.

Canon dismisses him with something muffled I can't quite make out. There hasn't been any water running. I don't really know what I will encounter when that bathroom door opens. He may be fully clothed.

He may regenerate suits like a T-1000.

But the distinct possibility he may appear in some stage of undress exists.

Alaric Canon. With skin exposed.

Must focus.

Focus, focus, focus.

He said to be here at 6:00 a.m.

I'm here at 6:00 a.m.

Do what he says when he says. Even though it doesn't make sense to me.

Some items still need packing up. Chargers and files. His laptop.

Not a chance in hell I'm going to do that now and rob myself of something to concentrate on when he walks into the room.

Be calm. Cool.

Cool as a cucumber…which sets my mind skipping down a dirty little path…

Sweet Baby Moses in a reed basket, it's happening now. The door is opening, and I don't know whether to sit or stand or turn around or look away or jump out the sliding door and hole up in a log cabin in the hills.

Calm. The. Fuck. Down.

This might be the closest I will get to the upper hand.

You're a reasonable man, Mr. Canon. You don't tolerate mistakes, Mr. Canon. When you set a time, it's not an approximation, Mr. Canon.

I breathe. Deeply.

It's like a dance, but I'm leading this one. I know why I'm here. I'm justified in being here.

One long leg breaks the threshold. I force myself to turn at what feels like half-speed. I'm ramped up on nerves, and moving too quickly will show it.

The leg and its friend are in black pants. I'm a bit more disappointed than I expected.

Bullshit. I'm super fucking disappointed.

But the point is, I'm not showing it.

He turns toward the main part of the room, toward me, and I begin wrapping the cord around his charger.

Hoping my movements still look natural and unaffected—like hanging out in a hotel room with one's potentially half-naked boss is a regular occurrence—my eyes flick up to see Canon stop mid-stride.

His shirt is open. The man is wearing a white dress shirt, unbuttoned, cuffs loose. Pretending not to notice has just become a Herculean effort.

"Explain yourself."

I barely glance up, even though staring would have been worth getting fired.

I start to pack up his laptop. I'm all business.

Pretending to misinterpret his words, I continue packing up as I rattle off the itinerary and my role in it. I'm to take notes, hand him hard copies or access reports as needed, watch for discrepancies. I omit "glorified nanny."

A few times it seems he's about to say something, to redirect me back to the situation at hand, but I plow through. Finally I close with describing the food that better not have gotten cold.

He nods once, mouth a thin line. The shirt is buttoned and tucked in now. I have missed the show.

"You failed to mention the dinner meeting tonight. I presume you brought suitable attire."

"The little black dress. Perfect for all occasions."

"Hopefully not too little," he says under his breath. He may have even rolled his eyes.

Do I seem like some sort of tart? Is this because I'm in his room? He shouldn't have told me to be here and given me a key then.

He takes a sip of the coffee, and the look is priceless. He was so ready to bitch and moan, and I have kept him from it. Despite the fact that he had to realize I've checked off all the boxes this morning, he remains somber.

"If orange juice is not okay, I can get you something else." Prune juice perhaps?

"A good rule of thumb," he says as he polishes off the eggs, "is not to make offers one cannot complete."

"Agreed. Thank you for imparting your expertise," I say. "By the by, I have grape, apple, and cranberry juice in my refrigerator, if you should feel so inclined."

He stops mid-bacon-chew. I think I'm getting addicted to flustering him.

If I can't be a blip on the radar, I will settle for being a fly in the ointment.

4:47 PM

❈ LOCATION: Office of Lawrence Peters, World's Most Tedious Man.

I FIND MYSELF THINKING about that scene in *Raiders of the Lost Ark* when a female student blinks at Indy, and her eyelids have words on them that read "I Love You" in black eyeliner. Maybe I can do that but make it look like my eyes are open. Even if I weren't already sleepy, this company's CEO would do me in.

He is ether in human form. I could easily keep up even if I handwrote everything.

In calligraphy.

Mr. Peters, on the downward slope to retirement, does not self-edit. Interspersed with the incredibly slow-spoken actual negotiations, we get it all. Some of it twice. The kids. The grandkids. The basset hound.

They're a hardy breed, seventeen years old before Peters had him put down last week. He will be missed.

Peters has prostate issues as well. Nothing's off limits, it seems.

During this, Canon doesn't even bat an eye. One would think he might be concerned about the health of his own prostate, given that it has been cohabiting with a very large stick.

He makes notes of this minutia as though it's as vital to closing the deal as the fine print in licensing our intellectual property rights.

Canon has remained stoic. Begrudgingly, I must admit I'm impressed.

Warm afternoon sun beats down on me from the window. There's a sunbeam on the carpet near my chair. I want to curl up in it like a tabby cat.

The morning was less trying. Three other executives had livened up the discussion. One was even lively enough to check out my ass. A pen jab to the leg he just happened to keep bumping against mine under the conference table seemed to give him the message that he was not my type.

"I must say, you have thought of everything. What do you need me for?" Peters chortles. Yes, chortles.

Canon smiles and raises his eyebrows infinitesimally; he doesn't need this guy in the least, and I'm fairly certain Peters is going to be enjoying his retirement sooner than planned. Mr. Peters doesn't notice and excuses himself to make a call. His meandering trek to the door takes about five minutes.

We're alone for the first time since his hotel room this morning. Canon takes out his phone then returns it to his pocket almost immediately.

I turn, shifting toward him just a little. I'm sure my eyes are a bit wider than normal due to my struggle to stay alert.

Our eyes meet, and I must be punch-drunk from sleep deprivation and three hours of Peters' monologue because I can't help the smile that takes over my face and, just when I think I might be able to rein it in, one corner of Canon's mouth turns up too. The shock wave ruptures the dam, and I can't help a single laugh escaping. He looks at papers he's holding, but even in profile I can see tell that his smile is bigger. Oh, good Lord, we have both been tortured for hours, and he's just better at hiding it. I clear my throat and shake my head, trying to resume professional behavior.

Not much longer. About 45 minutes, tops. Though it will seem twice as long since this Peters guy has tortoise nervosa.

"What?" Canon is looking at me.

The filter is broken. I've said that out loud.

Oh, crap. I'm mocking a potential business partner. I am so fired.

I own it. I repeat myself.

And Canon laughs. Hard.

Holy shit. I have actually fallen asleep on the job. Or died.

I hear myself laugh, too. It is a bit nervous and hollow. I need to get out of here. "May I get you a drink, Mr. Canon?"

He nods repeatedly, pointedly avoiding eye contact, regaining composure.

"Take a chance with their coffee or just a Coke?" Caffeine on an IV drip?

"Coke is fine." He clears his throat.

Over thirty minutes later, our drinks are gone and Peters has yet to materialize.

"Do you suppose he's left?" I break the silence. I'm concerned about running late to dinner; I had planned on being back at the hotel by now, and I need time to change.

I bet this is killing Canon, this waiting around.

"We will give him two more minutes, then we will leave."

I'm in the shower when I realize Canon said "we."

⁊:54 PM

🌢 LOCATION: Sierra De Touro Churrascaria.

🌠 ITINERARY ITEM: Dinner meeting with 4 top execs.

🌢 DRESS: Black. Littlest one I brought. Worn
   intentionally. Don't judge me.

THE FOOD IS AMAZING. Freshly grilled meat straight to the table again and again. Salad bar with items I can neither recognize nor pronounce.

We're dining with the comptroller and three VPs. There appears to be a shit ton of suits at this company; thinning the herd seems to be in order.

My recommendation is that we begin with one Diana Fralin, VP of Marketing. Tits on display and blatant, just blatant, flirtation attempts with the males. She's the embodiment of every negative connotation with female executives. Giant step backward for the women's movement.

It is an all-you-can eat restaurant. All you can eat meat. Meat.

Fralin wants the only kind not on the menu. Her attempts would only be more obvious if she stuffed her panties directly into Canon's mouth.

Most of the evening has been pleasant enough. Canon is beside me, so I'm spared his judgmental looks. I do get a few errant brushes from Fralin's heels when her attempts to play footsie with my boss go astray.

If she snags my stockings, I might have to cut a bitch.

"More top sirloin?" the server says, leaning a skewer of meat over Fralin and her décolletage. Making sure he gets a tip tonight. She's giving him two right now.

Others take slices, and I wave him off. Undaunted, he returns with chicken moments later.

"Beautiful lady perhaps prefers chicken?" He smiles down at me. Beside me, I feel Canon stiffen. All eyes are on me.

How unfair is it that this moment feels more unprofessional than all of the off-color comments made by others during the evening? I've listened to these company executives execute enough puns and double entendres to rival a sleepover chock-full of twelve-year-old boys.

"Look at him pound back the meat." Way to stay classy there.

"Don't choke the, er, I mean on your chicken." Been waiting all night to say that one?

"Well, hello, Sir Lion, so we *meat* again."

How exceedingly droll. Yawn.

Now, with the waiter orbiting Diana's omnipresent moons, I feel more like a chicken than like eating it. "No, thank you. I'm finished," I say.

"I will take whatever you've got," Fralin chimes in.

I just bet you would.

"We have glazed pineapple. Sweets for your sweet smile." He cuts meat for Fralin as he speaks to me.

I shake my head again. Canon clears his throat loudly.

Fralin's eyes narrow. "How sweet, Ms. Baker. Should I get his number for you?" she sneers.

Silverware clangs next to me. "Thank you for the dinner. We really must head out and go over those new proposals." Canon stands and pulls my chair out.

Sure. I don't mind leaving. I'm done. Thank you for asking.

Peters takes a break from his protein bonanza. "Well, well, well. Throwing in the towel already, are you, man?"

"Oh," Fralin says, crestfallen. "We will see more of you tomorrow, right?" Oh, she wants to see more of Canon, that's for sure. The thought is nauseating. Her...him...across the hall from my room... touching...each other. I push my chair in a bit too forcefully. The place settings clatter.

I should be thrilled at the prospect of someone keeping him occupied. I shrug it off. It's probably just the thought that someone so crass, so unworthy, might get noticed when I have failed.

11:10 PM

❋ PHONE: In bed beside me. Like a lover. Possibly better. Definitely bigger than some.

❋ VOLUME: On high.

❋ SCREEN: Dark. Continuously so.

I SHOULD BE FOCUSING on the lecture playing back on the laptop. Instead, my eyes keep darting to the phone.

I keep expecting him to call.

He doesn't.

A silent ride from the restaurant was followed by a silent ride in the elevator. Then I followed him down the hall to our rooms. Three paces behind at all times.

A couple of hours poring over tweaked proposals and highlighting differences with Bossy Pants. Now I'm alone in my room to thrill to the history of common-law marriages and other things only a handful of states still honor.

Back on task. Two days in and already seven hours behind in lectures. Not good.

At some point, I fall asleep with headphones on, listening to Professor Cameron explain the SEC's role in enforcing the Foreign Corrupt Practices Act.

It's as stimulating as you'd imagine.

DAY OF EMPLOYMENT: *377*

3:33 AM

"Noooooooo…"

Huh? Huh — What the — ? Oh. Oh, shit. It is me.

I haven't had this many nightmares in a while.

They seem to be stress-induced. Occurring more frequently now. Go figure.

In my youth they happened all the time. Always different, but with one important element often the same: Mr. Lincoln.

Dude is scary. Just picture him out in a field, stoic eyes and stovepipe hat, staring. Shudder.

Tonight he was in the closet. Not like that. Waiting. Breathing. Getting beard hairs on all my borrowed business clothes.

Then Abe made his presence known. Dumped thousands of pennies on me. Drank all Canon's coffee.

Yeah, I'm messed up. Other people get nightmares with mangy-furred werewolves tearing the shingles from their roof. I'm terrorized by Abraham Fucking Lincoln.

No point in trying to go back to sleep. I hit the fitness center.

⁊:00 AM

✤ CLOTHES: Black pantsuit.

✤ CANON: Dressed. Foiled again.

NOT GOING IN EARLY TODAY. He says there's no point if they're expecting it. Worrisome. He may be beginning to make sense to me.

"I will need those figures from corporate." He's straightening his tie in the mirror.

"They're in your email as well as hardcopies in my case."

The tie is not cooperating. "They don't do me any good in your case."

I bite my tongue and pull the stack of papers out for him. It's not really a stack so much as a ream.

It hits the desk with a thud. *Help yourself. Might wanna bend at the knees when you lift it.*

The sound draws him away from his battle with the rabbit and its hole. He looks like he's about to say something but then thinks better of it. He yanks the tie free in frustration.

Wordlessly I step around the desk and hold my hands out, offering to tie it. He pulls his head back slightly and seems surprised, then takes the step to me, to where our feet touch.

So close together. Close. The soft sound of his breath fills my ears. I work, then slide the knot up and linger near his throat for a moment.

Warmth. I'm aware of every hair on my neck. Slowly, I smooth the tie down over his chest with my hand.

"Better?" My voice is hoarse in my ears.

He glances in the mirror, gives a nod.

Computers and papers are packed in silence.

10:05 AM

"THIS HERE'S THE MAIN FLOOR for pick-and-pack. Four tiers high for the runners. The fork trucks can reach clean up to the top." Sean Becket, floor supervisor, has been the most personable of all the personnel.

Of course, we're scheduled to spend a whopping ten whole minutes with him.

Peters and Fralin, however, are practically shadows. Boring, whorish shadows.

The distribution center appears monumentally efficient.

If I listen closely, I can hear the gears in Canon's head turning. Copying it has become his plan.

Mine is still under revision.

Lagging behind, I film the operation with my phone.

I may or may not have filmed Canon's ass. Twice.

II:37 AM

❧ DELI DELIVERY DRIVER: Driving me mad.

"NO, NO, A DISCOUNT is most certainly not okay. Not only will you not be paid for this, but you will be back on these premises with a suitable substitute in under twenty-three minutes."

The deli delivery person does not seem to comprehend that some people cannot be bought with 15% off.

Wrong is wrong.

"But, ma'am, it's over ten minutes one way."

"Then you better call in an order to a nearby Quiznos."

He looks aghast. He hasn't read the COYA file. Seriously, dude. I'm not going down because your people slathered honey mustard on his sandwich.

Actually, I'm onboard with this particular preference. Honey is gross. Bee vomit. I have no idea why people willfully choose to ingest it.

The driver hustles off. Behind me, I hear movement.

"Mr. Canon. I didn't see you there. Are we headed back in?"

His mouth may turn up. "Not yet. Everything seem to be in order?"

"It will be." I hedge and hope Deli Man pulls this off.

Pursing his lips, almost pouting, he looks at me. Really looks. I start to feel self-conscious, flushed.

Is there something on my face? Something wrong I have not noticed? Without thinking, I tilt my head and look at him questioningly.

His eyes widen for a moment, and just when I think he's going to inform me that I have toured the facility and met a hundred-plus people with spinach omelet in my teeth, he coughs.

"Would you like a drink, Ms. Baker?"

Knock me over with a feather. "Yes, yes, actually I would."

"Good. Pick me up one, too," he says and disappears into the conference room.

My nostrils flare like a dragon guarding a pile of gold.

9:00 PM

❧ Location: Bed. Alone. As ever.

❧ Plans: Highly overrated as a concept, it seems.

❧ Homework: Untouched.

Boss Man wrapped things up early tonight. I have rewarded myself with sleep in celebration of removing the anchovy garnish from his room service Caesar salad without detection.

Deep in pre-dream fantasy about negative calorie brownies, my phone rings.

"Request the POs for the last five years." *Well, hello to you, too.*

"Will do, sir."

"Also, the older sales contacts lists. We will need to cross-reference."

"I'm on it." I smother my yawn with a pillow.

"There are spec sheets for the warehouse. I need them."

"Yes, sir." Anything, just let me sleep.

"Now. I need them now." Oh. *Oh.*

"I'll be right there."

Clara's robe is a beautiful black kimono. I don't own a robe, so it's better than none; however, I see now that it's rather sheer. Sheer, as in see-through.

My nightgown is pretty much a gray slip and covers everything, so that's not an issue, but this would not have been my first choice for traipsing across the hall to my boss's room. Well, there's nothing for it.

I knock, and his door swings open. Suffice it to say, Canon did not anticipate sheer anything.

While I'm standing in the hall, his eyes dart quickly to see if anyone else is there—as if that would make a lick of difference—and he yanks me inside.

"What do you think you're doing?" He starts pacing rapidly in the small space of the room. If he rakes his hair any harder, he's going to need plugs.

"Sir?"

"Why are you in my room like…like…like that?" His hands wave wildly around my frame.

"You said 'now' so I came now."

"I have to be able to trust you. Do the right thing. Tell me."

"Trust me?" Well now, doesn't this just frost my buns. "You're calling trust into question? You've said you're a fair man. I want to believe that. But you're not being fair now…sir." I want to spit.

"Is it fair to parade around in lingerie?" He paces, his shoulders brush against the curtains.

"This is not lingerie." I reach in the robe and pull out the very non-see-through corner of my gown. "Trust me—if I wore lingerie, you'd know it."

"You may have boundary issues. I should have redirected you after you showed up in my room the first day."

"You insisted we have access cards to both rooms," I point out.

He shakes his head and seems rooted to the floor over by his window. As if lingerie cooties are catching.

If Diana Fralin showed up in this, I bet he would pull her into the room and do something other than lecture her about trust.

I think maybe he's offended that he's been forced to look at me. Well, screw him. I'm not repellent. Many guys would be freaking thrilled if I knocked on their doors in this. Or less.

Calmly, slowly, I bend ever so slightly and set the files on his bed. Without the papers in front of me, I should feel more exposed. I don't. I am livid.

I smooth the fabric over my front. Pull the tie tighter.

"Mr. Canon, with all due respect, you have made it abundantly clear that I am to do as you say, when you say it. Without question." He starts to talk, and I don't know why I lose control of my persona and I sure don't know what possesses him, but I hold up my hand to stop him from talking and he actually does. "It is abundantly clear that seeing me like this is distasteful to you. In the future, I will take the time to fully dress and suffer your wrath for the delay rather than forcing you to look at me when it is evident you find the view so distasteful."

"Ms. Baker, I —"

"Mr. Canon, in the spirit of protecting you from things you don't want to see, I need to leave." I fight to keep tears from forming. "Good night, Mr. Canon."

9:21 PM

MY PHONE RINGS. IT'S HIM.

Has he called to apologize? I may faint…"Hello, Mr. Canon."

"We have been invited to lunch tomorrow."

Not a problem. I brought an extra outfit just in case. "Very well. Is there anything more, Mr. Canon?" My voice breaks. I don't want to examine why.

"No." His voice falls off. Pause. "Good night, Ms. Baker."

11:20 PM

THIS IS AN INCREDIBLY LUMPY MATTRESS.

That's probably what he thinks about my ass. That is, if he thinks about my ass at all.

Still…I think of the person in the next room…I want to be happy, to be grateful that I have this opportunity. I can surely use the raise. Perhaps of vastly more importance, with good reason, is to find a moment that satisfies this fixation I have about wanting him to "notice" me, so I can then get back to being a well-adjusted, contributing member of society. Or a reasonable facsimile thereof.

But seriously, the raise would come in handy, too.

Debts. Potential therapy's on the horizon.

Should have requested hazard pay.

1:14 AM

I'M ASLEEP.

It's not something of which I'm often aware, but this dream has that weird level of self-awareness.

Canon's silhouette breaks the doorway. A part of me feels a glimmer of hope.

And the part in which that glimmer is located has direct contact with a cotton lining.

My dreaming hope is that he'll ask something akin to "Will you let me show you how much better that lingerie looks on the floor?" and tilt his head back in invitation toward the open doorway. Back toward his room.

Instead, I cough softly as if to clear my throat. "I'm cold. I want to stay wrapped up."

At least in my dreams, I can be hard-to-get.

He pauses. His shadowed hand picks at the door frame. "I have another blanket. I saw it in the dresser."

My little glimmer fizzles, tucks itself into a ball, like an old television tube shutting down. "I'll be okay." Try to sound casual. Smooth the bedding out. Turn down the corner. "Thanks, though."

Even in my dreams, I'm disappointed. I have failed spectacularly at not letting myself hope he would offer to share.

As I tuck the sheet under the cushions, I notice him stretch to turn off my bathroom light.

"Oh," I say, my voice cracking for some reason I don't want to analyze. "Please...please leave it."

He looks at me, then the glow of the 75 or so watt bulbs. He shrugs and leaves it on.

I don't feel like explaining that I'm scared of the dark. Not to a guy who must give the boogeyman the heebie-jeebies.

He looks back at me. I fight my eyes not to follow the slope of his sides. "I can get the blanket now. Just in case you need it."

"I'll be okay," I repeat. I haven't even convinced myself yet. Fluff the pillow and drop it in back place. "If I get cold, maybe I'll knock on your door."

It's a comment I haven't thought about, and I don't know where it came from. I want to say it was a joke…not to acknowledge I was testing the waters.

Behind me, I hear him pad onto the tiles near the door. "Um…" His voice trails off in an unspoken question.

I scramble to save face. "J-Just for body heat. Not to snuggle or anything." I force a short laugh.

Yes, yes. Yes, it's all so fucking funny.

"I barely do that with my girlfriends."

Ack. My mental spine goes straight. Girlfriends. Dates. The kind of women he has voluntarily spent time with. Unlike me. Not ones he has been harangued into working alongside.

I'm still in panic mode from my slip into revealing how much I wish…

"Just for body heat." Fuck, did I already say that? "Like to prevent frostbite. Like to not lose toes. Plane crash in the Andes. That sort of thing. Not to cuddle." My God. Shut up. Shutupshutupshutup. Plane crash in the Andes? Really? That's harkening up some sexy imagery there, huh?

Hey, man, how did you first realize you loved her?

When I was starving and got her confused with a savory pot roast.

"Just kidding," I add a bit too quickly.

He's back at his door. Pauses. Looks back. Smiles. Smiles a smile that I can't decipher; it's impossible to tell if he thinks I'm funny or pathetic or insane. "Good night."

"Good night," I say, pulling the corner of the blanket away from cool sheets and slipping under. Under the blanket. Further under his spell.

Between the door and the floor, the air is pitch black.

Maybe his smile meant it's a unique situation for him to go to sleep with a woman so close and not be tempted to be intimate.

Not sure what time it is. Or how long I have been asleep. Or how long it took me to fall asleep rather than replay the past days' events again and again.

The calls. The complaints. The flayed pelt of panda bears.

Multiple nightmares revolving around our sixteenth president.

Look this over. Organize that. If it needs gotten, get it.

It. Yeah, I get it.

But I do not get him.

Now, hopefully not looking too much like an overeager puppy, I'm his PA. I'm still trying to let that sink in.

The dream shifts.

The room is decorated. It's still night, a tree is now lit, and the hotel room is dressed to the nines. Like an apparition, I open my door and practically float across the hallway over into his room. Garland over the doorways. Candles on the minibar. Greenery adorns his headboard.

The lights from his tree barely stretch to illuminate his bed, barely show the shadowy sheets which flutter and rise with his breaths. Barely light the contours of his face.

He's right in the middle, where I would have imagined him to be. Walking to him, my hand hovers above his form. I trace his frame, note the tug of his warmth.

Suddenly, his hand encircles my wrist, and I tumble across him.

I wish I could actually feel the scorch of his skin against my own.

His hand presses against my lower back, pulls me to him. Heat. And hard. And desire. And too, too good to be true…

…so I grab this little glimpse of REM heaven and stare and study and stake my claim. My thumbs learn the lines of his face. My chest mirrors his rise and fall. My legs entwine with his.

In darkness, my eyes see what I want to see in daylight: Love behind his eyes.

Warm. Mine. His. Real. Or as real as I can get.

Gasp. Echo.

Impossible.

He can't be gasping, simply can't, because this is a realistic dream—I insist, I insist—and my tongue is somewhere around his third molar.

But someone gasps. Moans. Practically purrs.

Again. But different. Low. Lower.

Shit. The spell breaks.

And double shit.

It's me. I'm full-on, unadulterated *moaning.*

Is it not enough that my every waking moment has been monopolized by this man and his persnickety patoot? Must he now rampage around like a prize bull in my slumberland china shop as well?

Rampaging anality. Raging hormones.

If I get any more regressively juvenile with these fantasies, I'm gonna need to invest in some Clearasil. And lube.

Pull the covers up to my nose. Cast a wary look at the door that stands between myself and Canon.

He's right over there. Asleep. Or recharging the lithium ion battery cell that runs his mainframe. Waiting for another opportunity to make me question myself, my choices, my sanity.

Unlike John Wilkes Booth, I may actually miss Lincoln.

DAY OF EMPLOYMENT: *378*

8:00 AM

❀ CLOTHES: Jeans and black turtleneck sweater.

❀ HAIR: Pulled back severely.

❀ BREAKFAST: Skipped.

❀ MOOD: Foul.

THE PLACE IS EMPTY. As it should be. Coming to an office for three hours to marvel at the wonders of meticulous bookkeeping on the Saturday before Christmas is not something most people would choose to do.

Alaricenezar Scrooge.

"Do you have access to the cleanser and toner market trials?"

"Yes. Here they are, Mr. Canon." *Enjoy them, asshole.*

"ETA for the POs?"

"They will be delivered to the hotel late today. They're stored off-site, sir." *Sir Asshat.*

"Does market data suggest —"

I hand him the market research analysis for each test product before he can finish. Final scores have been highlighted.

Lunch with the execs is early and casual. I say nothing. I point to my selection on the menu. I'm all quiet smiles.

Stepford Secretary.

12:15 PM

"Your coffee, sir."

"We will set up in my room and go through the POs."

All of them? Years' worth?

"Yes, sir. As you wish."

"Order room service."

"As you wish."

"Could you bring me some water?"

"As you wish."

"You do realize I have seen that movie."

"Sir?"

His eyebrows rise. *Oh, Buttercup, you smug bastard.*

4:00 PM

❧ Purchase Orders: Cover every flat surface of the room.

❧ Mood: About one purchase order from conniption fit.

❧ Ass: Asleep. As are both feet.

Been sitting for hours. Need to walk around.

Canon yawns. Even his yawn is magnificent. Sickening.

"Let's go for a walk."

"Okay," I say, perking up.

He stretches, treating me to a glimpse of skin between his shirt and jeans. "My ass has been mostly dead all day."

So you're gonna flash trail and throw in a reference joke, then still expect me to function? Hardest job ever.

We walk around the Plaza shops and admire this city's many fountains. Most are ornate and traditional.

There are several cow statues. Who knows why anyone thought that was a good idea?

The bronze boar statue reduces us both to fits when we spot it near to the hotel.

This is easy. Conversation. Interaction.

He's never been so attractive. That's saying something. I'm doing a terrible job of staying mad.

"Want some?" Canon points toward a little mom-and-pop donut shop. Rough around the edges. Needs a bit of paint. I bet they're amazing. The kind of place that outlasts corporate sprawl. Grandfathered-in equipment. My mouth waters. Canon motions again. "Want some?"

So tempting. Oh, we're only talking about donuts. "I better not."

"Do you have something against donuts?"

"Oh, no. I have something against walking them back off."

He shakes his head and mutters something as he heads to the doors. I guess I'm supposed to follow.

Painful. The display is truly fucking painful. Strawberry. Crunchy peanut butter cinnamon rolls. Apple spice cake.

"Ready?" He holds the door open, purchase dangling from his hand.

9:14 PM

❋ ROOM SERVICE TRAYS: In the hall.

❋ MY THOUGHTS ON PURCHASE ORDERS: #%*&^$#@!

❋ DONUTS: Gone. I caved almost immediately.
He had bought enough for two.

TIRED. I'M TIRED. And I do stupid shit when I'm tired.

"Would you like for me to put on some coffee?"

Canon is sitting on his bed. Legs crossed and barefoot. Stifling a yawn, he shakes his head.

Oh, please let that be a sign this day is nearly over. I mean, looking at him in faded jeans is a definite perk, but I am so over cataloging purchase patterns.

"Long day, huh?" His eyes change somehow. I nod. "Maybe you could find some Cokes?"

Oh. We're not done yet.

"Okay," I say, unintentionally laying a bit too long on the last syllable.

"I know this is taking forever. This is our only chance. It is the best way to make sure they are not fudging their numbers. Go change into something more comfortable."

More comfortable than jeans?

"I have pajamas," I say.

He sits up straight and rubs his hands over his face. "All right."

Twelve minutes later, I'm back with Cokes and wearing my "That is what I'm Tolkien About" PJs.

To say Canon looks relieved would be an understatement. He may have been expecting the kimono again.

In that case, I wonder why he would torture himself.

I'm thinking this is simultaneously the best and worst idea ever. Canon's wearing pajama pants and a white tee. All my theories are blown.

It is almost a foregone conclusion that I will embarrass myself by ogling him at some point. I can imagine what point: his point. The hold I have on my wandering eyes is tenuous.

He takes a swig of pop. Plunking myself on his bed and being careful not to scatter papers everywhere, I pat the mattress. "Let's do it."

Spit-take. Coke everywhere.

"You okay?" I ask.

Canon nods. And coughs. A lot.

SOMETIME...

"Hey...Hey, Emma. Wake up."

I feel hands in my hair. They shake my shoulder. I'm cold. I turn toward the warmth beside me.

"Emma. Emma?"

Just ignore them; they'll stop.

They do.

Then the warmth goes away.

Lincoln chases me. Through Walmart. I don't know which part is scarier.

DAY OF EMPLOYMENT: 379

8:30 AM

My PHONE IS RINGING. Somewhere. It's not on my nightstand.

Screen light shines through papers on the bed. Nothing seems right.

"H-Hello?"

"It is after eight. The day needs to start."

"Huh?"

"I need to get ready."

In a flood of revelation, it becomes clear this is not my room.

I fell asleep in his bed, and he…must have gone to mine.

Glad I never put up that dartboard with his picture…

"I'll be right out," I say and bolt from his bed. His really, really amazing-smelling bed.

Oh, shit. The video from the plant is still paused on my laptop…

Back in my room, nonchalance is a casualty. Legs still half asleep, I'm Bambi, stumble-bumbling for the computer.

The editing program appears to be paused in the same spot. He doesn't mention it.

11:08 AM

❖ CANON: AWOL.

WHICH IS DIFFERENT, since he's usually driving me up a wall.

He hasn't bothered to check in. Which bothers me. But I don't have the luxury of time to deal with it. I shrug it off and keep working from my hotel room.

On shrug number eleven, Canon materializes.

"You are on your own for lunch."

This floors me. Time to myself? "When shall I meet back with you?"

"I'll call you." Canon seems hesitant. For a moment, I'm drawn in to the tiny crinkles near his eyes. "Our trip has been extended for a few days. Through the holiday. Take the afternoon to make arrangements."

What? I can't be gone more. More 24/7 with this man? I don't have clothes or time or money or patience or ready access to happy pills to grind up into his coffee.

Or anything better to do.

He shuffles through some papers. "We will also be attending more functions with their higher-ups, so you will need additional evening wear. I can't imagine even you foresaw that, so use the time to purchase whatever you need."

Blinking rapidly, I try to compose myself. I'm failing miserably. Homework, recorded lectures, coffee beans, starched white shirts. Images flood my mind.

"Is there a problem?" He finally looks up at me.

Well, hell yeah, there is a freaking problem! "I, um, I…" I say and clear my throat forcefully. "I don't have the resources."

"I said make arrangements, did I not?" He looks at me like maybe I'm dense.

My cheeks heat. Coming up short doesn't sit well with me. "I mean… that is to say… There is a cash flow issue. This is, um, beyond my means."

After a moment of monumental awkwardness, he reaches into his wallet and places a department store card near my hand. "Give them your measurements. Purchase at least one more cocktail dress."

"You don't have to do that. I mean, I can recycle."

"No," he says, waving me off. "People would notice."

I nod, still processing all this.

"Branch out. Anything but black."

"Very well, sir."

From my hotel room's desk, I watch him leave. On the other side of the door, Ms. Fralin stands, bundled up in a heavy coat.

"Alaric, darling," she coos and ushers him out. "Finally I have you all to myself. Whatever will we do to pass the time?" The door shuts, her laughter muffled.

7:00 PM

❧ LOCATION: My room.

EVERYTHING HANGS IN THE CLOSET NOW. The tags and receipt mock me from the desk.

I took that card earlier today in a moment of shock. Extended trip. More clothes. What appears to be his personal department store card.

The company dime can roll right in and purchase whatever I need as far as I'm concerned. It sure wasn't my idea to go on this trip.

I really need to know if he's being reimbursed. Otherwise the tags go back on and the clothes go back.

Ideally, anyway.

I still need to wear them, regardless.

I just don't want to be indebted to him, to take any gifts from him.

Everything in me demands clarification of whose money I just spent. Hours of contemplating this situation has made me sure of only one thing: Ms. Baker cannot question Mr. Canon.

I've distracted myself satisfactorily with several school lectures, but now nothing is working.

Clara's chirpy voice mail gets my message about the delayed return. Never have I so desperately wanted to hear her voice, even if only to interrogate me.

It wasn't just lunch without Canon; I was on my own all day. Still am. I haven't heard from Canon; he's not come back. I've said, "Yes, sir," to everyone and everything I've seen. Even the shower.

It's like I've had something removed, and yet I keep feeling it. A phantom limb. A phantom pain in my ass that replaces the pain in my ass. Whatever. It's just not the same.

Why does this bug me so? Should I check on him? He could be hurt…

I'm not fooling myself. I want to check because he may still be with her.

It's not my business. He's not my business. I don't care.

Keep saying it. It might make it true.

I had a plan. This was not the plan.

Fully intent on flipping more channels, I dial him without thought.

"Canon." His voice is a surprise in my ear. Why did I call him? What's wrong with me?

"Yes, um," I say and look around the room for some non-existent guidance. Nothing. "Is there anything you'd like for me to be working on?"

"Are the purchases categorized?"

All the places he could be, the things…and people…he could be doing crowd my thoughts.

"Yes, all in order. Every pencil and enough Tyvek to furnish a clean room environment all accounted for." Word vomit. "We can only have these rooms until Tuesday."

He's quiet for a moment. "You did make other reservations, though?"

"Yes. Three places. When you have a moment, I can go over th—"

A crash, maybe something small breaking, on his end of the line interrupts me.

"Whatever you choose will be fine…Good night, Ms. Baker."

"Good night, Mr. Canon."

One bath, two room service desserts, and a nightie that makes me feel beautiful don't chase away the glumness.

I feel lonely.

I fall asleep reading a textbook.

9:22 PM

LINCOLN IS HERE. In my room. I throw the bedspread at him.

Lincoln is unfazed by bacteria. He uses my ChapStick. He paints my toes. He licks them. He sucks them in.

I twist and claw at my mattress and beg him to stop, but he—

"Emma! You have got to wake up."

Canon is holding me, but I feel jostled. He's been shaking me. I gulp down air.

"Shh." His hand smooths my hair out of my face and down my back. Pulling back, he looks at me. "I thought…oh, God, I thought you were being…and I heard you, and I could see the lights, and then and then and th—oh, my God, what the motherfuck are you wearing?"

He propels himself backward from the bed.

This is all so weird. I look down and remember the pity party that ended in donning a peach negligee with black lace inlays and fabric that makes Clara's sheer robe look like plaid flannel.

"This? This is actually lingerie."

I told him he would know it if I wore it. I don't do things halfway.

"W-Why?"

Deer in headlights. Yeah, that description works here.

And just to keep things straight, I'm sporting the headlights.

Maybe we could call them blips.

I may have just set off the radar…

There's something about flustered Alaric Canon I can't get enough of. I'm practically naked, yet he's the one uncomfortable.

"Why? What did you expect me to wear?" I stand to usher him out…and show off the cute little coordinating panties. "Did you think I sleep in the nude?"

"Good night, Ms. Baker," he calls behind him. He has already crossed the hall.

"And a good night to you, Mr. Canon."

DAY OF EMPLOYMENT: *380*

10:00 AM

❃ MEETINGS: All day. Shoot me.
❃ LOCATION: Conference room.

THIS IS OUR SHOW. Canon is in game mode. Proposals. PowerPoints. Power suit.

Sweet mercy, just look at him. Yum.

He points out that they seem to have "lost" an important sales area about the time this merger was proposed—a whole product category, just suddenly gone from the line-up.

His tone is smooth, his insinuation clear: he thinks they are attempting to retain an exclusive area.

Ms. Fralin adjusts her cleavage so thoroughly I begin to suspect the lost sales area is actually in there somewhere. She pulls an index card out from behind her neckline.

"That was part of a former associate's territory," she offers, glancing at the card. "Anyone have an explanation?"

Flustered, Peters shuffles through some papers. This guy knows zilch about his job. "Looks like LaCygne oversaw that most recently. Is he…let me see…he may be on site…" Peters flounders while clearly looking for who this LaCygne person might actually be.

Peters has forgotten to bring a file. He can't find his pen. Fralin fishes one out of her bra. It's like the damned Room of Requirement in there.

Canon is unimpressed. He's been working the room during his presentation; this breaks his stride. His fingers are in his pockets, his shoulders set.

The tension is palpable. "I can go track him down," I offer finally.

Looking down, Canon nods. He wants this info; he wants this deal between our companies to be on the up-and-up. This glitch was the principal concern that seemed to stand out to him in all those hours of research we logged.

11:10 AM

I FIND HIM ALMOST IMMEDIATELY. Just had to ask a non-suit. They always know the score.

LaCygne is Mitchell LaCygne. We went to undergrad together. Small world. Dated a couple of times.

Blue eyes and blue jeans. Baritone Scottish brogue. That is quite a perplexing family tree. Roots must span Europe.

My, oh my, why did we only go out twice?

Oh, yeah. Kellie.

Lucky ho.

"Hey, Emma, it sure is a pleasure to see you. You part of the new regime?"

I smile. "Yeah, I guess so."

"Well, what can I do for you?"

The next hour plus is spent at a break table. He's got records of everything. Looks like the line fell through because his predecessor had failed to deliver on time for the preceding several years. He had inherited a mess. A dying moose.

"I have no idea why. Just consistent bad luck...poor planning." He stretches back in the chair, popping his back.

We catch up for a bit. He's only been here a year.

"That's something else we have in common," I say, laughing.

"Ms. Baker." Suddenly Canon materializes in front of us. "If you can manage to tear yourself away..."

Mitchell lets the chair legs hit the floor. "You must be Alaric Canon." He offers his hand without standing.

Canon ignores him. "We're breaking for lunch early. Since you have been enjoying social hour, it seems we will have to catch up before everyone gets back."

I feel as though I've been smacked on the hand.

Mitchell tries the phlegmatic approach. "Emma and I went to undergrad together."

"One big, happy OU family." Canon scowls. "Ms. Baker?" It's not a question. It's a command.

Forcing a smile, my face on fire, I say goodbye to Mitchell and trail behind Canon. He leads us to our temporary office. I haven't been gone that long, but he's incensed. Quiet and fuming.

"Shall I go get your lunch?"

"Can you manage to do so without attracting a throng of admirers?"

"Excuse me?"

"You are paid to do a job. Why is it that at every turn, you are filling your dance card?"

"My dance card?" I don't even recall the last time anyone danced with me. Probably when Shady still had people imitating. "I went to school with Mitchell." One would think the instant rapport would be valued.

It occurs me that normally Canon would be grateful for something like this, for in-depth knowledge.

"Mitchell," he snorts.

"Mr. LaCygne," I correct myself.

"Expanding this trip is not ideal for me either, I hope you realize. Every hour is critical," he says.

Unbidden, I think of him leaving with Ms. Fralin yesterday. Spending some untold portion of his day with her. Just exactly how critical am I expected to believe a late night meeting with Executive Expando Bra is? I want to ask.

I don't.

Not that it should matter.

"Dinner is at the owner's home tonight," he says, tapping his pen. "Will you be able to make it, or will you be spending yet more quality time with the illustrious Mr. Mitchell?"

"I don't normally spend quality time with my former college roommates' husbands," I level at him.

His pen stops clicking.

We work in silence the rest of the day.

6:15 PM

❀ LOCATION: Samuel Dowry residence.

❀ DINNER: Pretentious dish. Name forgotten.
"Tastes like chicken" would be a marked
improvement.

❀ HAIR: Down and straight.

❀ DRINK: Rum and Coke.

LANCE ROWE, THE EXECUTIVE WHO ACQUIRED a new limp in the conference room the other day, thanks to my pen jab, attempts to ply me with alcohol.

Let us observe the mating rituals of the lecherous North American lounge lizard in his native habitat: The Open Bar.

He thinks he's being smooth. Suave. He tried handing me a Cosmopolitan at first. I told him that he might not wish to advertise that he digs *Sex and the City*.

Now he's operating under the mistaken belief that I have consumed three rum and Cokes.

Let's get something straight: I can drink. Hold my liquor. The table? That's what I put other people under.

It's a gift. The one thing I have inherited from my mother that I can truly use. Her favorite story is about the time a dive bar band challenged her, and whoever got drunk first had to pay. The night ended with her packing up the band's gear after every member passed out. Sounds more like a hassle than a victory to me. Mom is a little off.

Humoring the guy seems like the path of least resistance. Not rocking the boat, I take the drinks, smile, and then set them down elsewhere. Or tip them into a potted plant.

The fern may need detox.

I dump most of the latest drink. *Say hello to my little fronds...*

This is the largest dinner party I have ever attended. It's also the only formal one. There are about twenty people roaming around. Execs and a few spouses enjoying drinks.

"Ms. Baker, how long have you worked for the company?"

"Ms. Baker, how are you enjoying our fair city?"

"Ms. Baker, this is an exciting opportunity for us all, wouldn't you agree?"

"Ms. Baker, that is a lovely dress."

The banter is innocuous enough, but I feel the need to guard my words. Remain opinion-free.

My dress actually is lovely, I must agree. It's silk in a gradient fade from teal to charcoal with a neck so wide the straps sit on the very edges of my shoulders. Nothing revealing, but the way the air touches my collarbones feels sensual. Sexy.

My heels click across the marble floor as I position myself in the corner.

From behind the rim of my glass, as I pretend to take another sip, I watch Canon. He maneuvers through the clusters of people. Talking. He slides to another group when Fralin appears. A few minutes later—after she appears to count down to "not too obvious" parameters—she inserts herself into his new group. Shortly after, he moves away.

Their game begins anew.

Oh, his discomfort pleases me greatly. Enjoy, sir. Enjoy.

9:20 PM

IN MY HAND, I HOLD THE NINTH RUM AND COKE of the evening. All totaled, I've taken enough sips to equate one whole drink.

This guy thinks he's adding stains to my hotel bedspread tonight.

Moron. I'm not even acting tipsy.

"No, thank you, Mr. Rowe. Enjoy the veranda without me."

"Thank you for the drink, Mr. Rowe."

"Really, Mr. Rowe? Four touchdowns in a single game?"

Canon is looking at me from across the room. I may have been hasty in congratulating myself on how I've handled this situation. That is one heckuva scowl he's rocking.

Extricating myself from the lecherous delusions of Mr. Rowe yet again, I walk closer to Canon. Letting him know I can tell he has something to say. I stop a few feet away; I am not going to heel. He can come to me.

He does.

"I see your reputation for professionalism is undeserved," he hisses over my shoulder.

"If you feel I have behaved unprofessionally, please clarify, Mr. Canon."

"Drinking."

"I can handle it." I turn to face him. As punctuation, I take a sip. "You are drinking too."

"It seems Rowe thinks he is what's going to get handled."

"He can think what he wants."

"That is your fifth drink."

"Ninth," I say just to irk him.

His mouth drops open. "Do not move. I will say the goodbyes."

Before I can formulate a response, he's gone. He makes the rounds, shaking hands enthusiastically and thanking the owner for a lovely dinner. When he sidesteps Rowe's outstretched hand, I can't help but smile.

"Give me your arm."

"Excuse me?"

He rolls his eyes, grabs my hand and wraps it around his bent elbow. His pace is slower than normal as he leads us outside.

Utter silence until we're in the car.

"I'm not drunk." My voice echoes in the car.

At a stoplight, his gaze shifts to me. Silently assessing. His hands wring the steering wheel.

"I didn't do anything to embarrass you," I say in the hotel parking lot.

"Surely you're not implying I should've waited until after you did." His sentence is punctuated by the door's near slam. He escorts me through the lobby. I allow his flat palm at the small of my back to guide me. Our pace is quicker, closer to normal.

Mute elevator ride. He removes his jacket and watches the numbers climb.

The doors open, and he turns toward our rooms.

He's going to fire me. Maybe I don't care anymore. I have done my best. I have been his ideal. Even when I felt certain he wanted to find fault, I gave him nothing to complain about.

Well, fine. Have it your way, Canon. Enjoy the stimulating company of Lawrence Peters without me. Good luck with closing this deal on your own. I'm taking your coffee with me too, you picky bastard.

"Good luck," I say, seething as he watches me open my door. I'm so pissed I actually do fumble and miss the first two times I try to slide the card. Fantastic. "I'll catch the first flight out."

"Be quiet." He steps into my room.

"Quit telling me what to do!"

"Don't act like you need to be told."

"You can't boss me around!" I switch on the bathroom light in the darkened room.

"It may have escaped your notice, but I am your boss."

"Not anymore. You're firing me!"

"You're being nonsensical. Sleep it off." He towers over me, his breath smoothing across my exposed shoulders.

Sensory overload. I'm so exhausted I can't think properly, and I can't take it anymore. I put my hands on his shirt and push him. Even in the dim light, I can tell he's surprised.

"Either you are firing me or I quit. Either you fire me because you're convinced I was going to embarrass you or I quit because you actually did embarrass me." I shake my arms, but he must think I plan to slap him because he grabs both my hands in his.

"Emma," he says, jaw clenched. "You may very well not be intoxicated but neither I, nor any reasonably observant human for that matter, would be able to conclude differently from your antics. Also, for some unfathomable reason, you did not see fit to clue me in," he spits and lets go of my wrists with a shove, as if he suddenly realized he was holding an oven fresh Idaho spud. "Emma, you can hardly fault me for being rational."

"Antics? Fault you! You do the social equivalent of dragging me out by my pigtails and you think I shouldn't 'fault' you?" I step closer, heels stomping the carpet. "What I think is that there is an apology in order."

"See? And you thought we were at an impasse," he says and moves enough tower over me. "Proceed. I'm ready to hear it."

I bump my shoulder into his chest, curse myself for reveling in the treacherous warmth, and stand firm, pressing against him enough that his stature sways. "You enjoying pushing people, don't you? It's different when someone else is doing the pushing, isn't it?"

"Good night, Ms. Baker." He turns to leave.

"You think you're so superior to me." I'm hot on his tail.

"Ms. Baker, I'm not insulting you. It's simple biology: your body mass can't handle the amount of alcohol which you appeared to ingest."

This is it. This is the final straw—a drinking straw, no less—for my tolerance of Alaric Canon. These may be my final moments with this man, and I can't even see him properly in this damned dim light. Sometimes he seems to connect with me, but now he is so condescending. Who does he think he is? "Any reasonably observant human." Pfft. He won't hold me "responsible for my actions." He thinks I would embarrass him, that I would embarrass myself, by drinking too much at a business function, that I "can't handle that much liquor."

Drunk, huh? He thinks I'm drunk? Ha! If I was drunk with Alaric Canon in my room…well, let's just say this would go down differently.

An idea: it hits me like an eighteen-wheeler. Hell, what have I got to lose at this point?

He's such an ass. Underestimating me. Doesn't think I can handle things. I'll show him what I can handle. I'll show him I can handle an ass.

I reach out and grab hold of that glorious ass and squeeze for all I'm worth.

Air whooshes from him, and he wheels around.

If I'm going down, I'm going down in a blaze of glory.

I don't give him a chance to say anything, and I stretch around him with both hands and knead the ever-loving fuck out of his butt. It is motherfucking glorious, and I think the memory will keep me satisfied when I'm living off ramen for the next few months.

Off-balance and stumbling, he falls against me. Hard.

Actually, he falls against me gently. He is what's hard…part of him anyway.

Blip.

Ladies and gentlemen, we have blip.

"Mr. Canon," I whisper up to him, "explain yourself." My left hand runs smoothly along his hip, drawing ever closer to his…revelation.

I'm not sure where this boldness is coming from. My index finger traces his length. The fabric is rough under my touch.

He hisses. He hesitates. I feel his palms smooth over my arms.

"Some might say this constitutes an offer," I breathe. Warmth from his hands sears my skin. I'm calm; I don't let it show.

"One should not make offers one is not prepared to complete." I turn his words back on him and grasp him firmly.

His head rolls back. I watch his throat as he swallows repeatedly.

He's losing it. I want more. The power intoxicates me.

Watching him for a reaction, I pull his zipper. He doesn't disappoint; his breath ceases.

"Stop me," I say.

He doesn't. I slip inside and hold him. Grip. Fist.

Claim.

It is silk and heat and pulsing want. His body jerks, surges forward, and I can barely contain my shit because I know, I just know, this is a pure reaction. This is a human moment, and it is everything I wanted and more.

So much more.

My body sings. Oh, my—I am controlling him…I have him in the palm of my hand. Literally. Figuratively.

Fingers curling around, thumb in tight circling circuits, pressing his flesh. He rocks and pants into my hair, down my face. Power. Intoxicating power. This, this I could get drunk on. My free hand follows along the path of his shirt buttons. I release him, and he makes a noise that sounds like a pained whimper, but it dies on his lips when I grab his shirt and tear it open, broken buttons flying across the room.

"Didn't think I had it in me, did you?" I say as I press my lips to his chest.

"Em…you…you don't really want this…"

I shove him against the wall. The thud sounds through the room.

"Don't tell me what I want." I speak against his skin as I tongue and bend and descend...lower, lower.

"I'm sure I know what you want." My knees hit the floor. "I'm excellent with non-verbal communication."

A rhythmic beat resounds in the room. I think it's the blood rushing through my system, but then I realize he's banging his head against the wall again and again. He is losing it. I want more.

He's still nearly fully dressed; I watch his chest rise and fall between partially untucked shirt scraps and draw him out through his open zipper.

My mouth closes around him. He clamps down on my shoulders as if to steady himself, as though the wall is not enough to support his weight. He's leaning on me. Needs me.

Tapping on his belt buckle, I pull back and say, "Off."

He nods mutely and complies.

Now, there is an element to oral sex that might be called worshipful, and I'm a fan of it—and even in the pale light it's clear his cock is worthy of worship, praise, maybe some hymns—but that is not what I'm here for today. I suck him in, swallow around him, press my tongue flat and create enough suction to rival a Hoover.

His knees give a bit, and since his legs are so long, it actually puts him at a better angle.

One hand returns to his ass, securing him where I want him, and I stroke him with the other. He's moaning and writhing, and I know this is going to be fast.

Embarrassingly fast.

I want nothing more.

I pull out all the stops. Tongue his slit. Tight in my mouth. Hint of teeth. In unison, my hand moves from his ass to massage his perineum while I pull him to the back of my throat, hum, and swallow.

Whoo-hoo. Mind over matter. Deep throat. I have never been able to do that before.

I hum—sorta, it's not the easiest thing when your airway is obstructed—and only I know it is the opening bars of "The Battle Hymn of the Republic."

"I...I'm...Christ." His back is bowed out, arcing, as he twitches and swells. I pull back, and he spills onto my tongue and struggles to stop rocking.

He's gasping for air, and his hands are running through my hair, then along my face with...reverence?

That is unexpected.

I stand and spit.

"I will add pineapple juice to your breakfasts," I say and pat his tie twice, his chest heaving underneath. "Drink it if you ever want that to happen again."

10:10 PM

✿ EMMA BAKER: I don't give head. I claim it.

ROWE WAS ON THE MONEY about one thing tonight: I did get new stains on my bedspread.

Oh, my God. I sucked off Alaric Canon.

This is something we need to talk about. Discuss. Hash out. Cover.

What have I done?

I wonder if going to his room now is a good idea.

Oh, sure — now I worry about crossing a line. Knocking on a door now is not too invasive; I have tasted the man's semen, pinged his radar so hard I pretty much sank his battleship.

He would let me know if he wanted to talk, surely.

I'm definitely the sort of person who would want to talk about this...situation. Explain myself, if there is any explanation. Defend if it is defensible. Hear these same things from him. I want to understand him, this. He wanted it, even in a war with himself, he wanted...me?

Maybe this isn't such a mystery. What guy is gonna turn down a blow job?

I need answers. It's only natural. It's in my nature.

But...

I'm not me right now. Nothing I'm doing is natural. Today, the role of Docile will be played by Emma Baker.

And a docile Emma wouldn't go seeking answers.

She would make sure Mr. Canon's coffee was ready at 7:00 a.m.

She would turn the lights out and go to sleep so she had her head on straight and could facilitate her boss's schedule, and she would not not not fellate her boss's tool.

Since I am only acting like a docile Emma, the lights go out but sleep doesn't happen.

DAY OF EMPLOYMENT: *381*

6:47 AM

❀ BAGS: Packed. In case of hasty retreat.

❀ HAIR: Straight. Clipped back.

❀ COFFEE: Ready.

❀ ME: Not.

I HAVE BEEN STANDING in the hallway for a while. Mustering. Muttering.
Don't think about it. Don't think about it. Don't think—
My hand rises to his door to knock. Before I can, he opens it.
Make or break. If I make eye contact, it's going to break me.

"Good morning, Mr. Canon," I say, breezing past him and setting
his coffee down with a flourish.

I begin gathering up his things, focusing on them. "Rebecca sent
over the reports you asked for; Peters' assistant finally emailed me the
correct documents this time; they're catering lunch in from a pizza
place, so I requested thin crust for you; I have forwarded an email
from Mr. Dowry about some tickets to an event later this week; and
I will need time in my schedule this afternoon to relocate everything
to the new hotel." And...breathe!

I have packed up during this spiel and now have nothing to do
but look up at him.

He's standing across the room, ready except for the suit jacket still draped across the bed. He seems to have been motionless during my act, to have simply watched me.

I finally meet his eyes. He blinks away.

For over a minute, he says nothing while he fastens his cuffs.

"Is that everything, Ms. Baker?" Monotone.

"I believe so, Mr. Canon."

"Very well." He grabs his things and sidesteps the incoming breakfast cart as he exits.

A pineapple has died a needless death.

9:15 AM

❀ LOCATION: Office of Diana Fralin, Wearer of
Actual Wonder-Performing Wonder Bra.

"THESE CLOSING COSTS SEEM EXORBITANT." I shake my head, looking at the expense records for the deals Fralin has touted as the most profitable.

"You have to grease the wheels overseas for everything from getting your phone lines hooked up to filing government permits," she says. She looks at Canon and shakes her head. "I thought everyone knew that."

I do my best to ignore her and also make darn sure I do not see the look she probably throws Canon at my expense. He excuses himself to take a call.

"And these promo items?" I sift through voluminous printouts. "That's a huge line item expense. Do you have records for where these product samples went?"

"Our paperwork is in order." She waves her hand. "Listen, honey, maybe this is all new territory to you, but let me explain how things work in the real world." She sits on the corner of her desk. I feel my eyebrows disappear into my hair. "Sales reps do just that: sell. If they have to account for where every single individual magnet or trial-size cleanser goes, what nurse gets a pen with our logo, who might end up with a free T-shirt…well, you can see where they'd spend all their time meticulously documenting to please the bean counters rather than selling."

"I'm not suggesting the level of detail be anything that...stringent," I say. "But there are concerns with sales in foreign markets. Your international distributors, their tactics, expose the whole organization to scrutiny. If anyone receiving discounts or free items is a state official—"

"Maybe I was not clear, Emma. I am sure you are competent at what you do. This is what I do. Don't get me wrong. What you do is important; one can't undervalue the skill of making a good cup of coffee." She smiles too sweetly and smooths her already immaculate updo. "I'm also very good at what I do."

I think this is not about work.

"There are those who work for and those who work with." She traces her finger along the top of Canon's laptop.

Yep. Not talking about work.

"Listen, let's cut to the chase," she practically whispers. "I have an MBA and I earned my way to VP in less than two years. I will run this place when Lawrence Peters's slow, worthless ass finally retires. I know where I belong, where I fit. And with whom."

This may be it.

This may be my breaking point. Well, my daylight breaking point.

I may snap and get on the intercom and yell to all who can hear me that I have an advanced degree in technical writing, a law school scholarship, and a recently acquired mastery of my gag reflex.

I'm under attack. I want to tell her that I—courtesy of numerous hours of lectures from my professor who actually helped write NAFTA into law—have a tad more awareness than she does of the recent surge in Department of Justice and SEC prosecutions for things like giving free samples to anyone who works for a hospital in a nation with state run healthcare. Things are different. People are going to jail. Companies are paying hundreds of millions in fines.

But I don't. Because that is not my role.

I do not flaunt my divided priorities.

I do not assert myself.

I do not embarrass my boss.

And it hits me. I hadn't even thought about it. I've been focused on awkward, morning-after hook-up tension.

He may be embarrassed to have been with me.

Diana Fralin knows her place. I never thought about mine.

I have never before so thoroughly questioned something I have done or why I have done it.

Question myself.

I don't like that. I'm allowed to celebrate my womanhood, experience what I choose with whom I choose. I am not easy. I'm discriminating.

I have wanted him to notice me, hoped he might desire me. He might not always do so, he might do so and not show it, but there is no denying he desired me last night. I, literally, had proof in the palm of my hand.

The door opens as Canon returns to the room.

"Alaric," she says, bolting from her desk and bumping my shoulder on her way to him, "your Ms. Baker is quite the go-getter. So very concerned about our foreign trade practices."

"She is quite thorough," he says, sounding almost as confused by her comments as I feel.

Fralin taps her chin as though she is just now forming an opinion. It's for show; she's plotting.

"Well, she seems to have so much insight. Maybe it would be a good idea for her to spot-check some things."

Warning bells. They're ringing.

Canon turns to me. He must wonder what I have been saying. "What did you have in mind?"

Fralin smiles broadly. "Well, I can give her access to a few market segments, let her explain her accusations to the sales people whose records she pulls—of course you'd want to find more passive phrasing, Emma," she chirps. Canon's eyes look like they may pop out of his head at the word "accusations."

She doesn't miss a beat…or an opportunity, it seems. "I can lend you a temp while she's working on things."

She wants me out of the way.

Here is where I'm going to balk. I'm not playing this role under different circumstances.

I'm here for him…for my company.

"I really don't thi—"

"Mr. LaCygne would — "

She and I talk over each other.

"That will not be necessary." Canon holds his hand up, effectively cutting us both off. "Give her unrestricted access to everything pertinent. We will go over it. Together."

"Surely that would be a burden for you, Alaric," she backpedals.

I, on the other hand, may do a wee jig. Even my plan didn't fail this miserably.

Walking away, he punches keys on his ever-present phone. "I am not enduring a temp. Ms. Baker is the best I have ever had."

Suddenly, I'm fine if we're not talking about work anymore.

1:15 PM

✤ LOCATION: Hotel front desk.

✤ LUGGAGE TROLLEY: Stacked like a Jenga tower.

"BUT I SPECIFICALLY REQUESTED adjoining rooms or ones across from each other." I'm livid. Distraught.

My hands have taken to gesturing as if independent from my body.

"Our sincerest apologies, Ms.…Baker," the front desk clerk says after glancing to verify my name. "We can try to arrange for accommodations elsewhere."

"I have already checked. I gave up two sets of reservations in favor of here," I say as my hand swings, smacks, and threatens to topple our bags.

I'm both mad and scared. The rooms are in separate buildings at opposite ends of the hotel grounds. I will have to run back and forth. I will impact productivity. I will have to tell Canon. This is the first thing I have not delivered on.

Still at the counter, I call him. The clerk seems like she'd like to leave. *Oh, no you don't. You are going through this with me.*

"Canon." There are voices in the background.

"Hello, Mr. Canon." I swallow back my nerves and take a deep breath. "There is a problem."

"Such as?" The voices fade. He must be moving.

"The rooms are several minutes apart." I describe the grounds and room layout.

He's silent.

Then he's not.

"Unacceptable," he says, fumings. "Put them on."

I hot-potato my cell to the wide-eyed desk clerk. "This is H — ... Yes...It is an unfortunate mix — Yes, I suppose you are right...No, I mean, yes. Yes, there is no suppose." Her face is as red as the poinsettia on the counter. "Perhaps I could fin — I do understand, bu — I understand...one moment, please...I'm sure your time is valuable...I do need a moment to loo — but..." She's tearing up. I almost feel badly for her. The fact that she is the person who originally booked my reservation helps to erode my sympathy somewhat.

"Yes, we do. I will make the change now. Thank you." Thankful is not how she sounds. She hands my cell phone back to me.

"...is disgraceful. How does it feel to be so incompetent a customer has to complete even the most perfunctory of tasks for you?"

"Mr. Canon," I say after waiting for him to take a breath.

"Ms. Baker?"

"I take it that you resolved things, sir."

"Not ideally. You were right to call. Set up there and come back. We should be out around five."

At least it won't be a late night. I think of my email inbox once again crammed with unwatched lectures and the copious number of briefs I need to read or write. I feel like joining the clerk in her sniffles.

Moments later, I'm being handed two access cards and a signature page.

"Your room is here," she says and circles a corner room on the top of the main building. "Room service is twenty-four-seven with a limited menu after ten in the evening. If you need any special accommodations — " she looks up at me as if, having spoken to Canon, she is well-aware that this is a given " — please let us know."

I sign and wait.

And wait.

"Did you need help with your bags?"

"Well, yes, that would be nice, but we need to finish the paperwork for the other room." I manage to keep the irritation out of my voice.

"There is no other room. I…I had to…I bumped a late-arrival party and gave you their suite," she splutters.

"One room?"

"There are separate sleeping areas."

Oh, well, indeed, yes, that is a great comfort to be sure. I may swoon.

"One room?"

"There are rooms within the room. Separate sleeping areas."

"Yes, you said that. But we are sharing a room?" I say, and she nods. "I'm sharing a room with that man?" I will have no break, no respite from that man? She nods. I am not entirely sure she hasn't heard my thoughts.

I snatch the cards from the counter and glare at her as if it were all her suggestion. I barely remember to wait for the bellhop.

It is a lovely room. The nicest I have ever stayed in. Pale marble. Sage green silks. Soft cottons. Deep mahogany woods. One actual bedroom. Living area with glass doors to a balcony. In front of the doors, a sleeper sofa I will be calling home. Small kitchen. Huge plasma. One closet. One bath.

One friggin' closet.

I hang the clothes. His shoes on the floor, mine on the shelf. He gets the top drawer. I put my stuff in the bottom. His stuff was on the left of the sink in the old hotel, so I put it there and put mine on the right or out of sight completely. I order extra towels and blankets. The room already has a coffee pot.

One friggin' bath.

Plug his charger in by his nightstand. Make sure the in-room alarm is not set from anyone else.

One friggin' room.

I'm at a loss for where I can keep all my school reading material. It ends up in a suitcase.

One friggin'…*How the hell did this happen?* I have tried to take it in stride, to go about my business, but how the…what the…I can't room with my boss! I can't room with a guy I shoved around and dropped to my knees in front of and sucked the stuffing out of. Went all "wham, bam, you better call me ma'am" on.

Sweating. Not perspiring or glowing or any of those ladylike things. I am sweating. Even my ass cheeks are sweating.

I splash my face at the sink. My reflection seems foreign. These are not my clothes. Not my hair. Not me.

The reflection stares back. Judges.

Perhaps I'm berating myself too much over last night.

How am I going to study? Get dressed? Relax enough to sleep?

Maybe you should try talking to him about what happened...

Voice of Reason...do you have an invite?

I am not allowed reason in this room situation. I have to take it in stride. He set this up. If he is okay rooming together, I have to act like I am as well.

Do what he says, when he says, without question.

I leave for work. I need a raise.

5:25 PM

❋ LOCATION: Entryway of hotel room.

❋ PIN: If one dropped, you'd hear it.

STAGNATION GETS TO ME. "Shall I show you where everything is?"

His lips are pursed, tense. His eyes dart to the sofa, the bedroom, the bath, and back again.

"The bulk of your things are here," I say and beeline for the bedroom. He shows up in his own time.

I begin opening or pointing to everything. I'm like Vanna White if Pat Sajak had his sex appeal ramped up by infinity.

"I put your things in the top drawer. The rest are in the closet. Shoes on the bottom." He opens the closet and peers in while I rattle on. "Charger on the stand. Alarm is already off. I have sanitized the remote."

I think I hear him say "perfect" from behind the open closet door.

"You may notice a few things missing. I have sent them to the cleaners due to the extended trip. If you will follow me, sir, there is not much left."

Instead, he actually leads into the bathroom. My heels click across the tile. "I believe this is everything you had out in your old room." I touch near his things at the sink. He glances at them, then around the small room until his eyes fall on the few items of my own I have left out. For a moment, it almost looks as though he is going to pick up my perfume, but he doesn't. "If leaving this out here is going to be a problem, I can keep my things elsewhere."

"No, no," he says rather softly. It's a small space. Intimate. Something shifts in the air.

I cough to clear my throat and throw open the shower curtain. "I have noticed you are nearly out of shampoo. Shall I pick some up for you or will the furnished kind be sufficient, Mr. Canon?"

"You don't have to do that." His hands are in his pockets.

"Very well. Shall I order dinner, sir?" I leave the bathroom as I speak. Flee, actually.

"What I meant was that you really don't have to keep using 'sir.' And I feel like Mexican food," he says, still in the bathroom for some unknown reason.

Not good. I have already read it over, and there is nothing like that on the hotel restaurant menu. "I can run out and pick something up."

His tie appears on the doorknob. "Get changed."

"Sir?" It's a habit at this point. He flinches a bit at the word but says nothing.

"We will go out. There is bound to be a decent place around here. A chain or something."

He disappears into the bedroom. I sit on the sofa, fingers drumming my skirt.

Changing as fast as men tend to, he's out in jeans and surely a garment of some other kind. I'm fixated on the jeans.

Denim in long expanses. Barely contours to his thighs. Thighs I have leaned against but not touched. Bare feet.

Barefoot! Put some shoes on, already! How am I supposed to look unaffected and asexual with all this unfair fuckery happening?

He sees me sitting. He stops short, looks back toward the bedroom.

"Um, it is all yours." He pulls his shirt down and steps to the side. A gray, long sleeve, V-neck tee. I pass silently and close the door.

I really want to lean my back against the door and breathe deeply for a few moments. A few hours. Fill my lungs. Decompress. Instead, I grab out my jeans and a white pullover. If I were home, I would wear my favorite electric blue sweater.

As I slide on my clothes, it occurs to me I've missed the opportunity to search for restaurants.

It's getting to me. I'm slipping.

A quick search on my phone finds one within walking distance and several others nearby. Shoving my phone back in my pocket, I vow to keep my head in the game.

Grab door. Yank open. March.

"Ready, Mr. Canon?" My words are followed by a clatter in the open bathroom.

Canon walks out, nodding.

I check the mirror and think I might smell my perfume in the air.

6:10 PM

❧ LOCATION: On the Border.

❧ CHIPS: Basket #3.

❧ SALSA: Abandoned for queso.

❧ MARGARITA: Want one.

❧ HAD: None.

"IT IS OFTEN THIS WAY. You get on site and the whole proposal needs reinventing." He practically shouts over the music.

"Good to know." I'm smiling for some reason. I feel happy. It must be the cilantro talking.

He goes on a bit about contracts and even more about supplements and the new skin care line. I'm surprised; I would have figured he didn't involve himself in products, just deals.

"This was the best idea," he says and points his fork at his plate. I think we are both weary of stuffy dinners and room service.

Careful there, Canon, you'll dislocate your shoulder patting yourself on your back. I nod and take a bite of my black beans. Then stop mid-chew. Do black beans cause gas? I can't be playing a tune in my sleep. Not with him a few feet away.

"Yes," I say, cutting off a bite of chimichanga. "It is delicious." Without thinking, I offer him the forkful.

It's just suspended there. Hovering. He looks at it and me and then leans over and wraps those lips around my fork and pulls and takes what I have offered him.

And now I'm just supposed act like it is no big deal to put that fork that has been behind his lips, inside his mouth, touched his tongue, back into my mouth.

"What do you think of Lawrence Peters?" he finally asks.

What to say in a situation like this? Be professional or go for blunt honesty? "He is an ignorant bore."

Guess we're rolling with honest.

Canon looks like he might have horked a jalapeño into his sinuses.

"And your opinion on the owner, Samuel Dowry?"

"Well," I say, charging ahead, "I spent very little time with him. He seems shrewd but has...eclectic taste in personnel."

"Eclectic..." Canon repeats, smiling. "Lance Rowe?"

"Delusional, manwhore sycophant."

He laughs. "Diana Fralin?"

"You would know better than me," I say and stuff a stringy, cheesy bite into my mouth.

"But I asked you." His brows knit together.

Not sidestepping that landmine. Honesty. "Duplicitous skank."

"Wow. Not pulling any punches." He sits back and sprawls his arm across the back of the booth.

I shrug.

"What did she do to you?"

*I would like to ask you the same thing...*Scratch that. I don't really want to know.

"Got you to call her Diana," I mutter into my chimichanga.

"What was that?"

"Nothing."

"It didn't sound like nothing."

"You mean to tell me you haven't noticed how condescending she is toward me?"

"Yes, actually I have."

"So why would you ask?"

He studies me for a moment. "Why do you let her get away with it?"

"I'm not supposed to embarrass my boss."

He blinks. Repeatedly.

Yeah, put that in your picky pipe and smoke it.

He watches his fork swirl the rice around the upper corner of his plate. "I think we need to talk."

"If you say so." I try to look nonchalant.

"Don't you think so?"

"If you think so, sir, then I think so."

"Don't do that."

"Do what, sir?"

His fork clinks on the Fiestaware. "That. Don't you think we have moved past the mister/sir thing in our off-hours now?"

Oh, this is more to the point than I was expecting. Pointy. Thorny. This is different.

I swallow…which is different too.

He appears to chew on the word he's about to say. "Emma." Piercing stare. "You do remember, don't you? Because I really hope to hell you remember, otherwise I need to take a whole different tack here."

Our perky waitress appears. "Did you two save room for desert? Our fried ice cream is amazing." *With a pineapple garnish?*

Canon looks at me as if to say he is game. I think he is a puzzle.

"Does it have a honey-based sauce?" I asked her.

"Oh, yes. Cinnamon and honey. It's delicious."

"No, thank you, then," I say.

"Ugh. Bee vomit." Canon looks nauseated. I'm probably catching flies. Too weird…the same phrase I use.

"How about some margaritas? They're on special."

"No," we say in unison quickly. I shiver. Drinks. A reminder of last night.

"Just the check," he adds.

8:05 PM

CANON IS IN THE SHOWER.

No other status report possible.

…

…

…

…

8:17 PM

I'M IN THE SHOWER.

The same shower in which Alaric Canon was naked and touching himself mere minutes ago.

The water on the walls may well have splashed off his skin.

Showerhead: Does not detach.

Universe: Hates me.

Water beats down on me. Our conversation plays back in my mind.

Not the best of decisions...for either of us.

Not my finest hour.

Mine either.

You regret it?

Yes...no...

Me, too.

Friends?

With you?

He scoffs lightly. Friendly then...

For the best...

I do not feel better. Not even in the realm of better.

8:35 PM

♣ AWKWARDNESS: Tens all around. Off the chart.

IT TOOK A GREAT DEAL OF INSISTING that Canon keep the bedroom. I am not in the camp of people who think genitalia determines many things, one of which being who gets the sofa and who gets the bed.

I'm happier out here with the television to keep me company. Hopefully the ambient noise will scare Lincoln away.

I don my PJs while still in the bathroom. My skin is damp, and the fabric clings.

I step out into the quiet main area. Canon is in his room.

A sofa bed is not as easy to set up as one might wish.

I am determined not to ask for help. It's not the weight that is the problem. It's stuck.

It pulls free. Of course, a spring hook also digs into my '67 Impala pajamas and rips a huge hole as it scrapes down my thigh.

"Aaahhhhh!"

The bed legs smack the floor. I press my hands to my leg and will the pain away. It's probably not that bad, just shocking.

"What happened?"

I open eyes I hadn't realized I'd squeezed shut. Canon is down in front of me. He moves my hands to check.

I hiss.

At the sound he looks up at me. His fingers press through the tear in my pants.

"I'll be okay."

He shakes his head and tries to check for damage. Unsuccessfully.

Without looking up, he pulls what's left of my pants off and out of the way. Why the concern? I can surely still brew coffee and type even if my leg needs amputation.

"I said I'm okay."

All thoughts cease when his thumb traces a foot long red mark up my inner thigh.

"Enjoying yourself down there, Mr. Canon?"

The words are out of my mouth before I realize I've thought them.

He freezes.

It's like a switch flips.

My hands run through his hair. I don't know when I put them there. They move down his neck. To his shoulders. I fist his shirt and pull. Never looking up, he grabs the bottom of his shirt with his free hand. It goes over his head in one motion. It hangs in a circle around the arm he is still using to apply pressure to my leg.

"Move your arm and let the shirt fall."

His breath hitches. I'm shaking. I hope he can't tell. His shirt lands next to my pants, and he returns to my thigh.

"Surely you are familiar with the saying…kiss and make it better?"

Slowly—oh, God, so slowly—he leans in more and presses his lips to the bottom of the scrape near my knee.

Oh, yeah. I'm feeling no pain. Then his warm lips move up and press again.

Then again.

And up again.

If my knees don't buckle out from under me, it's going to be an unqualified miracle.

Near the top, after a dozen plus ongoing kisses, I touch his arm and bring it to my hip. To steady myself. I hope it seems like a reward.

His arm wraps completely around me. My hip at his shoulder, his palm pressing along the small of my back, stopping when his fingers encircle the other side of my waist.

I indulge myself. I run my fingers through his hair. Silk. Slide them over his shoulders. Satin. Trace the indents and sinews. Stone. The planes of his shoulder blades. Oak.

He hums.

I drag my fingers up his back, lightly scratching with my nails. Very lightly.

He moans.

It drowns out mine.

Here is a crossroads. A bridge. A defining moment. Run or succumb. Lead or be led. Live or be dead.

I want a lot.

I want to be more like the women he dates. The polished women. The ones on his arm.

I want him to not just be a fuck hot pretentious wanker who should drink pineapple juice so I can blow his beautiful cock more often.

Or something less whorish.

I want him to scoop me up in his arms and carry me to his bed and tell me he sees me for who I am and wants me and respects me, and he is only a hardass to get the job done and he will be the most patient and wonderful man on this green earth if I will only give us the chance.

But at the end of the day, I'm a practical gal.

He's practically the sexiest thing I have ever encountered, and I am going to practically do whatever I practically can for as long as he is willing.

He reaches the top of the red line.

I want him to cross it.

"Mmmm," I hear myself say. "I bet your lips would make everything feel better."

With my words, he bows his head against me. His grip tightens around my waist.

"Isn't there something in your way?" My voice sounds suddenly lower to my own ears.

"Yes," he whispers.

Oh, my…why is this actually working?

"What do you need to do? Want? Tell me." Slowly, I run a hand though his hair again and again.

"I need…to take off your clothes. I want…I want to…" he breathes into me.

I run my hand up under his jaw. "Want what?" My voice is low, slow. "Tell me."

His hand at my thigh moves up and twists around my panties. "I want to take these off and spread you open and taste you and tongue you and feel you come apart."

Gah. Thoroughly outlined. Well done, Canon.

I wrap a hand around the one he has at my waistband and encourage him to pull down. His other hand slides around to help, and I move my hands out of his way.

The panties fall into the ever-growing pile. I feel his breath. He kisses and slides his palms up my sides.

There is probably something I should say now to keep this little scene going, but I'm rather focused on not doing a header onto the sofa.

He presses his lips to my inner thigh, his breath swirls inward, and I pull his hair reflexively. He angles and does it again before he speaks. "Let me take you to bed." I think my ears trick me into hearing a "please."

The light hairs along his arm graze my palm as I travel from shoulder to forearm to hand. My fingers drag over his lifeline to reach his fingers, their tips. I curl and hold his fingers, and they curl into mine. Though I wish he would put himself out there, pull me, I pull him and step toward the bedroom, and I feel him shift and rise to follow me.

A half-naked Alaric Canon is following me to his bed. Forget buckling knees or not doing a header, this…this is a bona fide miracle.

I'm afraid to breathe. Afraid to upset whatever astrological align-ment has set this in motion. Wherever you are, dear butterfly, keep flapping your chaotic wings. Flap them. Flap them like your little life depends upon it…or at least my little death.

Save for moonlight filtered through the curtain, the bedroom is dark. His feet pad along the carpet behind me.

Next to the bed, I stop; I need to turn and face him. Face this.

I'm not able to make myself turn.

I reach back behind me and find him. Stretching until I feel his arms, then sliding down them until I can feel his wrists and hold them.

I can't get over the feel of his skin on mine. Warm. Smooth. Real.

I pull forward, and he steps flush against me, his every breath pushing against my spine. My hands travel to cover his, palm to back, and I place one on my abdomen and hold it there while I guide the other beneath the front of my shirt and drag it up my body until it brushes under the swell of my breast.

His breaths burn my neck. I press his hands into my flesh, then leave them there as I arch back and bring my arms around his shoul-ders and bend until I feel his hands stir. He twists to cup my breast as his lower thumb traces where my thigh ends and the rest of me begins.

As if I think he's asking needlessly for permission, I grant it. "Yes."

If I thought we were flush before, I was wrong. He pulls me against him, into him. Palms my breasts.

Yeah, just palms. I'm not big enough for his whole hand. Few would be. His hands are big. Huge.

Big hands include long fingers, a fact of which I'm reminded when the cupping between my legs turns to delving.

*Oh, yeah, well, hey now…there. Right there. Oh, please — keep going…or there…up there. Yeah, that works, too…Jesus, I…whoa…I guess there works too…I concede, you know better than…more…holy… wow…*All those times my knees threatened to give, to stop support-ing me, they weren't crying wolf; I would collapse if I didn't have my fingers entwined behind his neck.

I need to lie down. Before I fall down.

I break away and sit back on the bed, and he seems almost wor-ried, but I pull him to me and he drops and hits the floor and ends up looking up at me, hands roaming my skin.

Beautiful. He is gloriously, scandalously, incandescently beautiful.

I want to hold him.

And never let go.

It scares me.

Get back on task. I find a word. "Now."

He descends into the shadows.

Oh. Okay, so that is what we're doing. I can barely see his outline. Um, all right. I bless the darkness and hope it hides whatever shows on my face.

"This is not something I have ever been into," I hear myself say. That is a bit too real. A trip down a memory lane of lame lovers. Wow, over-share much? I know I need to cover my slip. Distract him. "Convince me." I pull his hair without reason. It spurs him.

*Oh, holy night…*I have been wondering about this. A niggling. Rooting around in my brain. Why would he need pushing? Act like he needs it? The concern has been there, but I have not wanted to consider it. It would be unfair to have such a pretty package and nothing inside. To look like a sex god but be sans skill set.

Not. An. Issue.

I don't know exactly what he's doing down there, and I don't really care just so long as he keeps doing it for a long, long time and—

Then he adds fingers into the mix. Where was I…what was I thinking?

Each pass and pull works together to remove and erase the fumbling of past visitors who should now, in whatever clouded corner they inhabit, hang their heads in collective shame. Adam with his kitten licks. Paul rubbing out a fire.

My feet on his lower back. Hands in his hair. I trace his eyes.

Now I'm fucking writhing. Writhing! I have zero idea of the logistics of what he is doing, and I think I've given up trying to figure it out. Just for all the peonies in Pennsylvania let him keep doing it, and I will endeavor to stay focused on that and pay no heed to how I'm beginning to tear apart at the seams.

Because I am. I'm going to lose it and start saying some pretty embarrassing, revealing things.

Like exactly who I have pictured when sealing the deal solo for the past year.

One hint.

I want to stay staid. In control.

When my hips start to surge forward, I force them back, deep into the mattress. I want to pull his hair and grind against his face and hope he has learned to breathe through his ears. I force my hands to the sheets, nails into the mattress.

It is a losing battle.

Then I am lost. I'm shouting and moaning and maybe channeling sounds I haven't uttered since sophomore year Latin class. *Salve o magister...Is est Olympus quod abyssus...*

The Latin word for male genitalia eludes me...

...it might be genitalia...

My breath remains gasps. He looks at me, eyes sparkling in the window light.

I want to kiss him.

But I don't.

That doesn't seem to be what we do.

My hand touches his face. The reverence he seemed to give me yesterday, I return to him.

I notice he is not still. Rocking. Rutting into the mattress.

I peel my shirt off, lean back on my elbows, and point to my chest. "Here."

His pants go away, and he moves over me, and I try not to be too damned obvious in my perusal—that is the polite word for it—as I devour him with my eyes.

He sits back on his heels, straddles my chest.

That's where his eyes are fixed anyway.

My tits.

He studies. His shadowed face looks nearly pained.

I hold his hand and bring it over where his gaze has frozen. "Hold me." As the words leave me, his hand envelopes, thumb easing across, teasing to a point.

I try to calm my breathing. Run my index finger down my sternum. "Paint me."

He growls, throws his head back, and strokes his length.

While he works, his head still back and one hand anchored to me, I roam his contours, his sinews. His thighs tense. I trace their definition. His hips and hand work in tandem, pulse and surge and simulate.

I want to, try to, feel all of him. Everywhere and all. Memorize his V. Wrap my hands around his waist, feel a hint of hipbone push into my grasp.

Ragged breaths. Sheen on skin. Everything about him has taken on an edge of feral, harsh focus…save where he holds my breast.

My lips are on his body before I realize I've moved and they run along his chest, teeth nip along the lower curve under his ribs, wrap my arms around him, fingers travel up his back, his muscles moving beneath my hands. He rocks and pushes and propels ever closer to completion, knuckles banging against me, silk teasing my throat.

"You are so close…I want it." My words echo in the tight space between us.

Sounds leave him in notes of strain and relief. It hits against me. Spurts. Trails. Hot.

I'm overwhelmed. Euphoric. And it was not even about me. My head rests against him, rocked with his heaving breaths, and he sags against me, drapes over me, chin at the back of my head, heart beating near my ear.

It is the strangest and best hug of my life. I never want to move.

Close. I have never felt so connected to anyone.

Joined without joining. Intensity.

Intense and real.

But not. Not real.

I need to get away.

In the shower, I scrub away what we did. He was still on his knees when I slid out from under him. When I pulled away.

The sofa bed sheets are cool.

I have no dreams.

3:10 AM

❈ Stealth: Is a bitch to bladders.

As quietly as possible, I tiptoe to the bathroom. Turn the knob. Close the door silently. Not even a click. Realize I was holding my breath.

Every brush of my feet is like thunder. And now, after my successful endeavor to reach the bathroom undetected, just how do I plan on peeing without him hearing me?

Oh, grow up. It's a basic human function. It's no big deal. It's nothing to be embarrassed about.

I turn the faucet on full blast. Congratulations, I'm a genius.

Afterward, I open the door and walk full-on into rock hard abs.

"You okay?" His voice is gravelly, confused. "Did you run a bath?"

Congratulations, I'm a goober.

"I'm fine," I say and duck around his body, trying not to inhale too much of his warm, sleepy scent.

"Didn't mean to disturb you," I splutter. I can't get under my covers fast enough.

He's quiet, motionless for a moment as I clamber onto the sofa. Then, he sounds almost apologetic. "I...I guess I didn't realize what a light sleeper I have become." He turns away. "Good night...again."

DAY OF EMPLOYMENT: 382

6:00 AM

❅ LOCATION: Hallway outside room.
❅ EARBUDS: Pandora radio. White noise.

I'M STILL BREATHING HEAVILY from my unscheduled visit to the fitness center.

The hotel door opens quietly for me. Pointless.

He's sitting on the end of the sofa.

I can't see his face.

"I thought you'd left." He doesn't look at me.

"I…I'm not leaving," I say. I don't know what else to say.

He nods and rises and walks to me. Our hands bump. Then twist. Then hold.

Squeeze, tighter. Then apart. The bedroom door clicks.

In the shower, I consider not shaving. Maybe stubble will help me keep myself in check.

It's all a bit more than I bargained for. That may be okay. I still feel out of sorts.

Out of control. How did I get so out of control?

I will fake it. Control.

It is a plan.

I am still contemplating the merits of Fake Control Plan 4782 while I dress.

I slide on black stockings and heels. Black panties. My bra doesn't cooperate.

My arm is bent back and arguing with the hook and eye when I feel him behind me.

His fingers brush my back. He fastens the fabric together. Runs a finger under a strap, untwisting it as he moves up my back to my shoulder.

"Thank you." My voice is soft.

He says nothing. I feel his lips against my hair.

Never mind. I think I'm no longer a fan of plans.

7:03 AM

❋ BREAKFAST: Most interesting eggs ever.

I AM STARING AT MY PLATE. He's in a tie.

I don't even know what to say. Uneasy. Almost…maybe…scared? I don't know if it is because he is so imposing elsewhere, or that I had him on a pedestal, or that this simply feels…different.

I remind myself I'm acting different than myself in every way.

I pack his things. The weather is turning. I hand him his coat. We leave.

I can feel him watching me. It's warm. Not unwelcome.

There's nothing I can think to say that will transition us.

Then he spares me the awkward move from night to day.

"Write up a temporary transfer proposal of Sean Becket to oversee our warehouse build," he says in the hall.

"Yes, sir."

"Rebecca needs a progress report." In the elevator.

"I will send it by end-of-day."

"Ms. Fralin has set up a dinner meeting with me tonight." In the car.

Oh. Lovely. "What would you like for me to do while you're at dinner, Mr. Canon?"

He switches lanes. "Wear whatever outfit goes with those black lace shoes and sit to my left."

I can't help but smile. His eyes flicker to mine. The corner of his mouth turns up just slightly, then he refocuses on traffic.

Incoming text: Just checking on you. You okay? —Rebecca

Reply: Fine. How's the betting?

Incoming Text: Bert will be so disappointed. He had down that Canon would eat you alive by last night.

Note to self: Never bet against Bert.

1:51 PM

❀ LOCATION: Break room.

❃ TASK: Fetching drinks. Arf.

CLICKS SOUND OUT BEHIND ME.

"Alaric tells me I need to change the reservations because we will have the pleasure of your company at our dinner this evening."

"Yes, Ms. Fralin," I say without turning around. "That is what he told me as well."

I stack cans and cups, pour coffee. Her nails tap the counter.

"Have you made any headway with your little foreign accounts pet project?"

"Not yet." The relentless patronization grates at me, my words are clipped.

"Perhaps tonight would be a good opportunity."

"That would have to be cleared with Mr. Canon."

"Of course, of course. Though…" I stir in sweetener. She sounds like saccharin. "LaCygne is the best man for working side-by-side on that particular project. That's his area, and he has the most flexible schedule. He might even be available on short notice."

"Again, whatever Mr. Canon says—"

"You do," she finishes for me. "I can tell. You're quite the dutiful one, are not you? He says 'jump,' you say 'how high,' and if he says 'bend over'—"

"I need to get back," I snap and walk past her.

"He's so focused." Her voice, shrill, echoes in the room behind me. "Last trip, he made time for fun."

My steps falter. Fun. I sincerely doubt he did any such thing. A vision of Canon wearing Mickey Mouse ears and holding balloons pops into my head.

Then, I recall his absence when she showed up the other day. But he has said every hour is critical. He doesn't waste time. A date would be a waste.

He couldn't get that time back from her. Unless ol' TARDIS tits can also time travel.

Not asking him questions has never been harder.

I just wanted him to notice me. This has been so much more.

I don't know what to do with all the "much."

Real? Convenient? Why do I care? Oh.

Oh. I do care.

I am going to ask him. Tonight, after dinner, I am going to ask him.

Maybe this is one plan that will not go awry. The others have sorta bordered on best laid.

I will probably berate myself all afternoon for letting Fralin get to me.

The atmosphere back in the conference room is oppressive. Claustrophobic. There are too many people and too many independent conversations being carried on.

11: Number of times Diana Fralin has found a reason to touch Canon during this meeting.

I suppose it's too late to say I'm not counting.

"Ms. Baker?" His voice breaks my concentration. Not good. Should have been concentrating on his voice. "The printouts?"

"Uh, yes, sir. Here they are." I dig out the papers. Fralin smirks and wraps her hand around Canon's to tilt the words toward her. He moves and sets the report out in front of her as his eyes turn up to me.

Don't mind me.

I'll just be over here. Enjoying a nice round of self-flagellation.

6:10 PM

✤ Location: Hotel bathroom.

✤ Clothes: Rebecca's black skirt. Clara's taupe,
  drape blouse. My never-worn taupe heels with
  black lace overlay. Unknown owner's citrine
  earrings.

✤ Hair: Up, twist.

✤ Makeup: Earth tones.

✤ Reflection: Not me.

"We need to leave," Canon says from behind the door.

"Yes, s—" I say, stopping myself. In the main room, he's messing with his tie in the mirror.

I step behind him. Straighten his collar.

If it were up to me, I wouldn't go to this dinner.

Neither would he.

At the restaurant, we are seated near a large, stone fireplace. Bottles of house wine line the tall, stone walls.

As requested, I'm seated at his left. He's right-handed, so either he doesn't want to spend all evening keeping his elbow out of my face or...

Under the white tablecloth, his palm glides long my forearm and down until it rests over the scratch I got last night.

A chair scrapes as it's pulled out from the table.

"Mr. LaCygne, I didn't realize you would be joining us," Canon says, his eyes narrowing almost imperceptibly.

"Call me Mitchell." He offers his hand.

After a pause Canon actually shakes it.

Then Mitchell steps in it. "Diana said Emma is anxious to begin working with me."

I'm about to clarify, but Canon beats me to it. "Anxious or not, she only works with me."

"Oh, Alaric." Diana slips into her seat. Across from Canon. Prime footsie access. "Don't give the kids such a hard time. I tried to tell you Mitchell would be the best person to look over things with her. He has been a veritable workaholic ever since his divorce."

I feel Canon stiffen beside me, but his hand stays on my leg. Seems Mitchell and I didn't get very caught up the other day...

"I suppose that's the upside of it. I'm flexible, Emma. Whatever works for you, works for me," Mitchell says.

"Traditionally that is the sort of thing one clears with an employer," Canon says, looking at them, then his menu.

I unfold my napkin. It's a task that doesn't take nearly long enough.

Mitchell's eyes meet mine. He looks at me as if he has just realized he's not gotten the whole story here. "If it's a problem, we can get together another time," he offers.

Diana smiles into her wine. She must've gotten a head start in the restaurant bar. Great. Fralin even less inhibited. "Oh, it's not a problem, is it, Alaric?"

"Why start asking me now?" Canon says without inflection.

The waiter appears to take drinks orders. While the others make selections, Canon excuses himself. He may never drink again.

When he reaches the far side of the room, he turns to look at me; he wants me to meet him.

I chug water down my dry throat and leave wordlessly while Fralin and LaCygne discuss something.

Canon is leaning on a thick wooden door frame. Somehow, he looks purposefully positioned. As if aiming for blasé.

"Yes?"

"You should know that I can tell what's going on," he says, jaw set.

"What do you mean?" With Mitchell?

He glances at me, then looks straight ahead. "With her."

This is new. Volunteering info of a personal nature. What a novel concept.

I look at him, encouraging him to continue.

He stands up and starts toward the table, pausing to speak low, near my ear. "I will handle it."

The waiter takes our orders almost as soon as we return to the table.

Canon stops him as he starts to leave. He waves a finger between Mitchell and me. "Box their food to go. They have urgent business, it seems."

"And bring us a bottle of this," Diana adds, holding aloft her glass.

Uh, that is not what I was expecting. At all.

6:43 PM

❀ LOCATION: Parking space near Buca di Beppo.

❀ MITCHELL'S TRUCK: Equipped with gun rack.

❀ FOOD: Going to waste. No appetite.

TRY AS I MIGHT, I could not get Canon to let me discuss anything privately with him before our orders arrived.

Mitchell opens the passenger door. "Your chariot, m'lady."

I manage a smile. Not a good one though. "He's a real piece of work, isn't he?" Mitchell says and offers his hand.

"Huh?" I step toward the door. My voice sounds foreign to me. "Oh, Canon? I suppose he can seem rather terse."

"Terse?" Mitchell laughs as I slip into my seat. "Does he have you bugged or something? I was just glad to get you an evening away from that asshole."

He pauses for a moment then shuts my door.

What is this I'm feeling? Oh, who am I kidding? I'm jealous. That bitch. "Handle it" as he said he would or not, she got me out of the way. She set this up, and I said nothing. Now Canon thinks I may have lied to him about Mitchell being married and maybe even that I wanted to be alone with him and I really was flirting with him. I was not, and I don't want to be alone with Mitchell, and I don't know why I don't want a break from Canon because he really can be an insufferable son of a bitch. I don't want Canon to be alone with Diana because I only want him to be alone with…me…

"How long?"

"What?"

"How long have you had a thing for your boss?"

What? "That's crazy talk." Crazy, crazy, craziness kind of crazy. Like post anti-helmet law Gary Busey crazy.

"Crazy or not, you definitely have feelings for him."

"Of course I have feelings for him. I feel he drips disdain and breathes arrogance and harbors standards designed specifically to ensure their failure to be met."

"Uh-huh."

"Don't 'uh-huh' me, Mitchell." It would not do me any good to have feelings for Canon. Sure, yes, he is proving himself to be capable of being nicer than I ever thought possible. But he wants the exact opposite of me: obedient in the day and some sort of aggressive bedroom role with which I am not accustomed, not comfortable with, at night. How crazy would I be to have feelings for someone who pushes me around during the day and then wants to be pushed around at night? Who confuses me with desire and doing up my bra?

"I won't claim it makes sense. But you have always been a strong person. Maybe this a good fit. I've never seen anyone affect you like this."

I laugh. It's weak. "What makes you think I'm so affected?" My arms cross over my chest.

He sweeps his hand exaggeratedly over the expanse of the dashboard. "Because we've been sitting here in your hotel parking lot for a good ten minutes."

What the...? I look around, bewildered. The hotel sign lights the thin layer of ice on the lot.

Cringing, I realize I hadn't even noticed we'd left the restaurant.

I have simply got to harness this. Get a lid on it. Control.

"I'm not in love with Alaric Canon."

"Um, Emma...I never said you were."

7:18 PM

❋ SOFA: Sitting on it.
❋ LIGHTS: Off.
❋ MITCHELL: Elsewhere.

I LEFT MITCHELL IN HIS TRUCK, crossed the lobby, went to the room, dumped my food in the trash, and sat on the sofa. About twenty minutes ago.

Canon could very well be helping Ms. Fralin make her way through her wine. Then, doubtless, she will want his help making a way through her.

I'm angry. Jealous and angry.

She has out-maneuvered me. Out-plotted me. Out-planned me.

I've let her. Because I'm not being me. Maybe if I was, maybe I would have put her in her place, called her out on her shit, schooled her.

More than that…more than that…the idea of her…him…

The thought is painful. I try to shut it down.

But I keep coming back to the notion that I'm not certain what it is that I — me, not this little PA part I'm playing — have on the line here. A romp with my boss? A couple of encounters?

A fling? A potential fling?

No, I don't even have that.

Ms. Baker has that. He's willing to give her the time of day…er, night…whatever.

I'm still unnoticed.

And — I think I've known all along — there is the distinct probability that I will remain that way.

I have made a giant mess of this.

If I weren't here, on this trip, in these borrowed clothes, ironing my hair, hiding my studies, holding my tongue, he would never have known that I exist.

But, for me, he definitely exists. More than ever. Intelligent and intuitive. Precise and passionate. Decisive and desirable, and I am desperate.

I have planned my way into desperation.

There are two choices here: Grab the bull by the horns and make some memories, or let it go and regret not experiencing more…whatever this is.

If this is all I get, I will take it, and treasure it, and make the most of it.

Bargaining stage.

If he comes back tonight, I will be whoever he wants me to be.

Just let him come back tonight.

God, I'm not just in the neighborhood of pathetic, I'm circling the block.

The door opens. The light spreads across the carpet, growing from sliver to spear, then snapping back to dark with a click.

"Ms. Baker?"

"Mr. Canon." I'm slumped forward with my elbows on my knees. I don't know if it looks quirky or clumsy.

He looks around for the first time, apparently not expecting me to be here alone. "Where is the illustrious Mr. LaCygne?" He flips on the entry light. His jacket is undone. The access card bends in his hand.

"I don't know. Not here."

"I gave you your leave for the evening. Why are you here?"

"Because this is where you want me to be."

A beat. "I never said that."

"You didn't have to."

I have been sitting here too long; everything seems bogged down, with the world trudging by in slow motion. He hangs his jacket. It feels as though it takes a whole minute or more. Without a sideways glance, he's gone into the bedroom. My train of thought has steamrolled down the mountainside as I've gone from nervous he would not come back to nervous he actually would, with a side track of the possibility he would come back covered in Diana residue, and then barreling into town with a load of he might very well not give a fair fig if I'm here or not, no matter who I happen to be.

This is crazy. I stand up on Jell-O legs — sitting on the sofa has taken its toll — and start toward the door.

As I wobble round the coffee table, Canon steps back into the room. Shoes and tie gone.

"Where are you going?" He stops trying to unbutton a cuff.

I look at the door and realize I have forgotten my card. "For a walk."

"If I wanted you walking around the hotel in the dark, I wouldn't have booked us into this single room."

A record skips in my head. While I would love to contemplate how and why anyone dug up an LP just to scratch it inside my brain — and it better be "Don't Worry, Be Happy" because God knows that song's just asking for it — I am a tad busy trying to process Canon's statement. Aren't we in this room for productivity's sake? The time to traverse the hotel campus between rooms and all that? He asked for that reason. Or wait…did I?

"You have given me my leave for the evening, as you say. I'm going for a walk."

He shakes his head and sighs. "If you insist upon going for a walk, I will go with you."

Him coming with me rather defeats the purpose of the walk.

"I'll stay in then."

"Because I would walk with you?"

"Because it's cold outside," I counter and step into the entryway with him.

"It has been cold all day."

"I'm not dressed for it."

"Change."

Oh, my dear Mr. Canon. That is the operative word, is not it? "This is what you told me to wear."

He winces slightly at my words. "I also told you to sit beside me, but you left."

"You told me to." I step closer.

"For someone who seems to pride herself upon knowing what I want, why did you pick tonight to insist upon acting to the contrary?"

Good question. "Why are your wants so contradictory?"

"They are not…" He wavers.

"You are quite the contrarian." Closer. More.

"To the contrary, my wants are not contradictory."

"That is a tongue twister. Did you reward Ms. Fralin for her efforts to get me out of the way tonight? She get your tongue all limbered up?"

His head pulls back, stunned. "What are you insinuating?"

I'm silent. I move again. Close.

"Answer me." He tries to huff, rakes his fingers through his hair.

"You need clarification?" I'm in his dance space. Breathing in his breaths.

His hands go out as if he is going to touch my shoulders—but he hovers there. Hands fold inward and skim above my arms and down, brush my skin.

"If I wanted her, I would be with her," he breathes. I press my hands to his shoulders. Warm.

"So…if you want someone, you would be with them." Sliding down his arms, I bring them to me, to my waist.

His voice is nearly inaudible. "Yes."

"You are with me," I say against his neck.

Beside my ear: "Yes."

Whoa. Hold up there, Buttercup. No fun storming the castle yet. We need to talk.

I need to clear my head. I step away. To the balcony window.

The lightest of snow falls. A thin layer of white. Reflected lights.

He moves the curtain out of the way. "Why do you always do that?"

We both watch the snow fall.

"Do what?" The bare glass is cool under my hand.

"Leave."

A car cuts through the fresh snow.

"When I was little, one Christmas, a cottontail visited our yard every day over break. Big, fat, gray. I would watch as it hopped through the snow, finding whatever little treats and treasures others overlooked. Some uncovered grass behind the bench. Last night's dinner in the compost.

"After a few days, it felt like my own. My pet. I looked forward to it every day. Its fat footprints in the overnight snow. Then I made the mistake of trying to pet it."

I turn to him, his arm still braced on the glass.

"Well," I say, "you can imagine what happened. I never saw it again."

He looks to me then returns to study the night. "But you know you are not you in this scenario."

His words shock. Can he know? Does he realize I'm not acting like myself?

"You are not the little girl." He drops the curtain. "Knowing how you felt then, why do you choose to be the rabbit now? Is it because the rabbit has all the power?"

He has a point.

Damn it.

1:18 AM

"PLEASE."

I hear myself repeat the word as I wake. No idea how many times I have said it asleep.

His troubled eyes lock onto mine, and he reaches for my hand. I don't have the will to keep it from him, to keep anything from him.

I think he's going to tuck blankets back around us, but he bends my hand to his face and presses his cheek to my palm. My whole being hums at the contact. He's so warm and real, the realest thing I've ever known.

I know I must be gaping at him, but he's unfazed. He hums into my skin and brushes stray hairs from my face.

He's actually very sweet.

I've been attempting to come to grips with that for days. Now, it seems, without reason.

He runs his lips up past my wrist and along my arm. He traces the faint blue veins. Half kiss, half taste. When he reaches my neck, he looks up, smiles.

And I recall why I care about this man in the first place. It's because he isn't changing to impress me; he's just letting me in. Letting me know him.

He isn't asking me to be any different, either. I'm doing that to myself.

He smiles, and I can see the best of me reflected in his bright eyes.

"Emma…"

Those same eyes that danced with light a moment ago shift, searing hunger surges in their depths.

I don't know when he grabbed my shirt, but if there were buttons instead of snaps, the floor would be littered with broken half circles. He pulls it open and free of my pants. He's tugging and pulling and pushing me to the bed, and it's all I can do not to step on his feet as they move near mine. My knees hit the mattress, and I fall back to sit on the bed.

He straddles me and wraps his arms around my chest, cocooned between my ribs and bedding.

Holy…should we do this right now…I was trying to take a night off. Get some perspective. Do I want it to happen like this?

Then he tears his sleep shirt over his head, pushing his chest into me. Arms high and bent. Looking like a classic Bowflex advertisement. And I don't care if that dates me, as long as this man does.

His arms come down around my shoulders. Slide and skim and skin.

Um, yeah. I sure do.

And I won't think about how we don't have a future, that there will be no more times for tender reflection. This trip will end, and there will not be nights for exploring and days for memorizing and, I think my heart momentarily stops at the thought, afternoon sessions in the copy room for come-what-may.

But this? This moment, this right here is about desire and claiming. Mine.

He lifts my head. I hadn't realized I'd fallen forward, melancholy moment held at bay. He weaves fingers within my hair. Slowly. Like spinning gold.

I don't know who moves first, or if we move together, but we are kissing, and I pledge I will remember him every moment of every day.

The rest of our night clothes hit the floor.

In another life, I must've been a Romanian gymnast because I flip and push him back on the bed in one motion. I waste a second wondering if his hair or the silk comforter feels smoother.

I hover over him, hair a shield, a shelter from anything but us.

I run my hands along his sides, across his ribs. He cups my breasts. Tongue. Lave. Mark.

I lean, move over, and run my tongue along his jaw. Stubble catches. Pulls. Drags.

Lower myself onto him.

He grunts, pushes forward. Holds my waist.

Moves and slides, and though the air outside is frigid, I'm sure not. It's like a sauna around us. The surface of the sun is nothing compared to here. Inside. Us. We pull apart, slowly, and nothing feels the same; it's a different, departing kind of pull. He leans up and claims my lips.

I arch back and stretch, and he meets me again.

We kiss. Deep and full, full as ever. He cups my face between his hands, somehow gentle in this moment. I feel safe. Never safer.

Like I never knew I needed protection before and will never be this peaceful, feel this safe again. Not unless we're together.

Another move and a moan escapes him. "Emma..." His voice. My name. Midnight velvet. Deep strum. Acoustic guitar.

I am lost.

I pull back, and he scoops me up. Picks me up as if I weigh nothing. Keeps us together. Never part. Never apart.

Flips me over. Reseats and resumes. The way my flesh grips, the way his length surges, it sears, it brands, it claims. I sigh long and low, a lament for whenever he is not deep within.

His hips go forward and pound against mine again, again. His chin drops down and near silent words pass across his lips.

He murmurs, looking down at my face. "Ung, is this how... you want it?"

He can give me more, if he wants. Not sure there's any room down there for more, if ya know what I mean (and I think ya do).

I want to give him more, too, if that's what he wants; I want him, however he will give himself to me.

I want to quit having these Deep Thoughts by Jack Handey moments when I'm in the middle of having as nice a time as is humanly possible.

We slide slowly, savoring, and I swirl my tongue around his nipple. Seems only fair. Mine spend enough time in his mouth. Draw it deep into my mouth, across my tongue. He moves against me, rocking, pushing me, pushing deeper.

I can feel my legs begin to shake as I border on desperation. I know we need more. My fingers play across the flesh of his thighs. Muscles tense and work beneath my palm.

Pull apart. Bend my knees behind him. Not enough. More. Want.

Sweat runs between us. His, mine, ours.

Ankles over shoulders. Find a way to make him slip further in. His hands freeze. Shudders wrack. Then his fingers dig into my thighs, find a way to make him slip further in.

"Oh fu—Emmmma." His eyes roll back in his head to where he stores how to do long division.

He bucks against me, and I feel myself begin to clench. He holds me tighter still, grinds against me. My new favorite move.

"Oh, please…please…" Even to me, my voice is soft and breathless.

He loses rhythm, but keeps pounding. Dedicated.

Wraps around my calves, widens my legs, and I really hadn't realized there was any of me left for him to discover, but I feel the difference, the pulse and heat where I've never felt anything before.

Limbs begin to shake. His, mine, ours.

Writhing. Over and under. Come apart. Pieces. Shards.

I cry out. My voice borders on a choke. He follows. Stills.

Blood pounding.

His.

Mine.

Ours.

DAY OF EMPLOYMENT: 383

5:43 AM

❧ LOCATION: Next to him.

I AWAKE TO THE SOUND of my own huge intake of air and sit up bolt upright.

He stirs but stays asleep.

I haven't stayed up late just talking in bed since Clara and I were in middle school.

I had asked him about Diana.

"I don't have anything with her, and I never have." He rolled onto his side to face me. "She's been more than clear with her wishes, but so have I. She is a necessary — well, I hate to put it this way — necessary evil for this process. She can mess up everything. I have told her I'm not interested. But she remains determined…maybe even more so since I expressly turned her down. Until we sign, I'm just trying to keep the peace, keep her at arm's length."

"Bet you wish you had longer arms," I said.

"And more of them. She's grabby." He smiled and reached out, almost touching me, then pulled his hand back and stuffed it under his pillow. "I don't think I like this 'no touching' rule."

"Well, it was your idea," I reminded him. My hand tingled; it really was hard to be so close and not touch him.

He huffed and pulled the bedding higher around us. "It seemed to be the only concession that would get you to stay in bed with me."

"You got me into your bed by offering to not touch me. Pretty sure that's the opposite of how it's usually done."

Then he'd told me about himself. The stuff I couldn't learn by watching him in a fishbowl.

His father raised him on his own after his mother had died. His father had asked him to be his best man when he had finally remarried last year.

"I'd rather not talk about my mother," he said, folding his arm across his face. "I barely remember her. Only little pieces. "

I left it alone.

I could remember my mother, but there still wasn't a lot to talk about. "My parents are okay. Just shuffled me back and forth after the divorce. Now they both have new families." It didn't really bother me to feel like an outsider around either of them. "But then, I don't have anything to compare it to. This is it. Just me."

It had been quiet for a while; I'd almost fallen asleep, when he spoke again. "Aren't you going to ask me?"

Disoriented, I wondered if I had missed something. "Ask what?"

"Why I'm such an asshole."

I blinked up at the ceiling. "Um, no. No, I'm not."

He sat up on one arm, his face surprised. "Really?" He paused for a moment. "I thought that might be the first thing you would ask. I've been waiting."

"You have no patience with distractions," I offered. "I get it. Besides, you've been slipping."

"How so?"

"You've been nice to me lately."

He burrowed down into the bedding. "Some distractions are better than others."

Now, hours later, I slide out from under his arm.

In the doorway, I look back at him. Peaceful.

I think about how frustrated I have been with him, but I can't manage to feel as angry now, even with effort.

My conversation with Mitchell plays back while I get into the shower.

But why would I feel that way about Canon?

"Stupid," I say into the spray. "Stupid, stupid, stupid." I spit the words through the water. My head rests against the cool tiles.

It has to be the oxytocin or endorphins or whatever those evil, mind manipulation chemicals are that surge during sexual activities.

In this case, really, really surge.

Reason it out. No big deal.

He's an ass. *You do realize I have seen that movie...*

He's judgmental. *What do you think of the owner, Samuel Dowry?*

He's condescending. *I'm not insulting you. It is simple biology...*

He's conceited...*she is the best I ever had...*

He's selfish. *Give them your measurements...*

He's incompatible. *Ugh. Bee vomit...*

He's secretive. *If I wanted her, I would be with her...*

He's impossible to please. *Wear whatever outfit goes with those black lace shoes and sit to my left...*

He's aloof and distant and cold, and who am I kidding with this line of bullshit, he is the singularly most passionate and responsive man I have ever known...

The water pounds down on me like the truth.

"I have been entirely wrong about him."

Shit.

6:45 AM

I'M STANDING OVER HIM. He's where I left him. On his side, tucked in.

Cutest little snore ever.

Stop it. I'm making myself sick.

I shake his shoulder, and he moves a little then settles back.

"Si...Mist...Can..." No, none of that seems right. I don't know what to call him in these evolving circumstances.

His hair is a mess. I run my hand along his face, into his hair to try to tame it. He turns into my palm. A small hum floats up.

"Please wake up," I whisper.

He blinks up at me. "Hi."

"Um, hi." I straighten up.

He sits up and takes in my clothes and the general condition of the covers that has him wrapped up like the savory filling of a bedding burrito.

"I've overslept."

"No, no. Not by much. I…I thought you were going to, so…I woke you."

He nods and starts to unwrap. I already know what's in that package—it's a different kind of package, go figure—and that is my cue to exit. Stage left. Turn and leave. In haste.

I hear him sigh loudly as I leave the room. The sunrise peeks through the curtains, and either the rooster crows or I can actually hear my own chicken shit soul.

I'm envious of how quickly he's ready.

I gather up our things and let the breakfast server in when he arrives.

"Over here." I motion for the cart to go near the sofa.

"Anything more, ma'am?"

"I don't believe so," I say.

Canon, suited, walks into the room.

The server turns to him. "You want anything more, sir?"

"It appears not," he says, slipping on his watch. "It seems that having more is a harder decision for some."

We eat and leave and drive and arrive, and I don't hear his voice again until Mr. Peters greets him at 9:18.

"Fine. And you?"

2:20 PM

✷ LOCATION: Break room.

✷ EMOTIONAL STATE: DEFCON 2.
  And I'm mad at myself about it.

✷ FUMES: Running on them.

HOT COFFEE OVERFLOWS THE CUP and pours across my fingers. After a delayed reaction, I hold them under cool water.

"Hey, Emma," Mitchell says, leaning on the counter next to the sink. "Just got my orders. Looks like I'm headed back to the old stomping ground to work with you guys."

"That's great. Really, really great." It's nearly impossible not to smile around him.

"So...any progress?"

Glancing up at him, I can't decide if he's inquiring about the foreign accounts or ribbing me about Canon. I play it safe.

"Nothing definite."

He turns the water off and hands me an ice cube. "Maybe you need a different approach."

"I need more time."

"How much longer is your trip?"

"Just a couple more days." I hear myself sigh.

"Is it definitely a now-or-never kind of thing? Or will there be a chance when you go back?"

"It would be too late by then."

"How are you going to handle it? Do you have a plan?"

Ha.

I shrug.

He cocks his head. "That doesn't seem like the Emma I remember."

Yeah, you're telling me. I shrug. Again.

"It's important...right?"

Yes. "Yeah."

"Yeah?" He leans with his back on the counter. "That is it? Just a 'yeah'? Maybe...oh, never mind."

I roll my eyes. I wish he would just get to the point already. Hypocritical, I know.

"Well, Mitchell, this has been...real. But I need to get back to him."

He smiles. "Get back to whom?"

"What? Work. I have to get back to work."

"You said 'him.'"

"Well," I say, pointedly avoiding eye contact and gathering up drinks, "I work for a 'him.'"

"Emma," he says, looking blankly at the empty microwave, "regret is a kind of cold forever."

4:18 PM

"Ms. BAKER?" THE UNFAMILIAR VOICE draws my attention away from my screen. A woman in a delivery service uniform stands in the office doorway.

"Yes?"

"Delivery for you. Signature required." She hands a clipboard to me and exits only to return moments later with a wide, flat box and a far smaller one on top. She's gone without notice.

It occurs to me—and I don't like the feeling at all—that I have not been asked to pick this up myself. It seems he would rather place orders and make arrangements himself than interact with me. I know I have brought this on myself.

It's a white box. No markings. No address. I look around the room, but can no longer find the smaller one anywhere. Opening the big box, I wonder if there's been some sort of mistake. Perhaps a different, heretofore unknown, Ms. Baker works here. Perhaps it's a present for Canon, from his family or something, and I'm expected to keep a secret from him until the official holiday. That should be handy and all, you know, since it's roughly the size of a Jetta.

Inside, beneath a sapling's worth of sugar-scented tissue paper, is a dusky rose evening gown. Halter neck, empire waist, no trim. Understated in every way, save the color. The color may not even be season-appropriate.

Not that I'm complaining; it is lovely and reminds me very much of my favorite lipstick shade, My Wish List.

I pull the dress out and a smaller, inner box tumbles out onto the floor. Inside is a pair of delicate chandelier earrings. Without thought, I slip one on and begin with the other only to stop and burrow frantically through the tissues in search of a card.

Tissues crinkling and earring tinkling near my ear—so different than the nothing I've heard all day. Or at least nothing I have wanted to hear, the one thing I have wanted to hear is conspicuously absent, I realize. I miss him.

I ache.

A small card, held between two long fingers, appears inches from my nose. I look up and meet Canon's guarded eyes. There was a time when I would've taken this look to mean detached and aloof; now, I know this is actually observation and caution. Wary.

Without breaking our gaze, I take the card. Quick glance and flip. It's blank on both sides.

I look to him again. "What is this?" I ask, smoothing the bodice against me.

His eyebrow quirks. Wordlessly, he sets something on the desk and leaves the room.

I stare at the spot where I last saw him until my eyes become unfocused. Only then do I look down. A pair of tickets sits on my desk. *The Nutcracker.* 8:00 p.m. Black tie.

6:30 PM

❀ LOCATION: Hotel bathroom.

❀ HAIR: Unruly. It is fuller and not at all flat.

How is a landlocked state so humid?

INTERNAL DEBATE AS TO WHETHER I wear lipstick that perfectly matches the dress or not rages on.

Which is better than the other things that beg for a turn in my obsessing. The delivery. The dress. The blank card. The earrings…they seem a bit more than I can attribute to needing me suitably attired.

The tickets. To the ballet. To *The Nutcracker*, of all things.

Of all the things that could simultaneously make me feel like it really was Christmas but also make me ache with longing, *The Nutcracker* would be the pinnacle.

My family was not big on tradition, or at least not any that were recognized as such at the time. Dressing up to see the ballet performed while my cousin played in the symphony was a memory I treasured. We didn't do it every year. Just enough. Enough to make it our sole tradition.

I have never gone since my family quit going. Well, since I quit going with my family. Different directions.

They have their families. I have me. Just me.

I haven't been in years.

Actually I'm not sure I've been since I got boobs.

Admittedly an odd segue.

But, right now, I've got boobs on the brain. I'm staring at the straps of my bra, and they are staring right back at me. Inches and inches of black straps. The dress is a halter. I don't have a Y-back or a convertible bra with me.

One reason why men buying dresses for women is not always the slickest of ideas: they have no frame of reference for necessary undergarments.

With no other real options presenting themselves, I take off the bra à la *Flashdance*.

Matching lipstick wins out. No one is going to be looking at my lips. I can't say as much for body parts that rhyme…

Final touches, and then I exit the bathroom. Canon is nowhere to be seen. Or heard. Still.

I slide on black pumps and catch my reflection in the full-length mirror. Panty lines.

Splendid.

Tonight, I will be wearing the matching panties to the no bra look.

His bedroom door opens, and I shove my underwear into the back of the sofa.

He's in a tux.

A tux is not that much different than a suit. That will be my mantra. I chant it internally as I now force my body to do things like blink, breathe, and remain vertical.

It seems tuxedos affect the cerebrum.

"Is there anything I need to be doing?" I squeak. *Anything besides proving the theory of spontaneous ovulation?*

He hasn't looked toward me yet. He shakes his head, opens the closet, pulls out my coat, and holds it up for me. Never once looks at me.

I slide into it, and he holds the door, silently ushering me out. When's he going to talk to me again?

The drive to the theater is accompanied only by the sound of the tires moving through the snowy slush. We may be meeting others there. I'm not sure what's expected of me anymore. I'm not sure of him or myself.

The valet line is long but moves quickly. He hands the keys over and takes my arm from the attendant who opened my door. I'm ridiculously comforted by the contact.

Inside, I check my coat. When I turn around, for the first time today, he is looking directly at me. Staring.

I want to say something, to get him to talk to me again, but nothing comes to me. What can I say here? Thanks for the dress that you had to get me so I could come to this with you? Did I ruin this? Can I start over?

"You look beautiful," I hear myself say.

Well, he does.

I think I see the whisper of a smile, but then it's gone. There is an alcove nearby, and I consider pulling him there to ask/demand/beg that he speak with me. We become part of the crowd streaming toward seats, and I can't make myself pull him there. I've stepped out of my role so many times already and I can't imagine he would be pleased to have attention drawn in public.

Mournfully, I look to the alcove as we move along. Then, suddenly, I'm in it. He's steered us there.

"I can't do this," he says. There is a faint echo.

I've lost my bearings. I don't know what to say or do, and everything is on autopilot. I reach out and touch his back. "Do what?" I whisper.

He looks toward the ceiling, sighs heavily. I rub my hand along his arm, hoping it's comforting.

We're inches apart. He turns and looks at me in a way I don't understand.

"This." He gestures between us.

I've taken to breathing through my mouth. "This?" I repeat softly.

"Ask me."

I'm sure the look on my face is confused. I'm good, but I'm not that good; I need more information than this.

Without looking any tenser, which may not be possible but I choose to take it as a good sign, he expounds: "About the card."

I didn't say he expounds greatly.

Oh. I have so many questions about the card, but I go for the obvious. "Why was it blank? Why have a card at all, if it's completely blank?"

He opens his mouth then closes it. It seems he was going to tell me, but changed his mind. "Why do you think?"

Oh, heavens. The show is going to start before we muddle through this. Not that I care anymore. I thought I missed him earlier, but now that he is here and I can see him and hear and, oh, God, smell him, I really don't want anything else ever. The Sugar Plum Fairies can do the dance of the damned for all I care.

"I don't know." I trace his lapel.

"That makes two of us." He touches an earring.

"They're beautiful." I brush against his hand near my ear.

His knuckles skim my cheek. Drag down toward my mouth. I turn and press my lips to his hand. His eyes shut for a moment.

"The signature was troublesome." He presses his forehead to mine. "What am I to you?"

I know he has to be thinking that I'm hung up on the fact that he's my boss, or he's powerful in my little universe, or that this trip makes him handy, or that he's a really smoking notch in my bedpost. It's none of those things. I won't work there much longer. But I am all I have got. I make my own way.

I can't risk anything.

This risks everything.

Here in this tiny space, with strains of prelude music in the air, our echoed breaths on the walls, I realize not another soul exists for me in this universe. If I never left this space, his side, I would be utterly content.

He is everything.

Wow. I'm pretty slow on the uptake.

His hands come to my bare shoulders, and I brace myself against his frame, run my hands up to his neck, his face.

"Ev —" I begin, but stop. "I lo —" That seems a bit much in the way of confessions. "Alaric."

It's like I said it anyway. He beams down at me, and I feel his grip tighten on my shoulders, like he's testing something or feeling it for the first time. I'm feeling more self-conscious than I expected, and I really just want to curl into him, to feel him hold me and be strong for me for just a minute because I'm allowed to be scared. I'm allowed to be scared when emotional epiphanies present themselves unbidden and unexpected.

I inch forward, and he does exactly what I hoped he would do. His arms wrap around me, and I want to press in even more, but I will probably smear makeup all over his shirt. I look up to explain. Our eyes meet, and I watch his flicker to my lips. Yes, please. Please do it.

But he doesn't move. I know he's tried to make the moves before, but I've shut him down.

I stretch up and brush my lips over his. Then, again. His hand moves, and I think for a moment that perhaps he is going to put a lock of hair behind my ear, and I'm fairly shocked to learn how much the idea of such an innocent gesture appeals to me. But he stops short. His fingers twist a curl around in my hair and brush a trail against my neck.

The pad of his thumb presses gently up under my chin. My face tilts up, and at once his lips are back on mine.

Soft, glorious pressure.

His eyes close and mine follow, and all that is left in the world is Canon and the gentle force of his lips on mine.

My breath ceases, and I can do nothing but take in the experience of him. The smooth skin of his lips. The brush of air along my cheek as his breath leaves him and plays across my cheek. The slight change in tension as his fingers curl and tangle deeper within the hair that's wrapped around them. Pulses pounding. I burn off an extra-value-meal worth of calories trying to prevent a persistent moan from seeping out of me.

And then he begins to move.

His lips alter, become my new altar. Stationary grows to soft, fluttering over mine. First one pass over my upper lip, then he shifts to kiss my lower lip alone, drawing it between his own.

The breath I hold will be contained no longer; it escapes me in a rush that parts my lips. Canon sighs in response. Tilts his head further. Warmth, wetness skim across my lips. Brush against the edges of my tongue.

Urge to taste. Fully. Overwhelmed. Slide further. Tilt. Completely experience whatever part of him he's willing to share with me.

I push my tongue back against his as softly as I can make myself. Our lips continue to press together, but I barely notice over the satin and slip of tongues slowly moving together. Then a second time. Then a third.

It seems a fourth circuit is about to begin when Canon pulls back. Bereft.

His hand skims from my neck to my shoulder. My eyes open. Canon blinks very slowly down at me. A lazy smile builds across those lips that have somehow taken on the role of sun in my solar system.

An encore.

His hands move up me again until he holds my face in his hands, and then he is kissing me back, and I'm kissing him back, trying to show him this is real and I am real, and please see me for who I am and let me taste your tongue already.

I suck in his lower lip, and he hums and brushes his tongue against the tip of mine. It's soft and sweet. My hands weave into his hair, anything to try to get him closer. To have him.

We miss being seated.

8:00 PM

❁ Seat: C12.
❁ Hand: C11.
❁ Loon: Grinning like one.

Darkened theater. We found our seats at the last possible moment. I may have skewered some toes.

He's holding my hand. My hand is in his, and our hands are on his thigh, and that means he is holding my hand.

Alaric Canon is holding my hand.

Sure, sure, he's been, um, *down there*…but this somehow feels different…more intimate.

Good thing I've seen this ballet several times, because I'm paying attention in the range of nil.

My lipstick is gone. Eaten off, as it were. All that pondering about whether to wear it or not a waste.

Smeared makeup would normally torque me off. But as long as I'm not channeling Tammy Faye Bakker after a cloudburst, I'm feeling pretty peachy about it. Hell, I have never been so happy about…anything.

Canon is fixated on the stage. Or he appears to be. His thumb traces my life line. Every once in a while, I feel him hold me tighter, press my hand between his own and his thigh.

Looking around, I can't see anyone we know. I've wondered if this was a work-related function or motivated by guilt about the extended trip making me miss the holiday with family.

Realistically, I know it might well be a date.

There was no asking, no explanation. I want to ask. I want answers.

But I don't; I'm now sure my reticence stems from fear of confirming that the demure-by-day-freak-by-firelight way I have been acting has been what he finds appealing enough to date.

In over my head here. I care about this quiet, complicated fucker.

I need to show him me.

In small doses.

After the curtain closes, we walk along the Plaza. White lights. Soft snow. Horses pulling decorated carriages *clip-clop* in the midst of the idling cars. That can't be healthy.

He hasn't said anything since we left the theater. Just held my hand and walked among the carolers and shoppers.

"What are you thinking?" I ask as we pass a store that smells of gingerbread and spices.

"As little as possible." He pauses in front of a bookstore. The glow from within clears any trace of shadow from his face. "For the first time in as long as I can remember."

On the surface, his words are dismissive; his face is not.

Still staring in at the books, he brings my hand to his lips and kisses two knuckles.

10:25 PM

❄ LIMOUSINE: Plaza Tour Circuit.

❄ BACK PARTITION: Up.

❄ RESISTANCE: Low.

OUR LIMO CIRCLES AROUND for a prime view of the fountains and Christmas lights for which the Plaza is famous. And the cow statues which defy justification.

The leather squeaks under us. A rustle, and he's flush against me.

Every cell is alight. My mind races. We need ground rules and limits and—

"You are…breathtaking," he says brightly, and miraculously evades cliché. I feel my ears tinge, and in the space of time it takes me to mentally form even the glimmer of an idea that I need to say words that would probably have been about "let's take this slowly" and "a single kiss and a *pas de deux* does not a relationship make," his arms are under and around me, my hair draping around us to brush against my exposed shoulders, and I swear I'm not going to let myself worry if he feels emasculated in the future when I recall that he gasps like a maiden when I grab the hottest part of him and stick my tongue past his tonsils.

My hands run under his jacket. Slide it off and toss it aside. Over his shirt, tracing his sides, skim his skin. Run his lines.

He hums and smiles and works so hard at kissing it seems as though he's making up for lost time. Like he's trying to get as much experience logged as possible before the ride is over and we have to stop.

Or should stop.

He presses my torso so closely against his chest that I can feel all the tension in his body. Every breath. Every tremor. I try to memorize every time he shudders when I touch a certain spot—behind the ear, under the eye, along the jaw—or move my lips against him a certain way—wet along his neck, pressure over his pulse—and file it away so I can make it happen again.

He tastes so good. If you left Santa a plate of Canon cookies, he would stuff the whole North Pole into his red velvet bag and lug it down your chimney.

I run my palm flat along his heated length. A shiver wracks his frame. I wrap one arm tightly between his back and the seat, fingers splayed just above the hem of his pants. I'm vaguely aware of my other hand as it skates lower. Thumbs rub circles. Fingers dig. I fist his shirt, stretching the collar to expose his neck. He quakes and holds me tighter as my tongue traces his collarbone.

Every gasp and touch is precious. We can't always be doing this, giving in. I have been afraid to start. He's like human Nutella: I'm afraid once I've started tasting I won't be able to stop until I've had all of him.

His fingers trace upward, along my face and into my hair, finding new places, each with its own color. The realness of it all assaults me. This is really him…in my arms, this is Canon…Alaric Canon…how he tastes of coffee, smells like sunshine and fresh linen, feels like… nothing feels as good as he does.

My fingers twist into his hair, and I kiss him with everything in me, the way I have envisioned for months, except now it is him. *Him.* Not the nice butt or the great profile or any other part that warrants its own centerfold, but the sum of them. The whole is greater because it is this particular man.

He stills, as if sensing that I'm in need now. My lips skim over his, soft fingertips pressing against his skull, and he opens and I explore his mouth. His body rocks against mine softly, hands sliding under my dress, bunching it up under my arms. Suddenly, the leather is deafening, and he's maneuvering out from under me. Greedily, I grab for him in protest. My mind whirls, tries to suss out what I could have done wrong, but before anything makes sense he's back and draped over my torso. All I sense is relief…for about a second until I realize there's nothing covering his chest.

I'm necking with Houdini here.

Dress shirt and tie: Evaporated.

His shirt must be a discarded wad somewhere in the back of this limo. The lights still flow rhythmically through the windows, but I can claim zero interest in seeing anything but this guy's very personal O-zone.

I bend forever and suck in skin. Break out the teeth. Gentle, but not.

The sound that escapes him would be frightening in any other situation. Guttural. A near roar. Excellent timing as I doubt I have much more patience for gentle left in me.

His one hand on my hip anchors me against him and the other drags up my ribs, skin lightly tugging to stay in contact with his, until he cups the swell of one breast in his palm.

So much skin. So much of us in contact, electric and raw.

Desire threatens to swallow me, consume me—and not just for him, for this—but the wish, the need to show him with every choice in how I touch him or move my lips against him or the whispered words that sneak past my breaking filter that he is valued and adored and *wanted.* This man wrapped up with me, that I'm wrapped up in, he doesn't understand that I often wake to thoughts of him, that it has become a small kind of mourning whenever we part.

Every part of him calls to me.

My hand grazes his inner thigh. He wants more. I want more.

I passed simple wanting somewhere around the Mouse King.

Softly, as softly as I can manage with what little blood is left in my head pounding in my ears, I cup his ass (again! finally!) and squeeze my fingers into the flesh I have watched walk away from me so many times. Savor it more than the first time when I grabbed it and everything was so different, so angry and intense. It's firm and soft at the same time. They're like cream puffs or stress balls or my God why am I even trying to describe them when I could just be feeling them?

I dare say: I relish his buns.

Pun intended.

I digress…

His heart races against my chest, pounding so hard I can feel it through my dress. Kisses and touches and discoveries.

Want. Want is all I am and all that propels me.

I wonder why I have been procrastinating on more intimacy. We can handle more.

Well, not handle it right here under the Mayor's Annual Christmas Tree.

Handling is maxed out at the moment.

He pulls my lip into his mouth, sucking it. Between his shoulder blades, his skin is smoother than silk. My leg bends across his thigh, and my hand slips along his pants just enough that my fingers unexpectedly land where his ass meets his thighs and excited heat.

Fuuuck. So warm.

I hear my moan in both our throats.

Ragged breaths. Fingers burrow into my shoulders, and he places tiny kisses on my collarbone this time. I sigh, try to make it deep and throaty to belie how nervous and exposed I feel. The only thought I can piece together is that I need to not fall to pieces.

His hands slide under, scoop me unceremoniously on top of him. Short, hard sweeps push, almost row like sailors in a galley, where our bodies meet together. So good. So, so good. My head falls against his brow and I pant, "God, yes…there, baby."

A gasp escapes me as he lifts his head away from me, and I panic because I may have just crossed a line here.

"I—" he starts.

"I-I didn't mean…" I say and make to slide from over him, but he holds fast.

"No, don't." His voice carries some form of desperation. "Don't… stop," he practically yells and begins to rock against me. He clings to me as if he were slipping from a high branch, his breath harsh in my ear.

Everything is warm and want and pressure. Grinding against one another clothed is not glamorous, and I know it, and we deserve better, and whatever this is we may or may not have deserved better, but there is no way I'm going to risk rejection at this point. I hold his face in my hands. Amid elbows and bumps and gasps and wholly graceless acts, I kiss him as gently as possible.

All of my thoughts flow together, overlapping. He rocks and we slide and I grip and pulse and it is all too fucking much. He is not even in me and I think it is the happiest my nether bits have ever been—the happiest I have ever been.

Through fog, his voice reaches me. "I want…I…"

It's a sentence he can't finish; he doesn't know what he wants.

I pull him against me and roll until he's over me and I'm under him. Feet tangled in the armrest, seatbelt digging into my back. I find I cannot care because there are only scant layers of fiber between him and where I want him so very, very badly. We move against each other, mimicking so closely what I want with him that it's all I can do not to tear at my seams and hope it can happen, too. A part of my mind tells me this is an excellent idea and that we are consenting and adults and have done plenty of intimate acts already and why not because I am so much in…so deeply in I—

"I'm…I'm…I…"

My plea's heard. Hands go under me. Hold my ass. Rock against me that much harder, that much faster. My feet dig into the backs of his knees, lifting and meeting each thrust. Hot and damp, he plows against me, over and over again.

More passes and he meets me every time and mumbles half thoughts against my neck, and damn, I want him inside so much it snatches the very breath from my lungs. A hollow fire inside. I tell him this in a ragged whisper, and his breath catches and his arms wrap around my neck as he groans out, low and coarse.

I want to feel every change, swallow every sound, but coals inside me burn white hot, my ears close, and then I'm gone too, saying his name and trying to find air.

When clouded edges finally fade from my sight, I remember where we are. Scant Christmas lights manage to filter in through the back glass. Canon's shed clothes barricade off ninety percent of it.

Maybe we need to buy some Dramamine. Bet that driver is hella dizzy from circling the block.

11:35 PM

❊ CAR: Hands folded in my lap.

❊ ELEVATOR: Hand in his.

❊ HALL: Other hand added over his.

❊ ROOM: Hands everywhere.

MY COAT SLIPS FROM THE HANGER and hits the floor. He looks at me as if to say it looks just fine there.

"You feel it, don't you, Emma? What's happening? You feel it."

I nod. Yes. So much I can't feel anything else.

Streetlights and shadows color the room. We're near the bedroom. Near the door.

He's waiting. For me. On me.

I loosen his tie. Feel him swallow below my fingers, breathe beneath my arms.

He's not moving. Waiting. Baiting.

I look at him and then to my shoulders, tilt my head, silently suggest. Strongly suggest.

His hands slowly roam me. Tentative. I step forward, and his arms go round to meet at the small of my back.

"You wanted me to wear this," I say as his fingers play at a dress seam. "So...take it off."

He holds his breath. I can tell because I'm holding mine.

The slow rustle of fabric fills the room. He pulls the zipper, looking down, watching me while each tooth pulls free. His hands slide under and graze my torso, along my sides. He slides it over my shoulders.

I wouldn't think this would be such a surprise. It was darn cold in that theater. And he was all but wearing my dress right along with me during our fun out in the limo.

But his breath hitches. Silk splashes on the floor.

I'm down to sheer, black thigh-highs and heels.

Okay, the man might pass out.

A panty-less warning might have been prudent. Noted.

His arms wrap around my shoulders. Thumb at the joint, palm around, fingers reach and press my back.

His hands travel down my arms, unhurried, drag. My wrists. Shoulders. Pale flesh inside my arms, almost tickling. Slower at the curve and swell.

I can feel him looking at me. Hard. Hands continue their trek. Soft.

Deliberate, measured, I bring my arms to him, to his shirt. His button's a puzzle. Hesitant and unfocused, I curse my nerves.

He doesn't seem to notice.

I don't remember the buttons being this difficult before. Probably because I tore them free.

Which seems like a genius idea, and I contemplate that method again while I push a fingertip under the rounded edge and thread it through. It's slow going. Maybe that's okay.

It is going to take forever at this rate.

I'm still in my heels, closer to his level. He barely bends to watch me, continues to feel me. Warm at my ribs. Heated fingers on my back.

Another button finally gives. Yeah, taking forever.

He breathes, shuddering, watches my progress. Roams me. Waits.

Waiting.

I take on another.

He follows my waist, my hip. The top of my stockings. Fingers dance. At the rim. Palms my ass, traces where thigh meets cheek. Dip and explore. Ready.

And I'm not holding my breath anymore. Not at all. I'm panting. Pants.

Pants. Oh, yeah…his pants. I start pulling at his pants and yanking, and I guess I will be going to the store to buy clothes for him after all because there is a rip that should be sickening, but instead I hear my laugh, a laugh like the sound you make when you see a car wreck and it is the exact opposite of how you feel. I'm frantic, desperate to not let on how very real, really real I'm finding all this.

Because I'm going to make love to him in a moment.

I just sorta realized that.

I start to step out of my shoes, but the change in height from the first movement makes me feel even smaller. I leave them on. He watches as I kick away the dress with my shoes still on.

I step into him. Run my hands down around his open shirt and start it over his shoulders and down.

He watches my chest rise and fall.

"You like?"

Corner of his mouth turns up. He might laugh now.

That will never do.

"Show me."

And I guess "show me" equates to "prove it" in his book because before I know what's happening he's pulled me by my butt and lifted me against him, bent himself to bury his face in my neck, arms encircling and cock—some hard proof right there—running near roughly between my legs. Somehow we get to the bed, and he is backed up against it and still moving and holding and oh-wow-that-is-pretty-fucking-amazing between my legs.

I finish pulling his sleeves down his arms and discover they won't come off as they're bunched up at his wrists where I have failed to unbutton the damned cuffs. Ah, screw it. Or him.

I give a shove, and he falls back onto the mattress, shirt under his ass, hands trapped at his sides. Eyes wide, not scared, something else. Something…I don't know.

I put my thumbs under the edge of my stockings and look down at him to ask if he would like them to stay. His head is raised off the mattress, watching me, gauging me, because this may seem more of a tease than a question—maybe he thinks I will take them off or not as I choose. He's wrong…I'm watching him for a reaction, to see what he wants. I trace the lace hem. He eyes the shoes, and I'm pretty sure he likes them.

Guess that's a yes.

Forcing myself to go slowly, counting to ten as I go, I bend at the waist and crawl up the bed. Slow and straight, trying for calm, trying for unruffled.

His eyes on me. Fidgets within his sleeves.

Fidgets until I start to hover over him. Then he stills. Then watches. Then breathes.

Kiss his thighs. Lips to hips. Tongue on shaft, base to tip. His turn to writhe. His fingers dig into the bed at his sides.

His chest raises in short gasps, and I want to touch it, to feel his heat on me. Knees astride and hands at his face, in his hair, I bend and slide the whole of myself against him.

Warm and welcome and…home.

So good it is bad.

Shift and bring my chest to his mouth. He watches me, and I'm not sure what I'm showing him when his lips press and his tongue slips along my breast, seeks and teases. Licks and nips and pulls me in, nearly biting.

He starts to object when I slide away, but my sliding stops. Abruptly. Because I'm there.

There, there.

Oddly enough, right about now I'm wondering about the mechanics of having sex with shoes on. How does that work in practical application? How do you keep from gouging someone with pointy heels, keep from scraping them? I'm already straddled over the expanse of his hips plus the hands that I have managed to trap there, and now there is the distinct possibility that I'm going to hurt him. Taking them off is going to be clumsy and awkward and not at all in-charge-looking, but it turns out all my concern is unwarranted as I feel his hands wrap around my ankles, fingers anchoring me, almost like I have anchored him.

And I feel secure.

I wrap my fingers behind his neck, thumbs circling below his ears. I slide down onto him. Just the head. Up again. Off again. And back. Angle, catch the ridge. And he's watching me. And I'm watching him.

Another pass and I'm going for broke, all the way as it were, this time, and he must sense it so he leans up and presses his lips to mine. Kisses me in a way I have never been kissed before. Kissed to my soul.

I sit up and slide him in to the hilt, until there is no more, until I have run out of me and he's run out of him.

Eyes locked and faces facing. It's intense and burrowing and connected, and I want to look away and but not as much as I want to feel this ribbon unspool between him, me, us, and see. Really see.

Forearms on his shoulders, hands behind his head, and feet held down at his sides. I move. He moves.

Tandem. Tense. Together.

Noise flows from him, the cadence alters when I do. Shift, he hums. Rock, he moans.

Full and hot and perfect and show me what you want, what you like.

Slick skin. Breath rasps.

Seems another shirt is ruined. His hand clamps down on me, splays across my back, pulling me down to him, and I keep moving, and he tastes my shoulders, my neck, holds me there, saying something. Low. I can't hear.

God, I want to hear.

I want to taste his secrets and feel his sounds and listen to his mouth on me.

Lick his jawline. Sweat and sweet.

Break away and sit up straight and he arches back as he thrusts up into my down. I bend back, my hands flat along his chest. I can feel his thighs tense under me, he is straining and feeling and hitting inside me and rubbing against me in the best oh-please-don't-let-this-end-too-soon-but-maybe-it-should-because-I'm-exhausted way. Because I'm nearly there.

Hell, I would be there and back again if I weren't over-thinking this whole thing, if I weren't determined to see him undone, to do the undoing.

His free hand is at my hip, helping and holding. I have grown so accustomed to the light that every change in his face shows. The blinks. The lip bites. How he watches me, more than looks, like he is studying.

Alarm flickers in me. Then, an idea. I move off him, and his hand holds fast. God, he is breathing so hard; his chest crashes, nostrils flare.

"No…please." He swallows. He snaps his hand away and looks at it likes it's done something offensive.

I take his hand and press my lips to it, reassure him.

Nothing is wrong. So much is right.

I spin over him — pausing mentally for a moment to congratulate myself on clearing my three-inch heel over his torso while I'm a hair's breadth from orgasm and teetering on a panic attack from the enormity of all the things I have not been letting myself think about, the thoughts scratching at the peripherals — keeping his hand in mine, to steady, to tether, together.

Backward, facing away, hiding somewhat, I can admit it, I reach between my legs with one hand and align him with me. It is wet, wetter than I anticipated, and I almost think I should be apologizing to him for some crazy reason — for what, him turning me on? — and I turn my head over my shoulder and watch him as he watches me sink back onto him. It's sneaky. I don't think he even knows I have observed. Pretty sure actually, because he didn't look cool about it at all. Mouth open, eyes rolling back, might've bitten his tongue.

I'm still holding his hand, and I bring it to my waist as I roll back onto him. His fingers entwine with mine, and he moves to meet me again and again, and I run my nails up his thigh while he moans and rocks, and then my hand smooths down to below where we join and cups him, plays at his base…and he is frozen.

"Oh…goddamn…" he breathes. *My dear, has no one done this for you before?*

Well, not that I have done this for anyone before…but I'm me and you are you and, well, I would think people would tend to roll out the red carpet and pull out all the stops…

I keep moving, his breathing changes and suddenly he's pressed against me, breathing into my hair, my ear, warm on my back I hadn't even realized was cold. His hand leaves mine and snakes down to touch me so near where I touch him, and then I hear myself, hoarse and breathy and burning, and I'm over the edge, complete. Our rhythm finally falters.

He swells. Curses. Drives into me at least as hard as I have pressed onto him and then throbs and pulses and pushes. Murmurs against my back. Whispers into my spine one of those secrets I want to know.

Time passes. I don't know how much. Our breathing slows. Finally, eventually, matches.

And I need to move. For many reasons.

I'm boneless, and my knees are numb. If I shift wrongly, I will tear into his skin with my heels. Wiggling, test my strength. It is lacking.

Then I feel him pull away a shoe and run a thumb up my arch. He leans and shifts and uses what was his trapped hand to remove the other. He rubs that foot too.

He pulls me up the bed. I'm spent, and it seems perfectly okay when he's wrapped around me. I'm tucked into him, and his arm is my pillow, and the shirt still hanging from his wrist is our blanket.

DAY OF EMPLOYMENT: *384*

10:00 AM

❊ RUDOLPH: Changing the old nose bulb.
Christmas Eve.
❊ LITTLE WHITE BOX: Haunting me.
❊ BUSINESS: Not mine.

THIS BOX IS MY PLIGHT BEFORE CHRISTMAS. I want to throw back the sash and chuck it out the window. Right after I accidentally back over it with a forklift three times.

It's not the box that has offended me really. It was just sitting there on her desk.

No, no. It's the tag on the little white box.

The little box that I have seen once before. The one that came yesterday with my dress, but left with the delivery person.

I lift the flap again, ever so carefully, as if I might trigger a remote spy cam installed to catch nosy assistants.

And, yes, again. I have already looked. I just want it to be different. To say something different.

But there, in perfect, pointed script was the source of my problems.

To: Diana Fralin

No "From." Just her name.

Not blank, but no signature. Do the same rules apply to her? He doesn't know what sort of sentiment to use when signing a card for her either?

I know what he said. I really believe him. I do. But the gift... Why?

The card is staring back at me. Mocking me. Making me want to take that damn box and wing it at her so it falls down into her abyss-cup bra and possibly aligns with Aslan in the battle for Narnia.

I can hear Ms. Fralin make her way toward her office. I picture her sauntering and laughing and adjusting and touching up her lipstick all at the same time.

I jump up and away from the box...but not before moving it a fraction of an inch, trying to imitate its exact position pre-nosy fingers.

"Oh, hello, Emma," she says, stepping into her office. "I had nearly forgotten about our little meeting."

I gathered as much since you're nearly thirty minute late for it.

"Do tell. What sort of illicit dealings are you here to meticulously detail for me today? A dinner meeting in Portugal? Free Post-its in Luxembourg?"

My jaw clenches. "Actually, I have generated reports of several now-questionable practices and cross-referenced them with companies who have been on the line for doing similar activities. The results are everything from heavy fines to disgorgement of profits. Some also result in jail time."

"For steak dinners with officials and palm money to set up phone lines? Please. You make it sound positively salacious." She rolls her eyes back so far I would expect she might have hit gray matter. Seeing as how eye rolling is about the fastest way to torque me off, I may crack a bicuspid. "We are hardly arms dealers, Emma."

I didn't really expect her to be receptive, but it was necessary to at least attempt to talk to her before saying she wouldn't listen. "I am not saying or even implying that you are deliberately breaking the law. It's just that the global business climate is quite different in the wake of the Wall Street failings. The SEC and the Department of Justice are now far more aggressive and far less lenient than in the past. You cou—"

"I will look it over," she says and snatches the papers from my hand. "Now, you will need to leave. I have to get ready for a party tonight."

She slings her bag over her shoulder. It's huge. I recognize the brand.

"Ms. Fralin, what a beautiful bag. Is that a Dooney & Bourke?"

She glances back at it dismissively. "Yes, it is."

I continue toward the door, then stop just before I exit. "I would hang onto that bag, if I were you. It's a potential collector's item. That Bourke guy thought what he was doing was no big deal, too."

There is no chance she's even going to bother to bend back the pages of that report. There is even less chance that she will Google Bourke and find out a whole team of high-powered attorneys couldn't keep him out of jail on bribery charges during this new crackdown.

Turning on my heel, I make for the door rather than waste more time on her.

"Emma," she calls out behind me. "Do tell Alaric how much I love his gift."

Oh, I'm sure he would much rather hear it from you.

7:25 PM

"It's a replacement more than a gift." The steering wheel turns fluidly under his palms. "And she is a shrew to imply otherwise."

I stare out the window. Christmas lights dot the landscape.

This is not a feeling I like. Jealousy. Especially since I think it's unwarranted. I remain quiet.

"I'm not used to explaining myself," he says.

I shrug softly.

"The other day when I left with her, we worked for a few hours. Then I left." He coughs and grabs the steering wheel a little tighter. "In an unusually optimistic move, I left to pick out your dress." He looks flushed, maybe a little embarrassed.

"I went back to collect things from her office, and she, once again, thought I was making an excuse to see her. That is when you called and between talking to you and thinking about changing hotels and Diana stalking me around her office, I knocked her business card holder off her desk. A hideous crystal thing. I replaced it. I am merely trying to keep the peace."

I nod a few times and glance over at him. He watches me nearly as much the road.

"Why did you put her name on the card? My card was blank."

"I had no desire to be with her when it was delivered or at any other time."

We twist a few miles further toward the hotel.

"How 'fun' were you on other trips?"

"Pardon me? 'Fun'?"

"She said you used to be 'fun.'"

"I'm the same life of the party I have always been. Though I didn't avoid her so much initially, before I knew what she was like. Emma, I have told you I don't want anything to do with her."

Big girl panty time. "I know you did. I don't want you to think I don't trust you. It was just so hard to understand."

He pulls the car into a space outside the hotel. "You can ask me anything, Emma. I'm never going to lie to you."

This knowledge doesn't make me feel better like I had expected it to. Of course he won't…but I feel like I have been play-acting so much.

I am not the least bit consoled. All I am is one big lie with him.

9:25 PM

✤ LOCATION: Hotel ballroom.
✤ DRESS: Last one. Blue silk.

CHRISTMAS EVE OFFICE PARTY.

I'm at least one "party" over quota for the year. I've begun to think no one at this company has children. Then Lance Rowe sidles up to a tipsy woman. He is a prime argument for asexual reproduction.

Dinner was hours ago, and now almost everyone is pretending they still want to talk to the other people here. As if everyone doesn't get enough of their co-workers during the week.

On the way here, I tried to talk more with Canon about the report I had made. His phone kept ringing. Then he needed to make a call. Then another. When we arrived, we were late and had to rush in.

Alaric went missing shortly after we arrived. I took up residence in the corner, holding up the wall, as that seems to be all I do lately.

After well over an hour, maybe two, I have actually begun to partake of the open bar. I have made a sizeable dent. If one considers the Grand Canyon a dent.

Blessedly, the occasions for small talk have diminished as the night wears on.

Now my primary companionship is in the form of a white poinsettia pyramid.

They actually are better conversationalists than Lawrence Peters. Plus, as an added bonus: poinsettias do not have prostates.

I weave through the masses but cannot find him.

Eyeing the crowd, I catch Mitchell's attention. He seems to understand who I'm looking for and nods toward a set of side doors near a champagne glass tower.

I smile in thanks and head that way.

1:15 AM

CANON, DIANA, AND THE OWNER, Mr. Samuel Dowry, stand huddled in the hallway outside the ballroom.

Hold back and wait. Do not draw attention. That is the name of the game. My role.

"Congratulations, Alaric," Diana purrs, placing her hand on his arm. He stiffens, moves, but continues to speak with Dowry until they shake hands.

"Closing this deal early is the ideal Christmas gift, don't you think?" Dowry booms as he leaves.

Wait, what? No. Not yet, this is too soon.

I didn't tell him. I didn't convince him.

I have been so busy worrying about my plans and my hormones and my concern with what it is about me that he likes, that I have ultimately failed. I have failed him.

I did not do my job.

"Closed? We're already done?" I steady my voice. Eyes turn to me.

"Oh, you didn't tell Emma our good news yet?" Diana giggles and rolls her eyes.

Alaric smiles at me and beckons me over, obviously counting on me to save him from her clutches.

I step forward.

"I'm out of champagne." Diana pouts toward her glass. The stem dangles and sways between her fingers.

"There's more inside," I say.

She rolls her eyes and walks past.

"Thank you for saving me." He pulls me to him once we're alone. "It is becoming increasingly hard to keep her at bay without resorting to tossing her off the roof." He punctuates his joke with a kiss to my temple.

I start to push away, refusing to let myself enjoy it. I need to tell him how thoroughly I have fucked up all that he has worked so hard for.

History repeats itself. He may not be married, and I may not be the other woman, but I have most likely just cost him everything.

Before I can form the words, glass shatters in a small explosion near our feet.

My legs are splattered in champagne. The broken pieces of a bottle lay swirled around our feet. Foam glugs from the broken neck like a thick, white tongue.

"What the hell, Diana?" Alaric glares at her.

I looked up to see him just as soaked as I am.

"Toss me off the roof?" Diana fumes and spins to march away. "Don't think I will be waiting be around for you when you finally get tired of screwing the help."

Yeah, that's how I like my bitches: Angry and butt-hurt.

Alaric starts after her to, I assume, confront her.

"Wait." I stop him. He turns and looks at me. Surprised.

"I need to leave." Liquid has already soaked through my shoes. My feet feel slippery, sticky.

Brow knitted, he returns with me to the ballroom. Diana is there. Livid.

There are so many things I want to say to her. Things I want to do. Things like punch her right in her Mary Poppins' bags.

Instead, I slide right by her and grab a final champagne glass from the tower. Liquid courage.

Alaric stops beside me. "Are you okay, Emma? You're not acting like yourself."

Too true.

Until now.

Diana appears. "You know, Emma, it is truly pathet—"

Her words are cut off when I suddenly toss the remainder of my drink in her face. All eyes on us.

"Let's go," Alaric says through clenched teeth.

Well, there now. I have embarrassed him. *Nicely done, Emma.* Jeopardized an entire company, his career, and embarrassed him in a single evening. Stellar job.

By the time I return the empty glass to the table, Diana has found her bearings. She grabs a full glass and starts to toss it at me. Everything is a blur, but it seems Alaric knocks her hand away as I duck to avoid it and irony descends in full force. My slippery feet give just enough that, instead of avoiding the splash of one glass, I bump the tower and everything rains down on us.

Covered. Soaked. To the bone.

Humiliation. Shock. Regret.

"I'm so sorry." I sniffle and look up at him.

Champagne runs in rivulets down his face. "It's okay. We just need to go."

That is just it. There is no "we."

There is him and me and someone who doesn't even exist. Someone who does his bidding and gets his drinks.

Someone nobody takes seriously enough to read a report that she's written. This mouse that I have become. This mouse that roars at night.

I am the other woman in my own relationship.

"I...I can't do this. I can't be with you. You don't really want me, and I have jeopardized everything you have worked for." My voice shakes as nerves and cool liquid wrack my body. "I will get a ride from Mitchell and pack up. I quit."

He tries to hold my arm, but I snatch it away.

"I won't always chase after you, Emma."

You won't have to. This is different. This is me leaving for you, not for myself.

The ride is quiet. Mitchell pulls up next to the hotel lobby door and nods twice in silent understanding that there are no words.

In the room, pale petals are strewn about the bed, the carpet. A bouquet of mixed, pastel colored roses sits on the dresser.

A single word written on the card: *Everything.*

DAY OF EMPLOYMENT:
372…381…MAYBE 495…SOMETHING.
THEY ALL RUN TOGETHER.

2:00 AM

- ❀ CHAMPAGNE: I'm covered in it.
- ❀ PETALS: Litter my entire room.
- ❀ BALCONY DOOR: Open.
- ❀ ROOM: Effing freezing.
- ❀ NIPPLES: Probably hard enough to puncture this silk camisole.
- ❀ MY HEART: Who the hell knows at this point?

THE CURTAINS FLUTTER OPEN. It's not the breeze. It's him. He steps into the room, watching his own feet move.

He barely resembles the man who makes grown men cry, who barters lives and livelihoods like wares at a flea market, who I have fantasized about for over a year.

His hair is slick and dark and drips champagne. A single, thick lock escapes, flipping forward as he rakes his fingers through it. His gaze never leaves the floor.

"Just tell me why," he whispers, barely audible over the street below.

Every instinct in me screams to run to him, to wrap my hands around him, to lose myself in his touch…in him.

But I would do just that. Lose myself.

It's all been make-believe.

"You don't know me," I say as softly as I can, as if for the first time I consider that I need to be soft, that he might actually be breakable.

His head snaps up, and his eyes — oh, God, his eyes! — they swim, an unfocused torment swirling in their depths.

"How can you say that? After all…after everything?"

"This is not me. I'm not what you think I am."

"You are everything I want." He moves to me. I move twice as far away.

"Alaric, I'm not who you think I am. I'm a liar. And I can't be what you want."

"Liar?"

"Yes."

"You have lied to me…"

"Yes."

"Lied…"

"Yes! Yes, yes, yes!" I would like to run my hands through my hair right about now — seems to be the thing to do in these instances — but the ol' hands are otherwise engaged in a rumba-like series of gestures about my head. Or maybe I'm knitting a caftan. "Yes. Lies. All lies."

"What is it you think you have lied to me about?"

"Think?" Frustrating! As if I don't even comprehend when I'm not telling the truth…which may actually be a fair assessment given my conduct of late…but I'm not feeling generous enough to not be mad at him for thinking as much. My hands find their way to my soaked hair this time, threaten to uproot it…until I realize this maneuver has pulled the sodden camisole tight across my breasts. Nothing left to the imagination.

They are practically staring at him. He hasn't noticed. I may be insulted.

"I don't *think* I have…never mind." Like weights, my hands drop. "These are lies." I point to the bland clothes I'd been packing until I heard him at the door. He had gone straight to the balcony. I suppose he was giving me space.

"This." I find a broken crescent of a button and hold it between my fingers. "I broke this lying. I don't get aggressive in bed."

He doesn't hide his surprise at these particular words.

"I have pretended to be the sort of person who will hold my tongue. Who will follow, and take orders, and keep her opinions to herself, and play nice—far nicer than the people we're dealing with deserve. I have made it so I can't be taken seriously."

"That is not lying," he says. "That is deception. An attempt to deceive."

"They're practically synonymous."

"For someone so together and determined, you certainly are being obtuse." He rests against the wall. "Emma, that is the only thing you didn't do perfectly. You did not deceive me."

He moves. Just a step. Then turns only his eyes in my direction. "Considering I have been nothing but forthright about my intentions, my affections…at the very least, you might trouble yourself to explain your decision."

"Explain…my…decision?" I ask, each word slower than the one before.

His agitation grows exponentially with each syllable. He is closer now. I don't know when he moved.

He searches my face for something. It is not there.

"You know…you must know how I feel about you." His words barely carry.

I nod. Yes. Yes, I know. Pretty sure anyway. I know how he feels because it is in every touch, in every look, in each breath and moment together and every ache when apart. I know it. I know it because whatever I feel leaving him, coming from him, it affects me in the same way or more.

"Answer. Me."

There is a broken thread in the comforter. Just a few pulled stitches, a tiny frayed bit at the end. That is my focus.

This is so much more than I was prepared for. I just wanted him to notice me. I still want it. I want it all. But I have made him fall in love with someone else. Made him want someone else. Someone who doesn't exist.

"Everything about me is a façade," I begin, and he starts to say something but, as it seems there is little point in pretending any longer, I talk right over the top of him. "I do not take orders, I give them. I'd never even brewed a proper cup of coffee before this trip. My hair is curly. My clothes are colorful. I have been neglecting the things I need to do for myself—the things I need to do to improve my life—for this trip. Contrary..." I laugh dryly at my word choice; he has rubbed off on me. "Despite what it seems, I do not generally shove men around or rip their clothes or..."

I stop again. Straighten. Deep breath.

"None of that really matters." I stand firm. "What matters is that today, when I needed to be myself, when you were on the verge of closing a big deal and making an even bigger mistake, I played my role. I sat quietly next to some flowers. Earlier, I didn't insist you speak with me before we got to the point of closure. I played my role, and now you're going to get hurt because I was so busy pretending to be this person that I'm not that I couldn't even step up."

"You think I have misjudged all that's been happening." He finally pushes wet hair out of his eyes.

"You have misjudged their practices. I have mislead you about me."

"So this is what you think," he says.

What I think is that I'm crying now. The room is blurry, and my cheeks are wet. "Please know...you are the last person—" I choke out, then sniff in a wholly unappealing way. "You are the last person I would have wanted to hurt."

He's quiet for a moment. I'm still fixated on the now very fuzzy thread.

"Why is that?"

He's going to make me admit it, label it. I knew since he stepped into the room. I knew since he first looked up at me from beneath those wet bangs. I dared to hope differently, but it is going to happen. Canon always closes.

My words are less than whispers: "Because...really...because I really, truly care for you."

He kisses me. Fierce and free. I rejoice in it. Memorize it.

Possessive and promising. I revel in it. And break it.

He looks unbelievably happy. Like there really is a tree and lights and that train set he always wanted but never got. Like someone knew what he wanted, exactly what he wanted, and gave it to him.

Then they took it away.

"Alaric," I say. "You don't really care about *me*."

He shakes his head, his laugh sounding like relief, and pulls me in. I'm greedy; I take this last hug.

"Don't attempt to tell me how I feel." His hands run along my arms, warming me.

"You care about a lie. I am a lie."

Pulling back, he runs a hand through my wet hair. Then steps away. Business mode.

"Ms. Baker, it's time for your review."

"Um, Al—sir, I tendered my resignation."

"Fine. Exit interview. Suit yourself." He waves a hand toward the bed, and I sit in spite of myself.

"As I was saying, Ms. Baker, we need to discuss the matter of your employment."

"Yes, that is what you said." And welcome to the weirdest break-up ever for a couple that never actually was.

Exaggerating each move slightly, he begins to pace the room with his hands behind his back.

"You did not apply for the PA position, correct?" Alaric asks, and I nod, taken aback by this question, but then I tell myself that he would probably do a check on any new assistant.

"Your primary reason for tendering your resignation?"

"Inability to perform my job effectively." I fidget. He continues to pace. "Also...impact on my personal life."

"Impacted—adversely or positively?"

"Um...just impacted. I have too many obligations...I don't have room fo—"

He cuts me off. "Were you given a poor performance review by your supervisor?"

"Well, no."

"Wouldn't your supervisor be the one to determine whether or not your job was performed satisfactorily?"

He stops in front of me, eyes bearing down, hands still behind his back.

I do my best to level my puffy eyes at his from my place on the mattress. "Failing to prevent a problem by sitting idly by is the same as creating the problem. I am guilty by omission."

"You put a great deal of stock in your ability to influence." He resumes his movements, slower this time. "Do you think so little of your supervisor? That he is incompetent at evaluating information? Unable to take precautionary measures? That he doesn't know exactly what his assistant is working on at all times?"

"No!" This is not what I meant at all. Does he mean…? Could he have…? "Did you alter the contract last night?"

He pivots and looks over his shoulder. "I'm not at liberty to discuss these matters with non-employees."

Oh, fine. Play that way. My arms fold across my chest.

"Did you receive a raise in the past year?"

"No."

"No, you say. But you seem to have had an outside source of income," he says and touches his chin.

I feel my head pull back. I'm not sure where he's going with this line of questioning.

"During your time with us, would you say that you were a dedicated employee?"

I nod. He must not conduct very many exit interviews.

"Consider your answer carefully, Ms. Baker."

"Alaric, I don't want to play this game any more." I start to stand. He stops short in front of me.

"Fair enough," he says. "No games."

I start to stand, but now he's directly in front of me.

"I know you. Don't tell me I don't." Serious. He looks dead serious. "Your name is Emma Jacklyn Baker. You attended OU for undergrad and had a three-point-nine-eight GPA. You retook chemistry only to improve your grade. You have worked for our company for—" Alaric looks at his watch, pauses for effect "—three hundred and eighty-five days. You took your current position as a favor to your supervisor, Rebecca, who is also the only person whom you have told of your return to school." He puts his hands in his pockets and leans back on the dresser.

I think I'm still blinking.

"You have a generous scholarship and will graduate with a juris doctorate next spring. You love movie theater popcorn, but hate microwave. You like Pepsi, prefer Coke, and never, ever RC. Your favorite sweater is electric blue; you wear it at least once every two weeks in cool weather. Since the day you started, there has been a woefully under-watered cactus on your desk. You have won approximately one thousand eight hundred and twenty-two dollars in the office's personal assistant betting pools. It appears you purchased taupe suede pumps with the latest winnings. You wore them for the first time on the day you came to my office, the day you took this job, the day we officially met."

SOMEWHERE BETWEEN 3-4:00 AM

SAME BAT-TIME. SAME BAT-CHANNEL.

In that moment, I knew the truth of what I would dared dream about. I couldn't deny it.

Alaric cared about me. The real me. Deeply.

What is this uncomfortable, foreign feeling unfurling in my chest? Logically, I should be rejoicing…but disbelief and confusion still hold court. He has been fully aware of me and my persona from the get-go. Everything from frizzy follicles to sarcastic retorts, he has known that tame was not the norm.

And he had noticed me. All along, he had noticed *me*.

I have been aiming for blips while he has employed state of the art stealth technology. He is the B2 of too-hot bums. Not so much a cyborg, but an aerial strike drone.

I note the still space around us and the scant number of cars that pass outside below the window. How long have we been silent? I move enough to see his face. He looks at me with such concern, as though he is assessing me for injuries. Injuries which I have, all imaginary or self-inflicted.

My hand rises up to cover, maybe to finally protect, his heart.

"My God, Alaric." My face presses into the hollow of his chest. For entirely different reasons than usual, it feels as though maybe I'm supposed to be here. Not that I could force myself to be selfless enough to move away regardless.

Barely audible over the blood pounding in my ears, I hear my voice waver and fall. "Alaric, what have I nearly thrown away?"

He makes a sound of understandable confusion. Perhaps he thinks I'm about to tell him yet more fuckery has been afoot. That I truly am someone else. I manage, miraculously, to not confuse him further by laughing at my own errant thoughts.

I rise from his chest. Trace a flat hand line from his heart up along his neck.

Up and up. Over champagne.

Over stubble.

Overwhelmed.

Just below his temple, a pulse pounds below my thumb. His or mine. Or both.

"Emma, you don't have to explain—"

"Shh." My lips find the corner of his eye and brush against it as softly as I can make myself. Because he is not invincible any more than I am invisible.

"Everything." One whisper to quote the card and carry the promise. My pledge. "There is nothing I don't want to share with you." Cheeks align. Heat radiates within. Across and through. Throughout. I hear him swallow as he nods softly in understanding.

And I begin to understand, finally understand, and to accept that something real is happening. Something real, for perhaps the first time in my life. That everything else has been the actual playacting before I would meet this man.

Tonight, there have been avalanches all around. Champagne. Emotions. Epiphanies. There are no more doubts left here. They are swept away.

Because, despite my long held belief that I have suffered from the depth of attraction…fascination…obsession I feel for the man standing here, I have fallen short. True, he has made ludicrous demands and behaved like an entire bright orange metal box full of heavy duty Black & Decker tools. And hidden a fair few things himself, it seems.

But that does not change stone cold facts: He cares. And knows me. And us. And is not running in terror from the prospect of commitment.

In fact, he seems to being jonesing for that "C word" like Cookie Monster would for a snickerdoodle. That's good enough for me.

Alaric has cared with purpose and direction and tethered patience. He held me fast while I slipped down the rabbit hole of my own daydream. It didn't matter to him that I have been faking subservience because he knew all along it served a purpose with the best of intentions.

And I know, when I look back, this will be "the" moment. The moment when it all flipped. Stopped holding back. Started holding on.

It is a celebration, a relief, a barrel of rum finding me in the freeze.

His hand slides over mine. I look out the same hotel window as last night. Same stars. Same night sky.

Everything else has changed.

Or has it? Wouldn't it be this life-altering, axis-tilting moment?

Where are the bells? Angels getting their wings and all that rot? Emma Baker, the man you have crushed on for over a year has admitted he really and truly loves you—what are you going to do now?

I'm going to The Knees Land.

Well, been there and done.

Outside where it is nearly empty, in the darkness of this Christmas morning, a silent pair of taillights disappears along the road outside.

He comes up behind me. Arms wrap warmly around my waist.

"So, um, you say you may have noticed me around the office once or twice," I say, not looking away from the lightshow.

He leans in. Whispers, so softly. "Red dress and my face full of your hair in the elevator on your first day."

Oh. That long, eh? So much for surreptitious behavior on my part.

I turn to face him. He's right here in front of me, hands on my waist, arms bumping against my own. So near me, and finally—finally—I see him level.

He had always felt beyond my grasp. Too beautiful. Too aloof. Too...asshole-y.

To learn this is, in a way, to learn that I have never noticed myself in the way he has noticed me.

I had hoped for a glimmer. A blip. A wink. Then I feared I had deceived him. Changed him in the worst, most deceitful way. Unmade the man.

Instead, somehow, some way, I have unmade myself through whatever bad choices and inane machinations had brought us to this point. I had not shown him. I'd not spoken up. I'd not been together or self-assured enough to just approach him openly.

It occurs to me that there is this woeful, yet distinct prospect: He's right. Which makes me wrong. I'm quite fond of being right, but I guess I'll give him his turn.

I have just never let *me* out before, but I know, now, with him I can do this. His mere presence does that for me. I'm me. Present and accounted for. Willful and strong. Passionate and right. Right for him. The reasoning of why we are right for each other is of no importance.

Those mysterious places in the heart will open their chambers only for so long and to so few.

"I want you to know…" I lean in and place a kiss near the front of his ear. *I can do this. I can put myself out there. He…we deserve this.* "…me."

It seems my words echo in the empty space of the room. Yet he listens, as if waiting for a cue. His still champagne-damp skin is nearly hot, humid against my own. "Just so you know…" I breathe. Move nearer still. Leave no room for pride. "I rather like your—" run my hand up his thigh "—taste."

His low gasp borders on a rumble. Heated breath rushes along my neck.

Suddenly, hands twist within my hair, draw me back, pull my gaze to meet darkened eyes. Eyes that focus, dart from mouth to eyes. Back again.

"Pure, stiletto wearing evil. That is what you are." He laughs in a broken growl. "Why would you tell me that?" He returns to a whisper. Loosens his grip on my hair. Looks a bit surprised to find his hand there. "Can you even begin to understand…what that does to me?"

I must shake my head in reply because a smile pulls at the corners of his mouth. "It is a dangerous effect." Then, maybe I need to contact Miracle-Ear, because I think I hear low under his breath some horseshit about me being the most beautiful woman and exciting lover and that he should probably consult a cardiologist.

There's a quake along my limbs as my body reacts to the tenor of his response. I hadn't thought about how he would take what I said, but if I had, I wouldn't have predicted something so…primal. He has always seemed so *satisfied* with my taking the lead. Not submissive to dominant, but aggressive to passive, if I were to classify it.

Our previous nights together: Me Jane. You Tarzan.

Those things are wonderful, precious.

This is different.

And I want to it happen again.

My hand runs up and along the planes of his face, trembling along its path. He leans into my palm. Eyes fixed on me. Intent. I cannot make myself look away from his mouth, his lips. Warm breath mixes with my own.

He is so beautiful, and though the term is over-used, his beauty is surreal. I run the tip of my index finger along his jawline and then to a perfect imperfection: a tiny scar near his chin. I will ask him about this someday. Someday in the future. Because, I realize, I am going to get more days with him.

Free of pretense, I want feel him, to kiss him. He is the man I have been thinking about for a year. Every waking moment and all the sleeping ones when Honest Abe would get the heck out of the way.

It would be in keeping with my newly minted sexual assertiveness to just lean in and go for it. It would be, but I don't let myself.

I will force him to take charge. And, yes, I realize that is an oxymoron.

Now would be a great time to grab him and kiss him passionately. That is what I want to do. That is what Scarlett O'Hara would do. Or maybe not. Did she ever get assertive? Well, I heard once Vivien Leigh didn't want to kiss Clark Gable. She complained he had bad breath. Her reserve comes across as coy on film. Do guys like coy? Rhett seemed to like it. What is coy anyway? Am I being coy now? Why am I thinking about this right now? Oh, my good God. Get a grip on yourself. The man of your (hot sex) dreams is leaning back and looking into your eyes and you are debating the outdated flirtation techniques of period piece cinema.

I draw in a long breath to try to calm myself. Problem is: I am not actually calm and I am freaking out about all this realness and newness, and my unrelenting staccato intake of air highlights that fact.

"Emma, I can hear the gears turning in your head."

What is the objective goal of coy behavior? Is it sex? Because I'm thinking that just might be a goal at some point here. Yeah, it is. Sex is my goal. Really hot, make-him-forget-his-own-middle-name sex.

Alaric's eyes narrow slightly, and he leans back and away from where we touch.

"Emma, are you…are you shivering?" His whisper makes the fine hairs along my cheek stand up.

My body goes full-fledged Benedict Arnold on me and answers him with a silent shudder that ends with a clench in my abdomen.

"N-No."

Yeah, I will not be taking home any statuettes for that one.

The window we stand by gives off a faintly cool aura, but I am surrounded, cocooned on all sides in his warmth, his scent. He kisses the top of my hair, and I feel him shake his head.

"Listen," I say, "I don't know why I overthink things. I want to be in the moment with you. I want to…want to be with you. I'm just…" I stammer, and his features relax momentarily then transform into contemplation, followed by concern. Just like me. That's what I am. "…concerned."

He shakes his head slightly. "Enlighten me: This is much different than scared, how?"

I fidget with the straps of my dress. He twists the thin strap around his finger slowly, then smooths it back down, creating tingling pinpoints wherever his fingers contact my flesh.

"Emma, I haven't treated you quite the way I should have." He brings his hand to my chin then tilts me up when I haven't even realized I have looked down. He holds me there and looks into my eyes. I feel myself swallow against the slight pull he creates along my throat.

"How can I be clear with you, to tell you what you need to know?"

I make to open my mouth but my voice fails me because at that moment Alaric turns his face to the ceiling. He kept his eyes fixed upward, suddenly unfocused and unblinking.

"I have never felt like this before…I think I have never *felt* other than with you. Is that what you want to hear? Or do you want me to say that I'm terrified, too?" His thumb and forefinger close lightly over my chin. "Because I'm not going to be able to give you that."

"Oh." My face falls.

"Emma, I am not going to tell you that because I am not scared about us or about being with you. I don't, however, relish the idea of *not* being with you."

My ears perk at a particularly appealing two letter word. "What do you want 'us' to be?" I ask.

"Is there even an 'us' already, as far as you are concerned? Is there a 'we' or…Hell, I don't really know where I stand with you." His voice holds a nervous tinge.

How much detail is too much? How in this am I?

I'm in all the way.

As ever. For always.

I run my hands up through the hair at the base of his neck and press his head down to me.

"This should be easy. Natural. It is…us," I whisper against his lips. "You are here, and I'm here…and we can only show each other the rest."

And I am done talking. Done thinking.

Done with everything but feeling.

Because there are no worthy words.

I press my mouth to his, and despite the smile I can feel forming on his lips, he presses back, kissing me for what feels like the first time in forever.

This has the potential to be just that: the first of forever.

He breathes in deeply, never breaking our kiss, always in contact. The intake plays along my skin, invisible feathers along my cheek.

As if my entire being exists only where we touch, I notice nothing beyond the silk of lips and heated pulse wherever we touch. All is recollection and recall. Smooth and satin. His tongue runs along my lower lip, then inside. Touches the tip of my own. Then further, further to skim sides, to taste me as I taste the sweet of him.

Yet this is different somehow. My moves are tentative, more so than when we were together before, more so than I have perhaps ever been before. This kiss carries the weight of a year's worth of acknowledged and answered longing.

Where he holds my face is soft. Reverent. Not so with the hand on my back. It grips. Tight. Nearly hurting. As if he thinks I might evaporate and leave him clinging to mist and air.

It's as though he is trying to remember and memorize me simultaneously. He seems to want to catalog this moment. Journal it. Hmm. Novel concept…

He's sharing with me that he is still afraid this will end, that we will end. His kiss tells me that he's as worried as I am, but that he's done the calculations. Risk versus reward.

My hands wind their way under his shirt and move along the skin of his back. He moans into my mouth, the sound sliding down my own throat.

We continue to kiss, tongues entangled, never parting. I mean to bring a hand around and run it along his chest — the same chest that has rendered me near mute on all my not quite accidental hotel room barging-in recon encounters — but, instead, I encounter the coarse hair that stretches from the top of his suit pants in a narrowing trail toward his navel. I run my fingers across it, and it becomes my turn to moan.

"Emma," he says, breaking our kiss and moving only enough to hover over my lips. His breath is warm, his voice a rasp. "Are you sure? I don't know if — "

"Shh," I say softly and place two of my fingers on his mouth to silence him. He kisses them quickly before his hand is there and his fingers close around mine, and then he brings our clasped hands to his side. He is still breathing against my mouth; each breath seems shorter, shallower. He seems to quit breathing entirely when he begins to walk slowly backward, gently pulling me by my hand, toward the bed.

By the time we reach it, we have separated enough that I'm able to truly see everything about his face. The point where his throat meets his sharp jaw. The slight turn of his nose. The faint, growing creases near his eyes that beg to be tasted. The light that plays and dances across his features reveals a mixed look of excitement and an unnamed something more.

The room is bathed in silver Christmas moonlight that spills in from the single window across the white sheets, leaving the rest of the room in shadow.

We near the bed. He glances away to gauge the distance and, still, I can't label the look I have been seeing, but I can't make myself dwell on deciphering it or anything else beyond wanting…and touching… and truly feeling.

And suddenly, it's happening. Hands in hair. Cradle and crush. Against his chest. Align. More than aware of every breath, of coursing blood, of crumbling walls. He kisses me with a level of intensity that distances itself from all our earlier kisses. I feel him breathe in deeply, as if he is trying to bring all of me into him. His lips, mine.

My mouth. His tongue. He delves, locates the deepest recess of my mouth, stakes his claim.

Fingers, thumbs in deep pressure circles, entangle within my hair. Flat of a palm, small of my back. Lower us to bed.

Us.

He bends, sits, then moves back more, pulling me on top. Unbroken kiss. Reassurance. And his desire for me strains against my stomach.

Tugging, not yet frantic, at sleeves. My dress is a splash on the floor. His palms skid across my waist, back to front. Hand and arms close around me there. Nearly encircle. As though his hands and fingers may stretch and reach completely from my navel around to my spine in glorious, hot pressure.

Moan into his mouth and, now, stunned when the sound returns to me tenfold from him. From inside him. I want him inside me.

Shift against him. Try to retain balance along his length, along his frame.

But, he shows me, it's not necessary for me to worry about falling off; one leg wraps around my own and secures me to him, his lean thigh aligns with mine, his calf braids against my ankle and foot. He pushes his other hand up between us, shoving his shirt out of the way. Pulling us together as if it hurt not to feel skin on skin.

He shifts our kiss, holds my locks back, presses his lips to me. To my face, my throat, my collarbone. Ripping, popping seams, he gathers what's left of his shirt in his fist.

"Emma, I need…to feel…to feel you."

I make a move, stretch up, yank at his clothes. His shirt peels most of the way off, but he holds me tighter yet. Relinquishes his grasp only when I can't suppress a giggle at the catch-22 of it all. He begins to laugh, too, but the sound catches in his throat when I have my camisole halfway over my head. Once it's completely off, I feel my hair spill down over my bare back and exposed chest. Reflexively, my hands cross over my breasts. His eyes narrow slightly, and he shakes his head once, slowly. He sits up and gently lowers first one of my arms, kissing its wrist as he displaces it, and then the other.

Never breaking the gaze we share, he reaches down and removes his shirt, making it as thin as possible before it slips over his head and lands in a distant corner. I grip his arm, trace the indentation where his shoulder and bicep meet.

Both his hands up my sides, thumbs pad under the swell of my breasts. Cups one. Rubs across. Tensing. Teasing. Taut.

Then his other arm slides around, draws me close to him. Close. Presses me into his chest, infuses.

His touch is no longer tentative; he blazes a trail.

Soft kisses along my neck are now nibbles, nearly bites along my collarbone.

Licks salt and skin between kisses. My fingers through his hair. He explores me. Again. More. Even when I think he knows all of me, he finds more. A spot. A pulse. A place that makes me quake, quiver.

Stealing moments, helter-skelter, whenever I can find my mind, I curve and kiss his forehead, the corners of his mouth, and the slight saltiness of sweat. Dew on breaking Christmas morn.

Of their own accord, my hands tug and pull his waistband. He notes my intent, breaks away from our embrace. Rests his head on my chest, panting and watching me work them down. Rise and fall, his chest heaves. He nods, head lowered. Some silent pact with himself, some secret I still yearn to know, wish to learn.

A monumental shift in our positions. He finishes removing his pants, leaves me for a moment. Bereft. I never knew its real meaning before. Then he's down beside me. I can feel my hair splayed out around me. Slowly, he combs the already tangled ends out with his fingers. Reverent. Continues to kiss me, forever kissing me. He is braced on a single forearm, moves his touch from my hair, to my face, and down. Draws a line along my body, pausing. Pauses briefly over my heart. He presses his palm flat there. Bends. Places open lips there, on the space that drums below him, that might now have fulfilled its dual purpose in life.

Yeah, well, open my envelope and call me a Hallmark card. He already said I gave the very best…

The rough of his hand slips lower, then lower. I cannot stop, don't want to stop my reactions. Hips rise. Plunging my hands into his hair. He slides a finger under lace, past the band of my panties.

I know if I shift ever so slightly I will be able to feel his erection, pretty much ride it. But he is trying to be gentlemanly about it. How very sweet.

But we will have none of that. None of that, I say.

It is touching…but I want to touch him.

His fingers skim the near flat of my stomach as he approaches… me. His focus on our kisses falters for the first time; while he continues to press his lips to mine, a greater portion of his attention is clearly elsewhere. As is mine. For, while he had been successful in keeping the physical evidence of his arousal somewhat discreet, there just is no disguising my excitement.

At this point, I'm pretty much a Slip 'N Slide. Like, a Slip 'N Slide with Wesson oil and the hot on full blast. Wheeeeee.

He grips the edges of the fabric, drags it down my thighs and legs. My flesh contracts where the fabric leaves a wet trail along my inner thighs. I feel my breathing still as I await his reaction to the effect he's had on me. My panties find their way onto the floor, and Alaric wraps one arm around me at the waist and the other around my shoulders.

His face buried in my neck, he continues to cradle me within one arm, the other drifts. Glides.

Fingers play along my hip. Thigh. There.

A gasp. Harsh and low. Resounding below my ear. Moment of stillness, and he stills momentarily, then his deep moan into the hollow of my neck makes my thighs clench together over his hand.

"My God, Emma," he rasps. Single finger slips inside. "You are killing me, lady."

Bite back a moan. Fight back all sounds, all words, not trusting what telltales may escape. Or shocking compositions of curse words. Like Beethoven found a late-life penchant for salacious symphonies. Alaric's been so composed, worshipful, while I was on the verge of shouting some incredibly vulgar things. He must notice what I'm doing, because he gently pulls my bottom lip from between my teeth with his own. Half suck, half bite. Watches my reaction through hooded lids.

"No, Emma, don't hold back." Throaty rasp. "Let me know how I make you feel." Then he slides a second finger. Stretch. I moan.

He curls them in me, searching.

My hands cling, dig. Fix to the contours of his back, then downward, and around to trace the V that has called out to me for so long.

He finds the spot. Brushes. Strokes. Then assaults. Crushes my lips.

Unable to aim. Almost on his lips. Kiss anything, all that I can find. Shout against him. Sounds, not words. The open ache of vowel sounds. No language known to man or beast.

Fall back together. Tangled arms. Foggy, I hear murmurs. Soft reassurances in my ear. Missing most of it in the thunderous blood rushing around my system.

"Always you. Only you."

My treacherous, trembling hand fumbles its way. Close him in my palm. Brush the tip. He hisses. Thick. He's wet, too. Coats my fingers. His hips move forward into my hand, and he's panting.

I wrap my leg around his hip, tucking my ankle against the point where his thigh meets his perfect ass, and encourage him to move over top of me. Which he does, then halts. His weight rests on his forearms, hands on either side of my face. His eyes dance…and since it is Christmas, I will allow the comparison to Fred Astaire, because I'm my usual Ginger Rogers, doing my dance in high heels.

Heat radiates from him. Near me, not entering me. He shakes above me, apparently awaiting some unknown cue.

I'm too busy with my turn kissing his throat, his shoulders, any part of him I can reach. A shadow of dark hair below his chin calls out to me; I swirl my tongue, roughness runs under my tongue, and draw his Adam's apple into my mouth in a long suck.

"Christ."

He speaks, and my suction breaks with the movement. He bends and curves over the top of me, bringing my nipple between his lips, pulling at it, drawing it deeply into his mouth. He moves, repeats.

Lick, and touch, and draw long breaths. Pull back, survey his landscape. Look for something more. More connection, as if I need another sense to take him in. So I want to give him the single one left: hearing.

The problem is, I don't know what exactly to say.

The high ceiling is invisible in the current light, only acoustics of reverberated gasps bounce back down upon us. In a room already filled with our soft moans, he needs words.

In this moment, I recognize my power. Because, for once, I can say how I feel without reservation. He needs to know, and I need to tell him. Where earlier words had seemed trite, in this space and time I accept that they can, they will, they must—must—make everything right. I conjure strength and force myself to break away and speak.

"You are who I'm meant for."

Lowest groan. Eyes close. Breath holds. Touch lips. Tremor. Enter. Lightning strike.

The unspoken words "Take me" rattle around in my brain. The sentiment seems insufficient somehow, perhaps embedded in patriarchal notions. The idea that there is a penetration, a plundering, an invasion, so there must be a taking. It's somehow off to me...for I am taking him. I am claiming. I receive. There will be just as much of me when we are done. If anything, he might be the one leaving himself behind. I will be the same...but more. I envelope, encase, claim. I accept.

I take him.

There is a responsibility in that notion that I never saw before. Take care of as well as care for.

He trusts me to be as strong as the both of us need me to be. We are but two short steps from loneliness, longing.

Trust gives way to thrusts, and I find I can no longer contemplate the intricacies of the universe.

He's being so careful and slow. It's touching, torture. Both.

Braced on his elbows, hover and touch and rasp, shallow breaths. Move, slip. Flat of palms beneath my shoulder blades. Wet along collarbone, neck. Water drips, rivulets beyond my ear. Kissed away. Pound. Harder. Harsh. I want him at the spot inside me all his own. Again. Beyond count. Fuck, I don't even know anymore. More. More. Fuck, please just more. Thunder, shudder. Body wracks. Hair clings, slick locks.

With each movement, each in then out, he moves fractionally further. Slow and paced and acutely aware of each new stretch. He continues, quakes so much and me, maybe more. I think, perhaps, he's resisting the urge to plunge ahead and finish the trek. I would be inclined to appreciate the need represented by such urgency—because I'm only human, heck, I want to feel that desired, that wanted—but it occurs to me that this inch-by-inch method has been going on for quite some time...and he's not done yet.

Move. Kiss. Slide. Farther. Further. Stretch. Again. Move...

And he's not there yet...

That is to say, Elvis has barely entered the building.

Holy. Shit. Am I that nervous? Or were those pernicious pineapples I've been sneaking into his meals really GMOs laced with super-conductor growth hormones?

I mean, I have been doing Kegels like a mofo, but seriously? This fit before? Just yesterday?

"Ungh…uh…uh…a…ric. I…oh, God—" I cry out as his hips tilt and thickness presses inside me against the spot his fingers had stroked earlier. My limbs leave my control, and I wrap around him, clinging. I clutch and grasp, fingertips pressing at the contours and sinews of his back.

Legs flail, and suddenly, I find I'm around him, past waist and hip, ankles entwined above. It causes a shift, a surge. Farther in, into me, much farther.

A shift that may catch him unawares; long, moaning curses fall beside and all around me. Progress and movement still. Only tremulous movements along his limbs. Strain and hold back.

I wriggle, then writhe, then learn to make his body beg.

Hands down the small of his back, smoothing one over his hip, press thumbs into bone. Will him, plead with him to continue. My hands slide between us, to where we meet. Near scorches, humidity, heat.

Partially sheathed, consume, complete. Hands run circuits along my sides, along my waist. Palm draws my thigh up, anchors him down. Transfixed, I don't have any idea why I note the soft webbing between his thumb and index finger as it presses against the back of my right knee. He holds fast, sounds so soft, kisses forming a line over my breastbone. They're unsteady. Tender whisper-laced kisses. Barely audible over the pulse thrumming in my ears.

These are the secrets.

Finally.

And I hear some of what he has to say for the first time.

Furtive, so much so it almost feels like I eavesdrop. "Only you…" His mouth press to the pulse point on my throat.

"Whatever it takes…" His lips smooth along my neck, open and moist. "Mine…goddamn it all….now…" The words are hoarse and dry. I feel him swallow against my breast.

My hands fly to his face and pull him to me and kiss him and never let go. I have never felt more. My palms rub against the scruff along his cheeks. Kiss and delve and swallow any more of these clandestine curses. Then I spread my legs, strain near pain, drag the hand he held me with along the way. Hips hitch forward. Manage a great deal more poise than I would have ventured I possess. Draw his length in. To the hilt. All of him, all that remains of him, of me.

He cries out into my mouth when his hips fully meet mine. I think he might have tried to hold fast and allow me to adjust, but I am having none of it; I raise myself and grind against him. Alaric breaks from our kiss and watches the space where our bodies join. Each joining, his breathing picks up more, and then yet more. Strong fingers wrapped at my waist. The fingertips of one hand feel as though they may almost touch the other, completely encircling me in his grasp.

Full, long, deep…complete.

Steady movements. Try to force my eyes to remain open. More than can be managed. Peek through foggy slits. Shadows, silhouettes move above me, within me.

He alternates in some rhythm I can't measure. Lips to mine. Then, watching himself in me. Slide. Disappear. Focus, gauge my reaction.

Vaguely, I register one of his hands moving from my waist, feel the drag along smooth sheets, past my body, my face, my hair, sliding until it extends over my head and, probably, latches onto the back of the mattress. Leverage. Heaving push.

I'm no scientist, but if this is what fulcrum or leverage (or, hell, thermal dynamics and industrial water technology, for all I know) do for intimacy, sign me up for the courses.

For a doctorate.

Pressure, and the hand he still uses to secure my waist tilts my pelvis up to greet his. He draws himself up on his knees slightly, slides his length into me. Slow. Rubs along my front wall, edges. All. Watching, ever watching my reactions.

I give up. Give in. Unmasked and no disguise, he sees it all. All that is me on display.

Draws back out, maneuvers me again. Forward plunge. Different path. Different point. Oh, more right there, and again, again and please. Air in throat, breath catches, soundless moan.

Moonlight glints off his smile. Finds what he's looking for. Takes a long breath, then draws back, then enters and pounds again, again. There. Just…there.

Scream. I want to. Need to. For all I know, I might.

Force. Extreme. Hold on. Ankles dig and ache. Feel my body, my back arc up and away from the point where we join. My head is weighted, too heavy, stays touching the bed. Back bows, mimics a flesh rainbow.

Might say his name. Might blaspheme. I begin to call out all manner of sounds. Some might even be actual words. Or the recipe for tuna noodle surprise.

Clutch at the sheets, pulling, arc further, and shake. He moves his hand from the mattress and drags a flat palm down the length of my torso to join his other one in holding my waist.

Breaths that are rough. He continues to pound into me. Thoroughly. Fully.

Completely.

All around, words spill. I hear myself saying things and can't stop. I tell him how I would think of him every day. Thrash and cool sheets and night air. Whisper nonsensical rants about cherry wood doors and white dress shirts and conference room C. How I can't concentrate except on him.

And still he pounds into me and still I keep pouring my heart out to him.

In shallow gasps I share with him how much he means to me and it scares me that he does.

Happy and terrified. I'm sobbing about how much he means to me when Alaric suddenly stops, his eyes wide. Stops, scoops me up. Flat against him, every crevice, every space. Fine hairs and cool sweat.

His hands run through my hair. Kisses my cheeks, my lips, corners of my eyes, every part of my face as if I've been missing and he has just found me. He lowers us both back to the bed. Lips tease flesh inside of one of my elbows. He places it on his shoulders, wrapping around him, holding him. Encased. He resumes. Long, full.

Maybe only moments and I splinter. Fall. Tense and clench. Lungs tight with confessions and courage and cowardice. He seems near the brink. His muscles writhe and contract. His words like whispers, inaudible through my haze. Breathes more secrets into my skin, and I strain to hear the tale, and he throws his head back, shouts, pours. Heat. Spasm. Full.

He shudders and continues to spill. Runs open-mouth kisses wherever they land.

I stay silent, and he continues to whisper, to respond to the confessions I have been unable to hold back. I begin to hear and understand the hum decoded through dissipating fog. His voice a low thrum. "I do…so much already…" He kisses my eyes and smooths the dampened hair from my face. "Already and always." He swallows thickly and runs his nose alongside my own. "Oh, God, Emma. You don't know how much…I do."

He wraps his arms around me and breathes his words into my hair. "I love you, too."

Say who with the what now? Well, Merry Christmas and Ho Ho Holy Crap.

Just what the hell have I been yammering on about?

CHRISTMAS MORNING

10:09 AM

WARM. EVERYTHING IS WARM, and I'm being jostled.

My eyes flutter open.

"Hey," he says, kissing my bare shoulder. "I couldn't wait any longer."

His lips are wet, soft. I stretch and kiss his throat.

"There is something I have to tell you…that you should know," he says against my skin. "I meant what I said earlier. It was not because of the heat of the moment or because I felt compelled to respond in kind. I want you to know that."

"Hmm?" So sleepy. Content.

"I love you, Emma." His lips brush the corner of my eye, my cheek, my own. "I love you and I know you. I know you in my soul. With everything I am, I love you for everything you are."

In my waking haze, no act, no filter, I say the first thing that comes naturally to me.

"I probably love you, too."

11:15 AM

❋ STOCKINGS: Hung over the lampshade with care.

❋ COITAL: Post.

❋ NOTE TO SELF: Find Cheesecake Factory suggestion box. Submit pineapple cheesecake.

❁ REINDEER GAMES: Is that what you kids are
  calling it these days?

SO MUCH SEX. I FEEL LIMP. Like I should move to a Boneless Chicken
Ranch.

5:02 PM

❁ LATHER: Rinse. Repeat.
❁ CONDOMS: Soon the way of the dodo.

AN ODD GRAY AREA NOW SETTLES BETWEEN US. Too intimate for small
talk. Not intimate enough for talk of bigger concepts like relationships, futures, curtains.

How do you start a casual conversation after you've been fornicat-
ing like the survival of the species depended on your successful efforts?

Hey, hun, did you like the mount up I did on you last night?

Yes, yes. I've been stretching. Trying to keep limber.

Today is a holiday. Canon is wearing Baby Jesus's birthday suit.

Well, at least he says it is. I recall some business about swaddling
clothes and something else about men being wise. And we know that
men are no such thing. But "holiday" with Alaric seems to translate
to some variant of "wall sex," so…well…who am I to quibble with
trivial matters such as accuracy and facts?

We have been enjoying a little celebratory SOS — Shoes-On Sex.

They say practice makes perfect, but that doesn't seem to apply.
If so, I'd have a doctorate. An FMP PhD.

It isn't Valentine's Day for a couple more months, but that doesn't
stop my heels from piercing Alaric's heart.

If by "heart," one means "dick."

"Are you prepping me for some sort of genital piercing? At least
let's discuss that sort of thing first."

"Do you mean an apadravya?" I try not to snort at the idea of
this stiff and proper man with such an ornamentation.

"Apadravya? Any intent to plunge a steel rod through…there…
best begin with 'Abracadabra.'" He exhales sharply, cupping himself
like a baby bird fallen from the nest, and shudders.

I snicker. He looks nauseated. If I ever broached the subject again, I'd be better off to just go straight for Avada Kedavra.

A piercing like that isn't anything I really want, but I can't help myself when he's like this.

"I hear it's very pleasurable," I say as innocently as possible, running two fingers over the sheet in slow, swirly patterns. His eyes follow their trek.

"It's done in one quick session when they pierce the mea—"

"Emma, I swear on a stack of balanced portfolios, if you finish that sentence, we are never having intercourse again."

Oh, dear. Instant mute. Just add threat of celibacy.

HOUR: LATE. OR EARLY. A MATTER OF PERSPECTIVE.

❄ SNOW: Sheets.

❄ ACTUAL SHEETS: Mostly near the lamp base.

❀ CONDOMS: Completely exhausted.

❄ US: See above, re: "Condoms."

I AWAKE TO NEAR DARKNESS, the moon's effects shy behind murky clouds. Fat snow obscures the silent cityscape. Norman Rockwell would be proud.

The only sounds I can discern are the soft, even breaths that accompany each rise and fall of his chest beneath my cheek. If there had been an actual zombie apocalypse and we were all that remained of humanity, I would still be content. Right up until the special of the day was my brains, anyway.

We're wrapped up in one another…finally. Not only physically—with his strong arms encircling me and holding me to his chest and my legs warm underneath the one he has draped over me—but emotionally as well. He had let me know as much in no uncertain terms.

I love you, too.

When he said the words, the feeling that overtook me was indescribable. Like the physical answering of a prayer unfurled in my chest and rapidly seeped out to the farthest points of my body. An incorporeal warmth in places I hadn't even known to exist within myself, as though my very soul heated and healed.

I'm still my whole person, but with this special new addition.

All that, but more, better. New and improved: Now with more sex.

At that time, for a split second, I had opened my mouth to tell him that I wasn't sure how I felt, that I wasn't sure I was ready to confess it was Real, True Love that had snuck up and came about when I was busy ogling his ass. But his phrase rang in my ears. *"...too."*

He wasn't waiting for a response; he responded to me.

"Um...Hey, Emma."

His chest vibrates with groggy words. I look up and can see that he's still bordering on slumber.

From between us, unbidden, my right hand ghosts up from beside me.

I want to touch him.

Everywhere and always.

I can see my hand's shadowed outline, fingers like dark tree branches against the window's scant light, Each one carved into the night with more distinction that would've been noticed under the midday sun. They rise above the landscape hills of his side.

The slope of his right shoulder is silhouetted against the midnight light that filters through the shade. The air warms briefly with each breath.

He shifts, momentarily restless, only to gather me up closer still and hum as he falls back under sleep's spell.

My hand remains aloft. I let it descend and trace the outline of his form. First, up his sculpted arm, then around the bend of his shoulder, across his collarbone. Still, he breathes softly. Then, emboldened, I smooth my hand down his side, his hip, thigh, and around to his butt. *Nice.* My fingers run along his curves, his flesh pebbled under my touch. The whole area is addictive and oddly comforting to touch. Like a stress ball. Or dough. Really, really great dough. I began to gently knead it like I'm baking bread for the troops.

Ass. It seems like a wonderfully crude word for such an amazing piece of...art.

"Um, Emma?" Alaric's voice, groggy but amused, breaks my musing. "What precisely is it you think you are doing?"

Whoops. "Oh, sorry…I thought you were still sleeping."

"I would be concerned if I — or anyone for that matter — could sleep through that." He kisses me with a practically audible smile.

"Well, I was just…doing a little impromptu exploring." I squeeze his cheek, and my index finger runs down the first inch or so between.

"Oh, well, so be it." He hums a bar and pulls me to him, my hand falling unceremoniously to his groin. He huffs. "I feel positively objectified."

My breath catches. He grows, more, under my touch, and he seems unaware, or unwilling, to stop his small tremors and rocking motions.

"Emma," he whispers and repeats and pulls me up into a kiss, his soft lips brushing over mine with every syllable as he continues to kiss me.

Alaric dips further, heat pushing into me. My head arches back into the pillows, I incline myself.

He slides fully. Throaty, deep moan.

Everything is hips…

and lips…

and real.

Only ever out partially, rejoin fully. A concentrated, delicious rocking motion. Scruff along his chin grazes my face and neck. I duck further into his embrace. Kiss the hollow of his neck; he tastes of sleep and sweat and…I can't imagine ever getting enough. I dive in, kissing and biting and pulling him into me as much as I can with my softening limbs.

Instantly, he stills inside me. All his movements halt, the caresses he had been trailing along my ribs, the rocking. He holds his breath.

Eyes clench. Face unreadable. I'm unsure what he's thinking, but I know I will remember this moment, that I will find the right time to ask what clamors inside his thick skull.

Moments pass, voice still AWOL. He looks down at me in what seems like relief.

"Oh, God…Em…Emma…" He rolls me over, holds me against him tighter than ever. Thrusts — frantic, possessive — names tumbling over then over again like a staggered ballad. We wrap around and hold on. Strokes, fan the flames.

I resist the urge to dig into his back, instead fisting the sheets in one hand and holding on tight across his shoulder blades with the other, straining my fingers straight to keep what little nails I had from scratching his skin, marking my territory.

Find my voice. "I'm...I'm..." Stars, novas. Pop and burn.

"Come on, Emma...Yes...let me have it."

Clenching, I cry out something close to his name. He falters. Shudders. Fingers clench hips. Stills. Moans low from the bottom of his lungs. His arms seem to fail him; his body crushes into mine, pressing. I feel covered, protected, even if I don't need protecting.

He flops beside me again, one arm still under me, his chest rising and falling rapidly.

"That was..." His free arm does a solitary, boneless flop.

"Uh-huh."

"Yeah," he breathes and looks toward the growing light of dawn.

After a few moments, he rolls to kiss my forehead. "Looks like it's about that time," he says and inclines his head to the window.

And just like that, our night is over.

Probably a good thing. With our stockpile depleted, unless the Trojan man makes house calls, I shall henceforth be looking all gift horses in the mouth.

"Emma, you are pouting." His thumb plays with my bottom lip, and I suck it in quickly. He huffs an almost laugh, shakes his head once and rolls, sitting up on the edge of the bed.

"Stay," I hear myself speak before I have even thought the word.

He leans back to me and sweeps what is probably a matted mess of hair over and behind my shoulder. "We will be together, right back here—together...in about ten hours."

That, actually, sounds like a dreadfully long amount of time.

I do my damnedest not to pout again; the entire concept of me doing so is shameful in the extreme, but I fail. Alaric shakes his head and runs the back of his index finger along my lip. "What can I do?"

"Stay." I reach up, peck his lips.

"Believe me, I want to. We can't just skip work, Emma."

"I'm sure Diana will manage to contain her disappointment." At least, better than she does her unruly bosoms.

He says nothing, just a nod and a shrug before kissing my cheek again and bee-lining for the shower, leaving me with only the view of the same ass that started all this to comfort me.

It does a fair job.

DAY OF EMPLOYMENT: *387*

12:45 PM

❈ Temporary Desk: About to become "former."

❈ Probably: Not the most romantic word choice ever.

❈ Canon: Alaric.

This company's foreign account processes are not terrible, but they are not safe. Not in the current climate, that's for sure.

There are too many payments to get things going in certain countries that could be construed as bribery. Small things, like taking clients to dinner. Clients who happen to work for foreign governments.

I know this info is not going to be welcome news. I know I'm not positioned as someone to take seriously on these matters.

That doesn't mean I'm not right.

I'm on page three of my detailed report. In the end, the evidence will be irrefutable. They will have to believe me, despite the source. Despite the fact that I'm just a PA.

"Just" associated with the term "personal assistant" doesn't feel right. I'm just the ring-bearer. I've just gotta keep the bus over 50 MPH. I'm just gonna go fishing. Oh, and by the by, it just so happens to be for an egregiously ill-tempered white whale?

Alaric has been in and out of the room all morning.

Fact-checking. Finalizing. Looking fine.

Now, he looks more relaxed. Open briefcase with papers scattered.

"Would you like something to drink, Emma?"

I know this game. "What can I get you, sir?"

He looks up, eyes bright. "Well, since you offered…"

I roll my eyes and push back my chair.

He laughs softly. "Since you are going…I would probably like a Coke."

"Coke?"

"Yeah, probably."

I narrow my eyes.

"Oh," he says, "could you probably get the transfer files?"

I'm at the door.

"And probably order lunch. Probably barbeque."

I spin around. He looks exceedingly pleased with himself.

I'm back with drinks in just a few minutes, but the air is different. He's on a call.

He paces at the far corner of the room. "Yes, I will, Dad. And a happy, belated merry Christmas to you too."

The phone closes, but he doesn't turn around. He studies the nothing of the wall.

Slowly, I go to him and nudge the can against his arm. He twists, smiles weakly, and nods slowly in thanks.

I'm back at my desk for a while when I hear him inhale deeply. I didn't even realize I was staring at him until I noticed the change.

"Cynthia."

I opt not to speak. I assume he knows I have no idea what he's talking about.

"She worked as my father's administrative assistant for only a few months before everything changed."

His eyes stay trained on the bare wall. "When I was five I went to my father's office building with my mom. Cynthia came out of his office looking haggard. Every hair out of place. Blouse half done."

His shoulders visibly tense. Even through the suit jacket I can see the change. I can practically see him dredge the memory up to the surface.

"I didn't understand the rage coming out of my mother that day. Cynthia was always nice to me. She was the lady who gave me candy and baseball stickers. I was enamored. So was my father."

I sit still, careful not to stop him.

"My family changed after that. I don't know how long it went on. It felt like forever, but time is relative, especially to a child. It might have been only a day or two. Every time a door closed, they screamed. They screamed and screamed. Every day. Every damned day, until my mom left. To go for a ride. I wanted to go for a ride too. She always took me. But not that time. I understand now. But then…then it felt like she didn't want me."

He shifts and finds his chair, but never looks to me.

"Then they called. I suppose it was something as simple as 'There has been an accident.' They said she may have been 'distracted.' I don't know. What I do know is that all I can remember of my mother was her yelling…and then dying to get away."

His fingers drum without rhythm. "My father brought Cynthia around a few times later. I couldn't even bring myself to look at her." He looks up, at nothing in particular. His gaze cold. "I learned to hate when I was five."

He begins shuffling papers, and I try to focus on an appropriate response.

Since it doesn't look like one was coming, I go with this: "Are you telling me this is why you are a…um, demanding and hate distractions…why you are an…?"

"You mean *asshole?*" His voice is lighter, the mood leaving with the memory.

"Well, yes."

"No, I don't think so. Maybe somewhat." He stretches back in his chair. "God, who sits back and analyzes themselves like that?"

"It might not be a bad idea…in some cases," I say as playfully as I can manage.

"There is a lot riding on my shoulders. People's jobs, futures. Nice gets you friends. I don't need friends; I need results."

I pop my can open.

"So, Emma, maybe you would care to enlighten me as to why you seem so hesitant about us?"

"You mean beyond the obvious drawbacks of being involved with a self-proclaimed and unapologetic asshole?"

His mouth turns up. "Well, when you put it that way…"

I take a swig. "No, it's mostly me, I suppose," I say and breathe deeply. "I'm used to being on my own. I control that. It's comfortable. I never cared much if anyone came or went before."

He smiles, shuffles some papers. I think he's trying to act nonchalant. "So you *probably* care now?"

"Okay, fine! It was a ridiculously inappropriate way for me to say it, and you deserve better, and I'm embarrassed about it if that makes you feel any better, but if you think you're going to get me to declare I love you for the first time in the middle of this crappy office with printouts and empty Coke cans everywhere, you are going to be sorely disappointed."

As I rant, the smile on his face grows wider. The man is on the verge of openly laughing at me.

"Oh, I'm not disappointed." He folds his hands behind his head. "That will do nicely."

I huff an imaginary hair away from my face.

DAY OF EMPLOYMENT: 388

8:15 AM

❉ LOCATION: Terminal B, KCI.
❉ BAGS: Holding my own.
❉ CANON: Holding his.

"SO YOU ARE CAPABLE OF CARRYING your own things," I begin and pull my suitcase along behind me. "Good to know." Not that I've given much thought to such matters since throwing off the PA yolk. Canon has so very many great places to visit, but I don't want to work there.

He keeps pace beside me as we near security. "I have no choice in the matter, as I find myself currently without staff." He's closer to business mode today, but his voice, with me anyway, is markedly softer.

"This process could not take any longer. It is as if we are all unwitting participants in a study for inefficiency." He talks to no one in particular while we take off our shoes at the checkpoint. "Procedures implemented solely to instill a feeling of security in paying customers. There are too many reported accounts of items still being smuggled aboard to indicate that any of these measures are even the least bit effective. Has anything…" He continues to bemoan the sorry state of airport security while our bags are checked. One guard seems about to comment but sees something in the look Canon shoots him and thinks better of it.

I've decided to consider him "Canon" when we are doing anything remotely work-related.

I've decided transitioning back to business-as-usual at work may be tricky, but not impossible.

I've decided the only running I'm going to do might be to catch a connecting flight.

I'm the first of the two of us onto the plane. I toss my stuff overhead, and he does the same. He spends some time reestablishing the bond with his phone prior to takeoff.

As the plane climbs higher, I offer him gum. He smiles and takes it.

"So how did you know about me?" I try to sound casual. Inside, I'm salivating. "I mean, some of that would be in my HR file, but the pop? The bets?"

He looks to me for a moment, then to the turned down tray in front of him. "Rebecca keeps a chart. It's right there in her cubicle for all to see. When I pieced together that you were always winning—you, the pretty girl I had spotted a while back—I became more curious. How would one person consistently win something like that? Luck? Strategy? A system of sorts?" He shifts in his seat, stretching as best anyone his height could in the small space.

"I was curious as to know how you knew. I became more aware of you. Where you were. What you were saying. By chance, I caught the ends of comments you'd made a few times. Complaining about popcorn the day a bag was burned in the break room, for example. The rest just cropped up when I made a conscious effort to pay attention."

I think about how I gleaned all my tidbits about him. We had similar methods.

"Then," he begins, "one day I realized I wasn't paying attention anymore merely for curiosity's sake. I considered going ahead and asking you out. I even walked up to you to do it. But I heard you talking about a man you were seeing, so I backed off."

"Really?" Shock is an understatement. He was going to ask me out. On a date. You know, one of those things where guys buy food and pretend to listen to you in the hope they'll get to see boobies. "You weren't worried about working together?"

"Until this trip—when someone decided sending the most distracting thing possible along with me was a stellar idea—we didn't work closely together."

"What about the fraternization policy?" I try to remember if we even have one. He looks as though he believes it to be a non-issue. I'm not so sure.

A flash of recollection. How distressed, terrified I was for him when the deal closed.

"Do I seem like the sort who would let an arbitrary rule like that matter?" His look is a bit more serious than earlier. "I'll go tell the appropriate people today, and they will just have to accept."

"Alaric," I say, still mentally stumbling a bit over the new level of intimacy in first names. "Maybe we…" I pause. My words sound like they are filtered through a long tunnel.

He leans over and folds me up in his arms, which won't make it any easier to vocalize this new, acute concern. I shift away from him. His outstretched arms fall in his lap.

"Maybe we should be low-key." I swallow around a swelling lump. This is not what I want, but it suddenly seems like the safest course of action. "Maybe we shouldn't see each other for a while."

I squeeze my eyes shut. Tell myself it's a prolonged blink.

When my damp eyes open, I am alone.

10:55 AM

☘ AIRPLANE: Final descent.

❀ CABIN: Pressure.

☘ NUTS: Bags—Attendants handed out.

✳ NUTS: Me—Suggested time apart.

THE SEAT NEXT TO MINE HAS REMAINED EMPTY since Alaric vacated it early in the flight.

I should be careful what I ask for. Might just get it.

To know that he's onboard, yet not with me, is excruciating.

It's now clear that the level of torture associated with working in the same office every day promises to be beyond comprehension.

We debark.

12:09 PM

❄ AGENDA: Locate baggage on carousel.

❀ OTHER BAGGAGE: The kind that puts me on the
  ol' emotional merry-go-round. Must be examined
  posthaste.

MY GRAY, SWISS ARMY SUITCASE sticks out among the ocean of black
roller bags. As I reach for the handle, a familiar hand pulls it off
the conveyor.

"Let me get that for you." Just over my shoulder, Alaric's voice is
like warm cocoa along my throat. "I insist."

The wheels *thunk* over the tiles, and I smile and, in spite of everything, find myself walking beside him toward a smaller alcove.
He spins the cases to a stop. His eyes move down to where we nearly
touch. The fingers of his hand flex and pull back fractionally. "I was
already on my way back."

He takes a deep breath. Seems to steady himself. "Emma, I know
you have suggested that we don't see each other for a while. It would
make professional sense. But I won't be willing to give you my word."
His hand brushes against mine. "Because I have no intention of ever
breaking my word to you."

Shoving aside all the familiar protective layers of doubt and fear,
some frighteningly real and others even more terrifying because I'm
finally forced to admit they are walls of my own construction, I move
my hand to entwine with his.

His mouth opens fractionally, and I noticed his chest rise as he
sucks in a long breath. Then, keeping our hands and forearms together,
he raises our mutual clasp up, and slowly, individually, brings each
of my knuckles to his lips.

He pulls our hands to his chest, and I look up in happy disbelief. He
leans over to lay his forehead against mine. "If you still think we shouldn't
see each other, then we'd better close our eyes. I'm not going anywhere."

1:30 PM

THE MAJORITY OF MY COGNITIVE EFFORT is devoted to not testing the
tensile strength of Alaric's pants or christening the backseat during
our ride from the airport.

Snow covers the land. It's even thicker here at home. Drifts and shoveled piles dot the roadways. Just looking at it all sends a shiver through me. Instinctively, I begin to reach for my sweater. Then stop.

Instead, I bend and drape myself across him and rest my temple against his shoulder. On one level, it feels unfamiliar and somewhat juvenile. On all the other levels, it is simply *divine*. My face against his chest, rising and falling along with each breath, our hands, fingers still laced between us. The arm he had around me alternates between pressing us in an embrace and his hand tracing light circles on my lower back.

My head is tucked safely away under his chin for most of the time we ride, until the car pulls up outside my home. Undisturbed, the car idles for a few moments. Alaric's fingers comb softly through my hair.

When he finally speaks, the deep cadence of his words echoes around inside my chest, soft tremors along my ribs. "We should probably get going."

1:37 PM

I SIT UP. SMOOTH MY SKIRT. I wonder what he considers "we," what he labels "us."

"What will you tell them?"

"We are together. That is all they need to know, if they truly even need to know that."

Suddenly, I recall his earlier comment about me seeing someone.

"By the way, I'm not sure what you overheard, but I think you heard wrongly. I haven't had more than an occasional, casual date in at least a year."

He looks uncomfortable. Like he doesn't particularly enjoy discussing other men. Big yay for him that for the last year I have embarked upon a self-imposed penis boycott.

"It sounded serious and long term." He shifts again, clears his throat. "Some guy named Abe."

3:15 PM

❀ CLOTHES: Unpacked. Sorted. Ready for cleaners.

❀ BOXED: Taupe shoes. Receipt included &
ready to return.

❀ ROOMMATE: Inquisitive.

❀ WITHDRAWAL: Already.

DIFFERENT. HOME FEELS DIFFERENT SOMEHOW.

Little knickknacks Clara has had out forever now seem different and new. I have not taken notice in a while.

Commonplace.

I had watched the driver pull away after dropping me off at home a little while ago. Alaric had muted his call with our company's owner and kissed my temple as I opened the car door.

Unlike the last one, this driver actually helped me with my bags.

Through the windows in my living room, I saw Alaric tap the front seat once, and they sped away.

Everything gets unloaded on autopilot. Shoes. Toiletries. Cosmetics. Clara helps put away all the miscellaneous crap we packed.

Tea.

Glue.

Needle and thread.

Duct tape and bailing twine.

"So tell me again, why did you quit? I thought the idea was to endure this and get a bonus or something," Clara says as she stretches to put Q-tips away.

I dump my hair-clips into their basket. "It was a raise, and it's complicated." I cringe as soon as the words are out of my mouth. "Complicated" invites clarifying questions.

Clara is quiet as we continue to unpack. Unusually quiet.

I sort through a stack of papers and tickets, and Clara dumps out the contents of the Late Night Emergencies bag. Then she eyes me.

"Emma, where are they?"

"Hmmm?" I keep sorting.

"The condoms. The pack of condoms I put in there as a joke. You know, since you were going on a trip with Corporal Asshole."

"Major Asshole."

"Whichever." She waves me off. Glares at me. "Oh, my God, with him? Did you?"

"Did I what?"

"Nude up."

"Fine. Yes," I huff and look skyward. I had every intention of sharing this with her, but at a point of my choosing. This will have to do. "I did. I used them. We used them. We barely left bed yesterday. I will be soaking in the tub tonight until I am indistinguishable from a shar-pei."

It's rare to catch Clara off guard. I have done nicely.

She gapes at me like a fish. A guppy. "I thought you'd tell me you met someone, or that the SOB needed them and you actually gave them to him. Or that maybe after a year of lusting after the man, you'd snapped one night and just had your way with him once." She folds her arms. Indignant. "Once."

The unpacking process always outlasts my patience. Cities are built in less time.

As we finish, amidst a stream of bubbly expletives from Clara that decry how "keeping your best friend out of the loop is big bullshit," she announces she's going to her room and that tomorrow I owe her both a manicure and, as she puts it, "a detailed account of all the damned pipe laying" that she vehemently maintains I should have already told her about. By her estimation, I was supposed to shag, hose off, and promptly Skype from the mountaintops.

I really don't know what to say. I'm on the verge of the bomb drop that we are actually together, an item, involved, when my phone rings. It's him.

"Hello?" I hold my finger up to Clara, letting her know I have every intention of full disclosure and that we're not done here.

"Hello."

Pause. Okay. Blink. Blink.

"Is everything all right?"

"Yes." He clears his throat. "Everything is in order."

You bet your firm, beautiful ass it is; I had everything set up.

I try to think of why he would be calling me already. There seems to be only one conclusion. I smile at Clara in apology and excuse myself.

"Alaric, I miss you."

I can practically hear his smile. "Good."

And whatever felt like it was stretched thin, like it might've broken when he pulled away in the car, is back.

Everything feels warm and welcome and home again. I sit and play with one of Clara's throw pillows while he and I talk about everything and nothing.

8:10 PM

"Emma! Can you get the door? That should be my pizza." Clara is painting her toes, which she always seems to be doing whenever her food is delivered. I think she may have a delivery driver phobia.

Grumbling, I point out to her we are a bit too old for pizza this late at night, and she is cruel for tempting me so. I scuff my way to the door in fuzzy slippers and sweats. "Coming!"

I'm ready to shove the wad of her cash at the driver when I open the door and suddenly decide we need to order pizza more often.

"You really eat this?" Alaric is standing in his overcoat and holding the box more like one would a football than a pizza pie. He follows me in and makes a face when I open the lid. Then I make a face.

Hawaiian. Not my favorite.

"No, not this kind." I shut the lid. "You can have my share." *Actually, please, please do.* My grin is salacious.

He hangs his coat in the hall, shoes by the door. We're a "no shoe" house.

He sprawls out on the sofa, arms stretched across the expanse of the back. Freshly showered, hair still wet.

Sleeves rolled up. Relaxed and stuffy at once.

Clara, after having waited long enough for a driver to have safely left the premises, shows up.

"Oh, you must be him. I'm Clara, the roommate." She says *him* with a fair amount of disdain, but extends her hand anyway.

Alaric's eyes flicker to me, but he moves and shakes her hand. "Nice to meet you, Clara. I'm Alaric, the 'him.'"

The conversation is somewhat stilted while they eat, and I contemplate who first thought hot tomato sauce and fruit would taste good together. Perhaps the same type of person who first looked at a cow's udder and thought, "Gee, I am rather thirsty…"

Clara leaves, a bit warmer with Alaric, and I make a mental note to thank her for being gracious as I have done very little explaining at this point.

"I know it is getting late," he begins, "but would you like to go for a ride?"

Not if you mean in a car…

"Do you need to go?" I place my hand on his leg.

"Not particularly. I just…" he says, shifting on the sofa. "I came here to see you. I got used to you being around."

I smile at him and kiss his jawline. He didn't shave this evening.

I breathe him in. He smells like want.

"Emma, I didn't come here with any expectations," he whispers near my ear.

He shifts again under my touch. Only then do I realize my hand has drifted to the top of his thigh. Down into heat. He grows.

My head shakes softly.

Run my nose down his throat.

Breath changes. Pulse quickens.

The sofa squeaks under us. Leather and denim and skin.

His hands close around my waist, almost encircle. Held.

His shirt untucked, my fingers run a path through light hairs.

His tongue knows my lips, greets them. Wraps around my tongue and pulls me into him.

"You are a dozen feet from your bedroom, Em—use it!" Clara yells from down the hall.

We do.

Clothes on the chair. The floor. The foot of the bed.

Two hands entwined. Landing at our sides. Our fingers knot above our heads.

Other hands explore. Visit and remember and trace and learn and memorize. Commit.

I touch his hip. Finger pads and grasp behind. He moans and shifts into me.

He likes when I grab his ass.

Lucky, lucky me.

Pull him to me. He rocks, our mouths together, his heated head presses into my stomach, then between my legs, then finds inside.

Oh, God, his breath is so harsh. He rocks into me. Squeezes my hand. Pulls me closer. Presses.

My thigh is over his hip now, calf against his cheek.

I feel it flex and tighten and move. And move. And move.

I shift and angle and slide. He's there. Again and again. Hit and meet and press against that spot until I shake. Then scream down his throat. Then shake some more.

Shove him over and take him in all the way. Feel the change. The length. All.

His neck arches, head into the pillow, eyes behind closed lids.

Our hands still clasp near his head. He kisses me and opens his eyes to watch me ride.

Hands on face. Then neck.

Nails down his chest. Light.

I shove my hand under his waist and move more. Faster.

He slams up, meets me. Again. Hits what might be a new place. His.

Rasp and pant and sweat and more. I want more and I want all.

He strains, near roars, and I know he's close. We have gotten there. Arrived.

"Yes," I breathe. "In me. I want to feel." I bend near his ear, keep the pace. He paws at me, keeps me close. "It's mine." I blink away the words. Too much. Is it?

He grabs my face, fingers in my hair, wrists under my chin, practically yanks me in.

"Yes." His voice hoarse, low.

And it's in me and mine.

We should shower. We don't. We sleep. Together. Complete.

2:47 AM

✽ BED: About half as warm as it was mere
   moments ago.

"ARE YOU SURE YOU HAVE TO GO? Your clothes would be okay just this once." I yawn into the pillow that now smells like Alaric and pull it close.

The zipper makes a series of quick clicks. "I know you are not suggesting I wear jeans to the office." He sounds both teasing and aghast.

I want to pout, and I want him to stay. I am not proud of either. I may feel needy.

"No, you're right."

"Of course." He's dressed and tucks the blanket around me. "I hardly think waltzing into work in jeans for the first time coincides with our goals. We're going for low-key." He kisses me goodbye quickly. "That is what I assured the board yesterday."

I nod. I was not really expecting him to stay. Just a thought. A snuggly thought.

It turns out, Alaric Canon is not the greatest of snugglers. Shocking, I realize.

Hard to imagine someone so warm and fuzzy doesn't just snuggle right up like a big ol' baby.

He likes his half of the bed. But we have held each other until I sleep. When I wake up, he's always holding my hand. Often with our feet braided together.

I think that means more.

DAY OF EMPLOYMENT: 389

8:03 AM

❀ CLOTHES: Favorite electric blue sweater and coordinating skirt.

❀ HAIR: Down and untamed.

❀ PA DESK: Empty.

❀ CACTUS: Dry. At home on my old desk.

MADELINE IS LEANING OVER MY CUBICLE WALL. She wants answers. Explanations. Details.

Rebecca is not much different. She's sitting on the edge of my desk, arms folded, looking rather terse. I was not prepared for her to be so upset about my quitting the PA position.

"I suppose you expect a raise for lasting a week." Rebecca huffs and crosses her arms. She's clearly miffed, but exaggerating and not truly, truly mad.

I continue to arrange my stuff. Stapler by monitor. Pens and highlighters in upper left drawer. "That was the offer you made."

"I think it's amazing you lasted a week, Emma," Madeline says. "Bert came closest, but he never said you'd quit. I almost can't believe the day has come when I get to pay-out the special pot."

I'd almost forgotten about the side bet for a PA who left without tears.

"Um, I didn't earn that," I say over the rapidly forming lump in my throat. I choke it back. There is no way this is going to show at work.

Both are silent for a moment. Rebecca unfolds her arms and places a hand on mine. "Really? I didn't mean to give you a hard time...I just thought you got fed up with him jerking you around."

"I'm fine. It was just an emotional moment when I gave up." I smile quickly at them both and focus back on putting things away. "Just trying to be honest."

I would like a raise even if I'm only working here until graduation. I'm almost relieved I didn't go the month and wind up being offered a promotion. "I did still earn the raise though," I say and look pointedly at Rebecca. *Pay up. I owned that position.*

And a few others.

"Yes, fine. I suppose you did." She huffs. Her reaction is off somehow. I look at her with what I assume is apparent confusion.

She rolls her eyes slightly. "Never mind me. I'm just mad that I finally found a PA for myself that I like, and now I'm told that it is more important that Mr. Canon have an assistant immediately. So I'm without again."

"You can always take back what's left of them when Canon fires them," Madeline says, moving back to her desk to gather the winnings from the traditional bet. I have technically won since no one guessed that I would not end up fired.

Rebecca nods thoughtfully and stands to leave. Then she sits back against my desk with a thud.

"Rebecca." Canon's voice fills the floor. I feel my eyes go wide.

"Good morning." Rebecca nearly covers her surprise. "I take it your trip went well."

"Yes," he says dismissively. "Ms. Baker, I will see you in the break room at noon."

Turning, I nearly beam when I see him standing there, imposing and somewhat larger-than-life. His face alters ever so slightly, a hint of smile cracks at the corners. He taps the top of the cubicle wall twice and leaves.

"What was that?" Rebecca asks, her voice higher with each word. Madeline has materialized back at my desk. I cannot hear a single keyboard click.

I shrug and smile. It is best to just get things out in the open. Less time expended on speculation.

"That?" I move to watch him walk away. I watch him because I can and because I want to and because he is beautiful in ways that I'm just discovering even after a year of studying him for other reasons. "That was my boyfriend."

Rebecca looks surprisingly self-satisfied.

Madeline's mouth drops as well as the envelope of cash.

I bend and pick it up. They both give me their own versions of a you-are-so-telling-me-everything-later-in-private look.

The envelope quietly finds its way to Bert's desk.

12:03 PM

❁ LOCATION: Break room.

❁ LUNCH: Cobb salad. Chicken and rice soup. Cut tropical fruit (which I plan to share).

❁ MADELINE: Bemused. Trying to see Canon as human.

❁ BERT: Confused. But $347 richer.

❁ REBECCA: Pleased. She had a plan.

❁ NEW PA: Familiar. Very familiar.

❁ CANON: Late.

WHEN HE ROUNDS THE CORNER, the atmosphere changes. The break room's unusually quiet; people move softly, trying to hear. To understand.

His suit and starched shirt also looks very incongruous among the plastic chairs and microwave dinners.

"You are late," I say and kick an empty chair out from under the table for him. "You should endeavor to attend future lunch meetings more promptly."

Smiling, he shakes his head, then opens up what looks to be a freshly delivered, hot sandwich.

"Did you have trouble finding me? Already lose your edge tracking my moves?" I tease.

"Oh, yes." He snorts. "I stalk you."

"I stalk you right back."

We begin eating. After a moment, I nudge the fruit toward him.

"You are nothing if not persistent." He looks from the cup to me.

"It's up to you," I sing-song.

"I will have you know there is probably less pineapple at your average luau than in my system at this moment." His voice is flat, the straight man to our comedic duo.

I smile victoriously. It's still fun to fluster, to influence him.

I move on to soup just as a familiar form appears near our table. "The report from Rowe is on your desk, sir."

Alaric swallows but doesn't turn. "Was I not clear to bring it to me as soon as it arrives?"

"Yes, sir," he barks and doesn't tread lightly on the sarcasm. "You were at your desk when you said that, so I took it to your desk."

"I am not my desk. It does me no good on my desk." He sets his sandwich down and turns to face his new PA.

"You also gave the distinct impression you did not wish to be disturbed at lunch." He looks to me quickly.

"Mr. LaCygne, I believe you know Ms. Baker," Canon introduces us without elaboration.

"This is a pleasant surprise," I say, taking the hand he has offered. I note that he has a daunting presence and demeanor even in servile mode. This may work.

"You will learn soon enough to do what he says, when he says it, even if it doesn't make sense." I offer my tried-and-true advice.

Canon returns to his sandwich.

"Thank you," LaCygne says genuinely. "Logic is a hard thing to abandon." With that, he's gone.

"Insolent little…" Canon grumbles.

"Not working out already?" That is too bad. He seemed feisty.

"Perhaps I shouldn't elaborate. It would give you an unfair advantage in the latest betting pool."

"I'm already excluded. Some unfortunate nonsense about 'insider information.'"

"Oh, however will you support your shoe habit?"

"You like my shoes?" I smile up at him and brush my pump against his calf discreetly.

He swallows. "I believe you are well aware how very much, and as I demonstrated for you yet again last night to what great extent I appreciate your shoes." He takes another bite to hide his grin.

I flush, recalling midnight last night, our post-ballet hijinks, a moment or two on Christmas…and a scenario involving a pair of red heels I just may have the nerve to try out tonight. Probably.

THE END

AND NOW FOR SOMETHING COMPLETELY DIFFERENT...

THERE ARE DEFINITE REASONS I arrive at work before everyone else, and this little sojourn into metal box hell is a prime example.

Marketing trials are 85% positive for the new labeling designs. If we...

Smashed into the far corner of an elevator — and forced to interact and *smell* people with whom I would cheerfully go to my grave never having encountered — is not a great start to the day.

Only 72% for the teen target market. There has to be a way to appeal more. Maybe a re-package...

Is that my phone? No.

But finding that my assistant had failed to bind the reports and distribute them yesterday was no way to start this day either.

That Nebraska printing company's bid was so far below everyone else's. Need to verify that they have the specs right.

That was definitely my phone this...

"Good morning, Mr. Canon."

I nod once. "Morning." *Whoever you are.*

I grab my phone and scroll through items while more people load and shift around like tiles in a child's puzzle game.

What would improve the percentages?

Conference at 4:00 today.

Dinner meeting at 6:30 with the Germans.

Need the counter bids for—

Everyone shifts, and I press myself flush against the back wall. Then they shift again, no doubt allowing yet another person onto the elevator. If we don't all plunge to the sweet release of our deaths, it will be a certified miracle.

Grand. The person now in front of me is nearly on top of me.

What the fuck?

Is that?

Yes, it is.

That is someone's ass pressed up against my dick.

A round, pliant, warm ass.

She's a brunette and comes up to my chin. That's about all there is to say. She is all wavy, long tresses and a red dress of the simple, elegant variety. I don't seem to recognize her. I also can't see her face. That doesn't really mean anything as I don't normally dedicate much gray matter to employees who sit in cubicles. They might as well work for any of the other businesses that share this building, as far as I'm concerned.

I might've willfully opted to reserve a few brain cells for this particular figure though.

"Sorry." I barely hear her voice. As the elevator starts its climb, her hand braces against my thigh, but I doubt she even realizes she's done so.

"Not your fault." I hear my own voice like that of a stranger.

Now, I'm at a loss as to why I would say that, why I would try to make her comfortable. It most assuredly is her fault. She is groping me and not respecting personal space. Crowded or not, there are some things one simply does not do.

One does not rub against strangers in elevators or grab onto legs in close proximity to dicks that have been in recent contact with lovely asses.

Lovely...

I shake my head and clear this train of thought, utilizing my phone as a suitable distraction while scanning and forwarding emails.

Percentages are—

Market tria—

It's hopeless. I can't think clearly with her pressed against me.

And it pisses me off.

The elevator ride with her can't be over fast enough. My floor is next and it is still taking far too long.

I resolve to never take the elevator again so that I can avoid this distracting person henceforth.

The doors open, and I make to move around her...but I can't. I can't move around her because she is already gone and has taken her pretty ass and what I now see are red heels along with her, passing through the doors onto my floor and into our open office area.

Well, this is terribly inconvenient.

The doors close, and we're up another two floors before it registers that I've failed to exit.

2:58 PM

Letterhead currently says "Limited Liability Corporation" not "Company." No such thing. Fix that.

KC Company is ripe for merger or buyout.

Conference call in one hour.

Dinner reservations confir—

That last thing I need to see when I leave my office is the first thing—the only thing—I manage to see.

She's standing up among the cubicles. Volumes of hair and her red dress practically a dead-center bull's-eye in my line of vision. Charts and banners and everything fade away, ceding to the contrast of porcelain skin against auburn waves. The whole room is mere concentric circles leading toward her face.

And, of course, even from this distance I can tell she is rather pretty. The fact that she's not a hag with a comely figure is, of course, par for the day.

She's probably ugly on the inside. I'll cling to that hope.

Crap. What was I leaving my office for? I keep walking steadily, not letting the thoughts tripping my mind find their way to my feet.

I realize I am still looking at her as I begin to turn down the hall. I blink away. Shake her image from my brain. It has more important things on which to focus. Fine. It is decided. The sooner I ferret out her flaws and irritating habits, the sooner I can get back on task.

I look back one last time.

ACKNOWLEDGMENTS

I am forever grateful for the support and inspiration of the collective of friends who were drawn improbably together over affection for one story, kept together through artistic efforts, and remain a constant foundation for one another now. They prove every single day that the coincidence of geography may be overcome to find the most compassionate, creative, and loyal friends that any person could be blessed to have. Look out world should they all be in the same room together one day.

ABOUT THE AUTHOR

Qwen Salsbury was born in Kansas and somehow keeps ending up back there. Raised on her grandparent's five-acre homestead within the city limits, her imagination was honed during long days of quiet play and spartan access to a TV signal. Now mother to handsome boys, she strives to ensure that they appreciate potential adventures found within the pages of a book, an honest day's work, and what ingenuity may yield from mundane objects like a string and a cup. The boys prefer a PS3.

After spending time in corporate America, she returned to school and received a BA in English—Creative Writing/Poetry from Pittsburg State University, the alma mater of Pulitzer Prize winning poet James Tate. She worked on a Masters there until going on to receive a juris doctorate from Washburn School of Law.

A seven-time Sigma Tau Delta writing award winner, she has had fiction and poetry appeared in literary magazines and has had stories selected by fiction communities as featured story of the month and year. Predominantly a writer of romance, her romantic fiction varies from contemporary to historical to fantasy, though often with a humorous slant and poetic undertones.

For reasons she can't even articulate herself, she decided to start writing fiction again while solo parenting and going to law school.

The writing of *The Plan* took on the form of a journal, which she posted online in "real time" over the Christmas holiday. It was immensely popular and many devoted readers still meet en masse online to read it in real time again each holiday season. Now greatly expanded to nearly double its original length, she believes that this book will be both a fun new read as well as rewarding to those who have already enjoyed the original story.

New Adult

Three Daves by Nicki Elson
Streamline by Jennifer Lane
Shades of Atlantis by Carol Oates
The Heart series: *Beside Your Heart* & *Disclosure of the Heart*
by Mary Whitney
Romancing the Bookworm by Kate Evangelista
Fighting Fate by Linda Kage
Flirting with Chaos by Kenya Wright
The Vice, Virtue & Video series: *Revealed* (book 1) by Bianca Giovanni

Erotic Romance

The Keyhole series: *Becoming sage* (book 1) by Kasi Alexander
The Keyhole series: *Saving sunni* (book 2) by Kasi & Reggie Alexander
The Winemaker's Dinner: *Appetizers* & *Entrée* by Dr. Ivan Rusilko & Everly Drummond
The Winemaker's Dinner: *Dessert* by Dr. Ivan Rusilko
Client N° 5 by Joy Fulcher

Paranormal Romance

The Light series: *Seers of Light, Whisper of Light* & *Circle of Light*
by Jennifer DeLucy
The Hanaford Park series: *Eve of Samhain* & *Pleasures Untold* by Lisa Sanchez
Immortal Awakening by KC Randall
The Seraphim series: *Crushed Seraphim* & *Bittersweet Seraphim*
by Debra Anastasia
The Guardian's Wild Child by Feather Stone
Grave Refrain by Sarah M. Glover
Divinity by Patricia Leever
Blood Vine series: *Blood Vine* & *Blood Entangled* & *Blood Reunited*
by Amber Belldene
Divine Temptation by Nicki Elson
Love in the Time of the Dead by Tera Shanley

Historical Romance

Cat O' Nine Tails by Patricia Leever
Burning Embers by Hannah Fielding
Good Ground by Tracy Winegar

Romantic Suspense

Whirlwind by Robin DeJarnett
The CONduct series: *With Good Behavior* & *Bad Behavior* & *On Best Behavior*
by Jennifer Lane
Indivisible by Jessica McQuinn
Between the Lies by Alison Oburia

Anthologies

A Valentine Anthology including short stories by
Alice Clayton ("With a Double Oven"),
Jennifer DeLucy ("Magnus of Pfelt, Conquering Viking Lord"),
Nicki Elson ("I Don't Do Valentine's Day"),
Jessica McQuinn ("Better Than One Dead Rose and a Monkey Card"),
Victoria Michaels ("Home to Jackson"), and
Alison Oburia ("The Bridge")

Singles and Novellas

It's Only Kinky the First Time (Keyhole series) by Kasi Alexander
Learning the Ropes (Keyhole series) by Kasi & Reggie Alexander
The Winemaker's Dinner: RSVP by Dr. Ivan Rusilko
The Winemaker's Dinner: No Reservations by Everly Drummond
Big Guns by Jessica McQuinn
Concessions by Robin DeJarnett
Starstruck by Lisa Sanchez
New Flame by BJ Thornton
Shackled by Debra Anastasia
Swim Recruit by Jennifer Lane
Sway by Nicki Elson
Full Speed Ahead by Susan Kaye Quinn
The Second Sunrise by Hannah Downing
The Summer Prince by Carol Oates
Whatever it Takes by Sarah M. Glover
Clarity (A *Divinity* prequel single) by Patricia Leever
A Christmas Wish (A *Cocktails & Dreams* single) by Autumn Markus
Late Night with Andres by Debra Anastasia